MW00328760

KALEIDOSCOPE

ALSO BY ELLYN BACHE

The Art of Saying Goodbye

Raspberry Sherbet Kisses

Over 50's Singles Night

Daughters of the Sea

Riggs Park

The Activist's Daughter

Holiday Miracles

The Value of Kindness

Festival in Fire Season

Safe Passage

Culture Clash

KALEIDOSCOPE

20 Stories
Celebrating Women's Magazine Fction

Ellyn Bache

Banks Channel Books

KALEIDOSCOPE. Copyright © 2017 by Ellyn Bache.
All rights reserved. Printed in the United States of
America. No part of this book may be used or reproduced in
any manner whatsoever without written permission of the
publisher, except in the case of brief quotations embodied in
critical articles and reviews.

This is a work of fiction. Names, characters, places and incidents are products of the author's imagination or are used
fictitiously and are not to be construed as real.
Any resemblance to actual events, locals, organizations or
person, living or dead, is entirely coincidental.

Library of Congress Cataloging-in-Publication Data

Names: Bache, Ellyn, author.
Title: Kaleidoscope : 20 stories celebrating women's magazine
fiction / by Ellyn Bache.
Description: First edition. | Greenville, SC : Banks Channel
Books, [2017]
Identifiers: LCCN 2016040879 (print) | LCCN 2016048097
(ebook) | ISBN 9781889199177 (trade paperback) | ISBN
9781889199184 (ebook) | ISBN Classification: LCC PS3563.
A845 A6 2017 (print) | LCC PS3563.A845 (ebook) | DDC
813/.54--dc23
LC record available at https://lccn.loc.gov/2016040879

Cover design: Carol Tornatore

Author photo: Sydney Webster

Cover photo of kaleidoscope design: © Migelito /Shutterstock

Banks Channel Books
bankschan@aol.com

"Our days are a kaleidoscope . . .
New harmonies, new contrasts, new combinations
of every sort . . . ."

– Henry Ward Beecher

Contents

INTRODUCTION

Until about the mid-1990s, and for most of the 20th century, women by the millions looked to magazines like *McCall's, Redbook* and *Good Housekeeping* not just for recipes and decorating tips but for the short stories that appeared each month. The fiction ran the gamut from sweet romances to thoughtful stories about unexpected pregnancies, career-versus-childcare decisions, the challenges of life after divorce . . . even the difficulties of handling a resident ghost.

I loved those stories. When I was about twelve, I began sneaking my mother's magazines out of the mail and furtively reading the fiction before returning the magazines to the mailbox. It seemed ages until I was finally allowed my own subscription to *Seventeen*, which in those days ran at least one quality fiction piece every month—a great thrill. When I grew up and became a writer, those stories were my model of what fiction should be like. I sold my first short story to *McCall's* in 1981.

Then, by the late 1990s, commercial short fiction had dwindled in popularity so much that magazines began dropping it. The late Helen DelMonte, fiction editor at *McCall's* for many years, told me she'd had a conversation with an auditor who said he didn't think a single issue of the magazine was sold because of the short stories. The stories were zapped.

From that time on, although readers still enjoyed the voice, the subject matter, the style of those stories, they found those elements in novels rather than short stories. Like many other writers, I began writing novels partly for the challenge and partly because there was no longer a market for shorter pieces. I learned that there are things a writer can do in a novel that aren't possible in short fiction. I enjoyed it. When my novel *Safe Passage* was made into a movie starring Susan Sarandon, I liked it even better.

But I always wrote short stories, too. I learned, gradually, to write what today would be termed "literary" stories—complex, often dark fiction, the language finely honed. If a writer is lucky (but doesn't make the cut at the few heady intellectual magazines like *The New Yorker*), he or she might be published in a prestigious journal that garners important literary prizes but pays very little (or, more commonly, nothing) and has a small but elite readership. Or she might do remarkably well. For me, as a non-academic, writing literary stories helped me sharpen my skills and provided a chance to tap subjects I might never deal with in my novels.

Then, recently, at almost every book event, I found myself being asked about my commercial stories that had been published decades ago, mostly in the 1980s and 1990s. Collections of literary stories were beginning to be published again after years of decline. "I really do like those stories," one woman told me, "because I can read them in the little bit of time I have and then go on. But I loved those women's magazine stories, too, and would love to read them again." Remarkably, younger women were also curious. People kept asking me if my older work was available.

Well, no. But I had kept copies of most of it and decided to take a look. The stories turned out to be more contemporary—and surprisingly, more "literary"—than I expected. They didn't seem dated. They were thoughtful as well as entertaining. They dealt with the universal issues (and not just "women's" issues) that we continue to deal with today.

And so I turned them into this collection. The twenty stories here were originally published between 1981 and 2003, in national periodicals like *McCall's* and *Seventeen* and *Good Housekeeping*; in regional magazines like *Virginia Country*; and in newspapers (yes, lots of newspapers carried fiction in those days) like *The Chicago Tribune* and *Encore Magazine* (despite its name, really a weekly arts and entertainment newspaper).

I think you'll enjoy these stories whether you remember this type of fiction from its heyday, have discovered it more recently in novels rather than in this shorter form, or never encountered it at all. At a time when our lives are ever more busy, I hope you'll find here a pocketful of thoughtfulness, a little taste of comedy, little jolt of joy.

Have fun!

BIRD OF PASSAGE

The first time Jon and I kissed we pulled away, a little embarrassed at our mutual breathlessness (we're in our late 20s, after all) and might have felt too awkward to continue except that Jon said, "Robin, for a bird you certainly have a mighty sweet beak." I laughed, of course, and the following Saturday moved in with him—the most impulsive thing I've ever done in my life.

Ten weeks later, soaked from the endless Miami rain, hair frizzy, reeling from the results of a positive pregnancy test, I came home from work to find not Jon but a note: "Sweet beak, I've gone to the library to rescue Resnik from the doldrums. Your love, your sweetheart, the Bird Watcher."

Needless to say, I am not amused.

Normally I am a deliberate person, a scientist, who likes things to go as planned—or at least I was before I came to Miami and met Jon. In the 77 days I've known him, Jon has made my name, Robin, into a metaphor for wonderful things. He has told me I have marvelous plumage (a reference to my thick, unmanageable hair), a great flight pattern (unstylishly wide hips that give a swing to my walk) and the typical fine red breast of my species—this after I got a sunburn while wearing a particularly skimpy bathing suit. I actually laughed at all of this, and have come to realize now that love is deaf as well as blind. Tonight I'll sit here alone while Jon makes his friend Resnik study for an hour, then buys him enough beers to make him forget that his wife is filing for divorce. By the time Jon gets home I'll be in the dead sleep I've been sleeping the past three weeks, which alarmed me at first and now has been explained, I suppose, by the pregnancy test.

None of this was on my agenda, and I've said nothing to Jon about my suspicions—but since the pregnancy is fact and I am a realist, I had planned to serve dinner on the screened porch as soon as the rain stopped (it always stops before sunset and remains clear all night) and tell Jon the news while there was still enough light to gauge his reaction. If he seemed distressed, I intended to say, "Of course I'll have an abortion." I have always wanted children, but I am prepared for the worst. Depending on Jon's reaction, I was even ready to suggest I find separate living quarters.

The only thing I wasn't prepared for was to find him out with Resnik.

Jon didn't know I had something important to tell him tonight, so I know I'm being unreasonable, but that doesn't keep me from being angry. I start switching off the little air-conditioners that cool the bungalow but make it sound as if we live at the bottom of

Niagara Falls. When I moved to Miami three months ago, the weather was part of the appeal—along with chameleons and exotic plants and anything else that spoke to me of the tropics—but no one warned me about the rainy season.

Tonight I opt for dampness and quiet. I start rolling jalousied windows open to vent my fury, only to find myself under observation by Penny, who is standing outside the door to our screened porch, in the rain, waving at me. Penny lives in the other half of our semi-detached bungalow, and normally she keeps to herself—unless she wants something, a quality that has earned her the rancor of our elderly neighbors and put Jon and me somehow in league with her because of our shared youth. In fact, Penny is younger than we are, barely out of her teens, the mother of a six-year-old son.

"Oh, good, you're home, I thought maybe you weren't," Penny says, twirling the end of her hair like a third grader. "I came to ask you a favor." Surprise, surprise, I think sourly. "The sitter isn't coming tonight, and I wondered if Polo could sleep on your couch. I hate to ask but I'm in a bind." Penny works nights and sleeps days. Polo apparently has no father and is often left to his own devices.

Penny sees me hesitate. "Polo trusts you," she says quickly. As the only child in our row of bungalows, Polo is much maligned. There's talk among the retirees of petitioning the landlord to restrict the bungalows to adults, and so my sense of obligation is called up.

"Sure he can stay," I say. "It's no problem." Actually, Polo trusts us because Jon feeds him. It's that simple. When we first moved in, we used to eat breakfast on our porch each morning, which might have been romantic except that Polo was always playing next door on his porch. Skinny, sullen, he would stare at our eggs so pointedly that I could hardly swallow.

"Want some?" Jon would ask.

"I've already eaten," Polo would say, eyeing the food. This went on for a week.

"Ate what?" Jon asked finally.

"A Ho Ho," Polo said.

"A Ho Ho! Didn't anyone ever tell you about the four food groups?"

"No," Polo said.

"Meat, milk, grains and fruit. Eggs are meat, toast is grain, orange juice is fruit. Very healthy. You better come have one of these omelets," Jon said.

"I can't take food from strangers," Polo told him.

"A stranger? Me?"

"Sometimes strangers put something in your food," Polo said.

"I could see putting something in a drink," Jon said, "but in an omelet? You could even watch me cook it."

Jon is relentless in the face of need, a quality I once found endearing. After that Polo ate breakfast with us every day until school started.

So it isn't that Jon is irresponsible, luring Polo into a life of balanced meals, trying to cheer Resnick.

It's just that he's unpredictable. It annoys me that I should be carrying the baby of a man who doesn't show up to hear about it.

Our first date—if you could call it that—was indicative of things to come, and I ignored it completely.

Jon and I met in the snack bar my first day at the hospital, where I run a research lab and he does part-time social work while he's finishing law school. He picked me up, bought me lunch and talked for an hour about his friend Resnik, whose wife had left him.

"I'm taking Resnick diving in the Keys this weekend," he said finally. "Maybe it'll take his mind off his troubles. You can come with us if you want." He sounded so offhand that I said yes. We left on Friday after work and stopped in every bar on the road, more to play pool than to drink.

The next day Resnik dived while Jon taught me how to snorkel, pointing out different kinds of brightly colored fish. Resnik showed off a scar on his stomach: "The mark of an angry moray eel I frightened from its cave," he said.

"Childhood surgery," Jon whispered, touching his mouth to my ear. There was a lot of this discreet touching. Later we ate sandwiches in another bar, nursed sunburns (Jon rubbed sunburn cream into my shoulders) and played more pool before driving home.

"See, I was right," Jon said when he took me to the door of my apartment. "Resnik doesn't think about his wife when he's underwater. Did you notice?" I smiled, and Jon kissed me. That was the first time he called me sweet beak. He said he'd feed me black beans and rice in Cuban restaurants, take me waterskiing and teach me Spanish. He leered and said he could also think of other tropical delights. I laughed. How could I refuse? But that was in July, when spontaneity seemed appropriate, before this pregnancy and the rains of September.

At ten o'clock Polo is still wound up, excited about spending a night away from home, unable to sleep. We are drinking hot chocolate in the kitchen, though it's too warm for hot chocolate, and Polo is talking nonstop.

"Jon's pretty old to be going to school," he says, watching me with the hooded eyes of the urchin he's fast becoming, fishing for information.

"A lot of men his age go to law school," I say. "He worked for a while after he got out of college. Now he still works part of the time and goes to school part of the time. Listen, don't you have to go to school tomorrow?"

"Where does he work?"

"In an office in the same hospital where I work. He helps people who don't have enough money to pay their hospital bill." He also spends endless hours worrying about these people and bringing some of them home for meals. I don't tell Polo this.

"Are you a doctor?" he asks.

"No, a scientist. I do experiments." He's not impressed, and I can't say I blame him. Once I ran my personal life with as much precision as I did my lab, and I wouldn't have gotten pregnant in those days, either. Then I interviewed for my job in Miami, for the perfectly logical reason that it paid more, and the moment I set foot off the plane I abandoned logic entirely. Common sense bleaches thin when you emerge from the throes of a northern spring into tropical heat, though I'm not using this as an excuse. Even the colors were brighter than back home—magenta sunsets, greens so rich they seemed more a philosophical concept than a color. The job interview lasted a day, but I stayed five, lying on the beach at Crandon Park, thinking about childhood summers when I was mindless but happy, suspended in the hot, still center of the year. I would have taken the job even if they'd offered only half the salary they did. Back home I gave notice and sold the furniture I'd bought, so sensibly, when I turned 26 and decided it was time to live like an adult. And later, when I moved in with Jon, it was not because I hadn't yet found a permanent place to live in Miami—though that was true—but because I woke up without him the morning we came back from the Keys and felt empty, felt halved.

"Listen, Polo," I say. "Finish your hot chocolate, and then you absolutely have to go to sleep." I am thinking about my pregnancy, the rain, Jon's absence, all the things I didn't expect when I moved here. The firm note in my voice makes Polo gaze at me with what looks at first like respect, then caution, then—very definitely—defiance. He begins to drink with tiny sips, pausing in between, dawdling. For a moment I am angry, and then I recognize the rebellion of a neglected child.

"Never mind, take your time," I say, as much out of guilt as charity. "What difference if you stay up late?"

Polo smiles, but my heart closes to him even as I grin back. I see in Polo my own son six years from now—the pathetic, fatherless product of my wild venture south. Even his name is a nickname, a throwaway, and it occurs to me that in Miami people are fond of aliases, of keeping their real names, their real selves, secret. Penny must be Penelope, Polo is a game people play, Resnik's first name is lost with disuse and, if Jon is short for Jonathan, I've never been told. But I am Robin. Unprotected. Featherless, Jon would say. And I have no right to consider having the baby of a man I hardly know, who disappears at odd hours, leaves me with responsibilities I don't want—and may leave me altogether before long. I was going to tell him because I held out hope, but what if he is gracious about the child out of charity? The sensible thing is to keep my mouth shut and have the abortion quietly. In the past I would have done the sensible thing without a second thought.

"I don't know about you, Polo," I say, "but I have to turn in."

He puts the cup down, bewildered because I have gone back and forth so often over this matter of staying up, and he looks at me with eyes that register—very clearly—betrayal.

In the morning Jon is asleep when Penny comes to pick up Polo. He is obviously disappointed not to see Jon, but I don't offer to wake him, partly because I don't want to have to talk to him. When he got in last night, his kiss roused me from my heavy pregnant sleep, wouldn't let me retreat into it again all night. My exhaustion this morning is like sickness.

At work I call the women's clinic and make an appointment for a consultation later in the week. If nothing else, I will bring order back into my life. Order always gave me comfort before and will again. But the tiredness clings to me, and there is a fullness about the way I feel that disturbs me, because I rather like it, this sensation of carrying a child. Even at lunchtime, when I leave the windowless lab and see the sun still shining, no hint of rain, I am not cheered. I leave work early, thinking it's just as well Jon will be in class when I get home. I don't want to tell him I'm pregnant. Whatever he says will only confuse me.

But when I reach the bungalow, he is studying on the porch, smiling as if nothing could please him more than the sight of me.

"What brings you home at this odd hour?" he asks.

"Exhaustion," I say sourly. "I had a houseguest last night—Polo. He wouldn't go to sleep. I thought you had a class."

"I missed it. I had a houseguest, too—this morning. Polo's grandfather is sick, and Penny had to go to the hospital, so she left Polo with me. I took him to school and picked him up. She just came to get him a few minutes ago."

"I didn't know Polo *had* a grandfather."

"Well, he does."

"You shouldn't be such a soft touch."

"I know, but what else could I do? Let Polo wander the streets? Believe me, between him and Resnik . . . I'd rather be with just you." He does look tired, but maybe he is saying this to please me. I don't know what he's thinking, and I realize that I never have.

"Polo ought to have a daytime sitter, " I say—unreasonably, I know because, Penny can't afford one. "What a fate, to get stuck with a name like Polo—the name of a game. Like naming your kid Trivial Pursuit." I sound vindictive, but I am still angry about last night. "If I ever have a child," I yell at Jon, "I want him to have a perfectly ordinary name like David or Stephen. Nothing weird like Polo or horrible like Resnik's first name must be for him to end up being called by his last name."

Jon gives me a bewildered look, but manages to smile. "In other words, if you named your child Ignatius Wigbotham, you wouldn't want him called Iggy Wiggy."

"Precisely," I say. I am not amused.

"Resnik's name is Robert," Jon tells me. "Robert Resnick."

"Robert? Really? Just Robert?"

He nods. "Hideous name," he says. He is making fun of me, and I don't like it. "I don't even know your name," I yell. "I don't know if it's Jon for Jonathan, or —"

"Hey . . ." He starts toward me, but I move around the table, away from him. He follows, and I move again, as if we are playing tag. Jon is still smiling.

"Is it that funny?" I scream. "That I should want to know your name?" In our 77 days together—78 now—I have never raised my voice before. And now, in addition to screaming, I surprise myself by bursting into tears and am so embarrassed that I turn away.

"It's Jon," he says. "J-o-n. No *h*. No Jonathan. Just Jon. I thought you knew."

Now that he says it, I think maybe we had a discussion about this, but I can't remember. I start to cry harder.

"I'll tell you something else," Jon says. "Polo's name isn't like the game. It's Paulo, like Saint Paul with an *o*. His father lives up in Pompano."

Now I am crying so hard that I can't see to move around the table any more. I stop, feeling at once foolish and relieved that Paulo isn't named after a game. Jon's arm is circling me, and I have no energy to remove it.

"Personally," he says, "I always thought I'd name my own child something more avian. Oriole. Sparrow. Something like that."

He knows, I think. Then I realize there's no way he can know; he's just playing one of his Robin jokes. He is stroking my hair, and we stand there a long time. After a while I think: This isn't just another joke, he wouldn't be talking about naming his child bird names if he weren't trying to tell me something. Finally he shifts me to the other shoulder, where his shirt isn't so wet from my crying.

"I know you hate humidity," he says.

"What?"

"Humidity. You know . . ." He points to the damp spot he's moved me away from. I don't know anyone else who talks like this, and I know I'm going to tell him.

Of course, it may not work out.

Maybe he'll get bored with me. Maybe I'll get tired of his nights out, his giving all his time away. He will never be entirely reliable. But he is not the sort to abandon a child. And the worst I could end up is a well-paid scientist with a child who will make me laugh. The prospect seems not so terrible.

"Now that I've missed my class and you've come home so exhausted," Jon says, "let's take advantage of the situation and go to bed."

"It's four in the afternoon," I tell him.

"Love is not always a logical decision," he says.

"So I'm beginning to see." As we walk into the bedroom, I am thinking I ought not to tell him directly. I ought to paste a mock headline onto tomorrow's *Miami Herald*: Robin Lays Egg, Expects Baby Bird. The idea is so corny that it would have made me cringe three months ago, but Jon will like it. I don't mean to laugh, to give myself away so soon, but I do.

꒰

THIS APPEARED IN *MCCALL'S,* NOVEMBER 1985

KALEIDOSCOPE

The children were at each other again. Round and round went Melissa, brandishing a kaleidoscope that had sat, untouched until now, since Christmas.

"Give it to me!" squealed Peggy, the 10-year-old, scampering from living room to den after her sister.

"No! I want a turn!" Into the kitchen, around the table.

"Enough!" said Laura sharply, snatching the kaleidoscope away. "Nobody's going to have it if you can't share."

She shooed them away, wiping bits of unfinished tuna sandwiches from the table, wondering why the lunch wove no magic on their temperaments. She had taken off work to be with them during their spring break, hoping to do some cleaning while they played outside and her husband, Stan, was away on business. What she hadn't counted on was non-stop rain, the three of them being housebound like prisoners.

The phone rang just as Laura turned to the dirty dishes. It was the part-time girl from Taylor's Interiors where Laura worked in the art department.

"You know the batik project of yours I was supposed to finish? I think I ruined it. I guess I put the wax on wrong."

Incompetence, Laura thought.

"Happens all the time," she said, wanting desperately to see the damage, knowing it was out of the question. She should have finished the batik before she left, a long golden wall-hanging of sailboats in the sun.

"Mommy, Melissa bit me!" Peggy wailed, limping in dramatically, clutching her leg.

"Melissa, don't!" Did other eight-year-olds bite? Was her mothering that inadequate? "Be good for one hour. Then I'll make you a sundae."

She slammed the dishwasher shut and carried the kaleidoscope into the den where they wouldn't find it. Slumping into an armchair, gazing idly into the kaleidoscope's ever-changing pattern of color, she wondered what was wrong with her. Only 1:30 and she was tired. Lately her energy seemed to be dissipating, melting away. All week, coming downstairs each day to the havoc the girls had wrought, she found herself fighting the urge to crawl back into bed. Spring cleaning, indeed. If she picked up—or worse, marshaled them to pick up, the mess would take perhaps ten minutes to reappear. She wanted order: wanted it to be there, not to be in the never-ending process of trying to achieve it.

"Get off!" Peggy screamed from the living room.

"You started it!"

"I'm telling."

Laura hoped they wouldn't find her. Her gaze traveled to a shelf where dusty knick-knacks sat askew on top of a haphazard pile of magazines. A perfect mirror of her madhouse life, she thought. One of the hard-won conditions of her job was that she could take off during these vacations, hiring sitters only for a few hours after school and all day in summer. Theoretically, this allowed her to work guilt-free. In fact, she often looked up from a project she loved —crewel pillows, perhaps—to see the clock inching toward three and yearn to be home staving off the girls' after-school hunger with something more nutritious than Cheetos. The situation kept her flow of creativity at a trickle, when what she longed for was a steady gush.

Melissa, alone, slunk into the den. "Mommy, I'm hungry."

"I said I'd make a sundae in an hour."

"Now," she whined.

Laura had no energy to fight. In the kitchen she dished out globs of vanilla ice cream, doused it with chocolate syrup, and contemplated her ambivalence toward her offspring. It disturbed her because she'd always wanted children. She'd carried a vision of herself pushing their strollers, reading them books, mothering as eaily as she breathed. She also carried a picture of her career—as a ballerina, a pilot, an artist. What she had not had was a sense of where the visions would overlap.

"Here!" she said, setting the bowls on the table with what she hoped was enthusiasm. "Peggy, when you're finished put the dishes in the sink, okay? I'm going up to clean the bathroom."

"Okay." Turning ten had inspired Peggy to feign more competence than she actually possessed. She shot Melissa an *I'm in charge here* glance as Laura left.

Kneeling in the shower stall, a spray bottle of cleaner in her hand, Laura found herself devising ways to get away to Taylor's, to see what had been done to her batik. Scrubbing, she was reminded of the irony that aside from her twin visions of herself as career woman and mother, she had always believed her life would lead to one perfect, climactic moment of work. At some undeniable instant, she would dance the ultimate dance (in her ballerina days), land the plane despite insurmountable odds, paint the perfect stroke.

Now, with her happiness hinging on the inaccessible batik, she feared that even when the girls were older, the perfect moment would fail to materialize. Or if it did, she'd be too exhausted to enjoy it. Face it, she was half exhausted already.

Peggy, her face twisted with disappointment, wandered into the bathroom. "Look what I did." A streak of chocolate syrup wended its way down the front of her white T-shirt. "Do you think it'll come out?"

"Probably. Try rinsing it with water at the laundry tub."

"Okay." Peggy was forever spilling milk and breaking dishes. When worried, she contorted her face into gnome-like bumps and crevices. Laura's bitterness dissolved: she loved her children. It was only that, right now, she would rather be at work.

The shriek rose from the laundry room high and piercing, instantly recognizable as terror rather than mirth. Laura froze with her finger on the spray bottle, then bolted down the steps.

"Mommy! Peggy's got bleach in her eye," Melissa screamed.

Peggy was leaning over the laundry tub, clawing at her face with both hands. "I can't see!"

"Don't worry, we'll wash it out."

Hands shaking, Laura pulled Peggy's curly dark hair back until she looked skyward, then turned on the cold water full force. With her free hand she sent a stream of water directly into her daughter's eye.

"Ouch. Ouch! Don't!" Laura's heart thudded, but she held on so Peggy couldn't wriggle free and kept the water coming. "We're going to see Dr. Williams," she announced when she finally turned off the tap.

Peggy pulled away, frantic. "Why? It's bad, isn't it? I still can't see."

"Not as bad as you think." Laura's heartbeat was a storm, her voice a sunny morning. She led Peggy out of the laundry room, toward the car, Melissa following. Peggy curled in the front, no matter that this wasn't allowed, moaning with pain as Laura steered with one hand, stroked her daughter's head with the other.

"Is she all right?" Melissa, too, was now in tears.

"I'm blind, aren't I?" Peggy wailed.

"Of course you're not blind. Look out of your other eye." This sharply. Then, very softly, "Don't, honey. It'll be all right. Now tell me what happened."

"She tried to get the syrup out of the blouse," Melissa said.

"With straight *bleach*?"

"She was going to surprise you."

* * *

Lou Williams was not only a fine ophthalmologist; he was also a trusted friend. He peered at the eye so calmly that Peggy stopped moaning.

"How much bleach did you get in the eye?"

"Just a couple of drops."

"Okay. Here's my hand over here. What do you see?"

"Everything's fuzzy."

"Well, that's to be expected. We'll fix you right up."

When the eye had been dressed and the girls banished to the outer office, Lou turned serious. "It's a nasty burn. Going to be painful for a day or two."

"But there'll be no damage to her vision?"

"Too soon to say, Laura. All I can tell you is, you're lucky you got to her right away."

"Yes, lucky," Laura said. But her mouth was so dry she could hardly get the words out, and her palms were wet as tears.

Peggy was home the whole next week, with a gooey ointment over her eye and a patch over that. Stan had returned from his trip, but he went to work as usual so Peggy wouldn't think the situation was particularly grave. Laura took off another five days. Peggy brooded, dogging her mother's steps.

"When you take the patch off, I can't see," she complained. "Only light."

"That's because of the medicine. It's too thick to see through," Laura said, hauling the vacuum into the den.

"You're just saying that."

"Why would I? You'll be fine. Look, here's that kaleidoscope you and Melissa were fighting over. Now you can look at it all you want."

Briefly, Peggy pressed the tube to her good eye, turning it to change the design. Then she lost interest. "If I'm not blind, why does it still hurt?"

"Because you burned it. A burn always hurts," Laura sighed.

On the third day, the art director from Taylor's dropped by with some sketches for crewel work Laura had left on her desk. "Think you have the energy to fool with these while you're home?" To her surprise, Laura did. She found herself drawing as Peggy worried, functioning as if her fingers were a separate entity—"You're sure I'm okay, Mom? "Absolutely"—even as the spectre of blindness haunted the room like another presence. Laura felt at once selfish and grateful that she was able to take pleasure in her work.

On Friday Lou Williams washed the last of the ointment from Peggy's eye. "Read the letters on the chart now," he told her. Laura held her breath.

"E . . . F . . . P . . ." Peggy read tentatively. Then

more quickly: "T . . O. . .Z." Her face began to transform itself from gnarled gnome to ten-year-old girl, as if it had been ironed smooth with steam.

"All right!" she said, reaching the bottom of the chart.

Lou winked. "Now you can start making up all that school work." More seriously, he turned to Laura. "You know, I was a little concerned. With a burn like that, it's hard to be sure. But there's no damage."

Laura felt as if all her muscles had unclenched at once, after a week as a human fist. Twenty-twenty vision! Reprieve! She was actually trembling.

In the parking lot Peggy seemed genuinely penitent. "I guess that would never have happened if I'd washed the shirt with water like you said."

"It certainly wouldn't." Laura tried for sternness but couldn't mask her smile. Could this be her daughter speaking? Sounding so mature? "Next time, leave the bleach bottle alone."

In the back of the car, Peggy fell instantly asleep, exhausted from her ordeal. And Laura, after weeks of weariness was suddenly wide awake. She drove to Taylor's Interiors, had her assistant bring the batik outside so she could look at it, and surveyed the damage. Not hopeless after all. The fabric had ended up so pale . . . perhaps it could be redyed?

Driving home, Laura saw herself putting the finishing touches on golden sailboats against an azure sky . . . arranging with Peggy's teachers for make-up work . . . going to the grocery to restock their depleted pantry. There was no way to do all of it, and all of it well. But behind her, Peggy began to snore, her mouth wide open in ridiculous and fearless abandon, and Laura felt nearly content. Perhaps all lives were fragmented. Perhaps even turning the batik into a genuine work of art would be just a small moment among many—not the great climactic one she'd imagined. In the brief instant before she remembered she was late for Melissa's piano lesson, the pieces of her life danced before her as bright as the pattern in the kaleidoscope—each with its own color, constantly moving—as perfect, in its way, as her daughter's sight.

꒭

THIS APPEARED IN *ENCORE MAGAZINE*, MAY 9, 1991

THE BABYSITTER

There was something bizarre about the house right from the beginning, but bizarre in a cheerful way. The rooms echoed, yet their high ceilings muted the boys' shouting, which was a pleasure after the din of the apartment. And though Susan was alarmed when they disappeared for hours into the extra rooms, still she was pleased to have them fall asleep instantly at bedtime, after so much running around. Maybe her sense of oddness was only that the place was so big compared to what they were used to or that she was so enormously pregnant and trying so hard to get things finished before the baby came. If Susan had the sense of being watched from time to time, she told herself that the eyes were friendly, protective, and gave her company on those long evenings when she painted the kitchen alone.

It was unusual that they'd bought the house in the first place—a farmhouse now engulfed by suburbs, more than a century old and affordable only because of its poor condition. With two young children and another on the way, they were lucky to find it. Greg took an evening teaching job to help pay for the remodeling, and Susan spent hours sanding the woodwork.

On weekends, when she and Greg worked together, her uneasiness went away. Only during the week, on the nights when she was alone, did the eyes seem to be following her, assessing her, more curious than threatening.

Of course it could have been the kids. At four, Lucas was not above sneaking downstairs after bedtime, peeking at his mother from the staircase around the corner, then sneaking away when Susan looked. Or Ronny, wound up from the excitement of first grade. But both boys slept so soundly after exploring the house that she doubted they had the energy to spy. Besides, Susan had the feeling it was not a child watching her but some intelligence, older, more responsible. A crazy notion, but there it was.

*   *   *

Then the baby—Mindy—was born the second week in December, and Susan had no time for her imaginings. When she came home from the hospital, she was too busy to dwell on the possibility of curious, watching eyes.

Mindy's nursery was tiny, a narrow sliver of a room. When she began sleeping through the night at less than two weeks, Susan decided the room agreed with her very much.

What a child Mindy was! "Did you ever see a baby whose pacifier never falls out of her mouth?" Susan would ask Greg. "Did you ever see a child who never kicks off her covers?" Susan was certain that her daughter was the most contented baby she had ever known.

In April, when financial necessity demanded that Susan go back to work, she knew it would be all right. Carolyn Westfall, a patient, trustworthy woman who lived nearby, was happy to have Mindy with her during the day.

"You won't have a bit of trouble with the baby," Susan boasted. "She's really exceptional." So when Carolyn mentioned that Mindy would never stay down for a nap, Susan was surprised. At home the baby slept two or three hours at a stretch and woke cooing to the mobile over her crib. When Mindy continued to nap fitfully at Carolyn's, Susan wrote it off to adjustment pangs . . . until the night of the storm.

It was early May, unseasonably warm. The sticky heat had left Susan feeling especially drained, and it was all she could do to check the children before turning in. The boys were all right, but she had to open Mindy's window against the closeness and remove her zippered blanket, leaving her to sleep in just her light pajamas. She placed the zip-up blanket on the rocking chair across from the crib. Then she fell into her own bed, exhausted.

She didn't know what time it was when the thunder began and lightning flickered against her eyes, dragging her toward wakefulness. The wind was wild in the yard. Old oak limbs clawed against the windows, and rain came in little bursts through the newly installed screens. Beside her, Greg slept on.

Still half asleep, Susan got up, shut the heavy window beside their bed and then padded down the hall to tend to the boys' room and finally to Mindy's.

The silence hit her as she stepped inside the nursery, a silence so deep that she was startled. Then she realized it wasn't silence so much as that sense of storm cushioned by walls and layers of windowpane. She had expected the wind and rain to be howling through the window, but when her eyes focused she saw that the window she had opened earlier was securely closed. And Mindy . . . Mindy was zipped into her blanket!

Opposite the crib, the rocking chair was moving slightly, as if set in motion by someone brushing against it moments before . . . removing the blanket Susan had put there, putting it on the baby. A scent filled the room, not of rain or even talcum powder but of violets. Watching her peaceful, sleeping daughter snuggled securely in her blanket, Susan did not know whether to be grateful or afraid.

She couldn't sleep for the rest of the night. She thought of the eyes that had followed her while she worked on the house. Perhaps they were also responsible tor Mindy's pacifier being always in place? For her never seeming to fuss at naptime? Even—oddly— for her perennial contentment? When the first clear light finally seeped across the sky, washed and golden after the storm, Susan shook Greg's shoulder. By the time she blurted out the story, he had managed to sit up, disheveled but fully conscious, giving her a look she could only describe as patronizing.

"Obviously one of the kids," he said in a deliberately level voice. "One of the kids went in there just before you did, closed the window, and went back to bed."

"Oh, sure. One of the kids. Why didn't they close their own window then? I was in the boys' room before I went to Mindy's, and they were fast asleep. Ronny sleeps like a rock. And how do you account for the blanket? But I'll ask."

The children stirred. Susan asked. Both of them looked at her as if she had lost her mind. Lucas shook his head. Ronny was more direct. "Why would we try to get the cover on her? It's hard," he said. "Besides, that's the mother's job."

That, Susan supposed, was when her uneasiness returned. Ronny had been right when he said that covering the baby was the mother's job. She supposed she had looked forward to comforting Mindy if she had been wakened by the storm. She supposed she'd been as much disappointed as relieved to find the job already done by someone, or something, else—unseen, kindly, but eerie. A ghost. She couldn't bring herself to fear this ghost, which protected her child and kept her cooing—but she did rather resent it.

At first, the jealousy was just a small twinge. Summer passed. Mindy sat, Mindy pulled herself up. It was ridiculous to be envious of whatever it was that made Mindy so happy.

Then, that fall, when Susan and Greg were

invited to a party, Greg's teenage sister came to baby-sit. Beth was the boys' favorite aunt, cheerful and young and as enthusiastic about junk food as they were.

Greg had forgotten to turn on the porch light, and it was dark in the driveway when he and Susan came home. In the dim glow of the bulb from the upstairs hallway, they could see a figure standing in the baby's room. Beth's long fair hair fell against her white shirt, and the outline of her arms was just barely visible as she held the baby to her shoulder.

Hurrying into the house, Susan made directly for the stairs, but the sight of Beth sprawled dozing on the family-room couch stopped her. The television buzzed, tuned to a shopping channel that must have put her to sleep. Then who . . . ? Susan and Greg bolted for the steps at the same moment.

Upstairs, the hallway was quiet, the door to the nursery closed. Greg motioned Susan to stand behind him. With a swift movement, he flung the door to Mindy's room wide. And there she was . . . curled up on her belly, breathing softly as if she hadn't moved for hours. The room was peaceful, empty . . . and filled with the scent of violets.

"Beth always falls asleep to the TV. She's probably only been out for a minute," Greg insisted as they walked downstairs. "She was probably up there checking Mindy right before."

But Beth was hard to wake, and, when she lifted her head from the couch, there was a mark on her cheek where the fabric had cut in, as if she'd been lying there for a long while. "Beth, try to wake up," Greg instructed. "When did you check the baby last?"

"I put her down about eight and looked at her at ten." Beth looked sheepish. "I guess I fell asleep a while ago, huh?"

"Perfectly all right," said Greg.

Later, after Greg had dropped Beth at home, he and Susan sat in the kitchen drinking tea. "Beth probably went up and then forgot," Greg insisted.

"What about that smell of violets?"

"Must be Beth's perfume."

"Beth only uses—I forget. But nothing that smells like violets."

Greg was adamant. "It looked like Beth up there with Mindy. It had to be." But Susan knew it wasn't Beth. The girl in the window had hair longer than Beth's, hanging loose on her shoulders. Beth was always careful to toss her hair back. And Beth had been wearing a loose beige sweater, but the girl in the window seemed to be wearing a nightshirt, or a gown, and it had been not beige but . . . so white.

"Well, you can think what you want to," Susan said. "But I know it's a ghost."

Susan recalled the smell of violets and imagined Mindy's small form, Inside her, waves of relief mingled with anger and irritation. It's *my* job to comfort her, Susan thought. *Mine.*

But how could she be jealous of a ghost? It must be the *weirdness* of it all that bothered her—the dark, nagging sense that the *thing*, whatever it was, was watching over Mindy because it didn't trust Susan.

Still, her resentment was simple enough. Her work already took her away from Mindy most of the day: when she was home, she wanted to be responsible for her daughter's well-being all by herself.

The incidents became more telling as Mindy grew older. Once, when she was a toddler, Lucas's friend Pete teased her until she cried. Susan was just about to intervene when Pete announced he was going to the bathroom. Seconds later he came rushing out, pale and distraught.

"Somebody pushed me!" he screamed, though clearly there wasn't anybody there. They didn't see much of Pete after that. Nobody was really sorry. It was just that Susan would have preferred to handle the situation herself; she should have spoken to Pete for teasing Mindy.

She was the mother, wasn't she? Wasn't that her role? On the day Mindy lost her balance at the top of the stairs, Susan raced up to break her fall. Then the oddest thing happened. Suddenly, in midair, Mindy seemed to shift position and actually float, until she was close enough to the banister to grab hold. Mindy laughed, as if it were a great joke. But Susan, reaching her, found herself trembling—not just for Mindy's safety but at the idea that the long, protective arm that had caught her had been not Susan's own but the ghost's.

Inevitably, the story of the strange happenings began to get around, She and Greg were careful not to talk about them in front of the children, but the boys knew and found them funny, The only one who really seemed oblivious was Mindy, who had learned to talk and seemed to regard "the lady in white" as perfectly natural,

With the story out, Susan should not have been surprised when the local paper called, wanting to do a feature on the ghost. Two days after the article appeared, the phone call came.

"We lived in that house from 'seventy to 'seventy-five," a no-nonsense woman's voice announced, after she had identified herself as Mrs. Singleton. "You're absolutely right, of course. We had an incident ourselves when our granddaughter came to visit. Afterward I did a good bit of research. I thought you'd like to know."

"Oh?" Susan said.

"Belinda, our granddaughter, came down with the most awful virus. It was very frightening—she was only five at the time. We had her in the same room where your daughter apparently sleeps. She kept asking for the lady with blond hair who kept coming in to put her hand on her forehead."

From the land records in the courthouse, Mrs. Singleton had learned that the house had been in the hands of the Farney family for years during and after the Civil War. An old library book about the town's early settlers had yielded up more. The Farneys had farmed the acreage surrounding the house, and the place had had a singularly peaceful history during those troubled times. Except for one thing: The young bride of one of the Farney boys had died in childbirth there in the 1880s, in the very room where

Mindy now slept At the time of her death, the girl had been only 15.

"They used certain rooms for birthing rooms in those days," Mrs. Singleton said. "And married those girls off so young, poor things, it's a wonder most of them survived. I'm not one to believe in spirits, but one can quite imagine the ghost of a young girl grieving for her lost child and her lost life."

"What was her name?" Susan whispered, stunned by the transformation of suspicion into history.

"Hannah," the woman said, sadly, "Hannah Farney, dead at age fifteen."

"Did her baby live? What was it, a boy or a girl?" Susan asked urgently, fearing she already knew the answer.

"A little girl," Mrs. Singleton said firmly. "It died, too, the same day."

Susan could hardly breathe, but she managed one more question. "What did they wear, in those birthing rooms? Anything special?"

"Oh, those smock-like nightgowns, I would imagine. I'm really not certain."

But Susan herself was certain that the presence watching out for Mindy was the ghost of Hannah Farney herself.

Next it was the big metropolitan paper that wanted to write about the ghost. Susan felt that she should object, but since she had allowed an article once, how could she refuse? By now the boys enjoyed regaling their friends with ghost stories. Mindy, at three, was still a bit confused about the issue, but even she loved hamming in front of the photographer who came out to take a picture of the whole family next to Mindy's bed. The crib had been taken down, but the rocking chair was still in its place.

"It was the ghost that pushed me that time," asserted Pete, who had resumed his friendship with Lucas in the light of the new publicity.

"Yeah, and, if you don't watch your mouth, she'll push you again," Lucas said importantly.

"Boys!"

Only Mindy, listening, suddenly did not seem amused by the discussion. She retreated to her room, oddly quiet.

"She's the ghost, isn't she?" Mindy asked when Susan trailed her upstairs. "The lady in white."

Susan's heart beat unevenly in her throat. She'd known Mindy would make the connection sometime, but she didn't think it would be like this. Before Susan could answer, Mindy said resolutely, "She smells good. She does." Then she rushed out to find her Teddy bear, as if to keep Susan from speaking.

A few nights later Mindy woke in tears out of a deep sleep. "It's her," she sobbed to Susan, who had rushed in.

"Who, darling?" asked Susan, stroking her hair. "The lady?" But Mindy didn't answer. Susan held her, stroking her hair, until she fell back to sleep.

"Nightmares," Greg said, when Susan returned to their room. "Too many ghost stories. She'll get over it." But, as the weather grew colder, Mindy became ever more sleepless, waking often. Where before the ghostly baby-sitter had seemed to give her comfort, now the idea of "the lady" began to frighten her.

"Are there really ghosts?" she asked.

"Some people think so and some people don't," Susan replied lamely, suddenly unsure how to answer. Her lack of certainty only confused Mindy more. The child could not seem to reconcile the idea of "ghosts" with her knowledge of the white-clad girl who had taken care of her. Susan felt helpless. Suddenly the ghost could not protect Mindy anymore— and neither could Susan.

One cold night Mindy woke shrieking, more panicked than Susan had ever seen her. "She's here!" Mindy screamed. "Mommy, come quick."

Susan ran into her daughter's room, where Mindy sat up in bed, illuminated by bright moonlight, with terror in her eyes. A faint odor of violets filled the air,

"Mindy, what is it?"

"She's here! She is!"

"Where? What is it?"

"Over there. Don't you see her? Look." In the corner where Mindy was pointing, the old rocking chair stood. It was empty, bathed in moonlight, but rocking, ever so slightly.

"I don't see anything," Susan said.

"It's her! Mommy, make her go away." And Susan knew she must. There was nothing in the chair, but Susan began speaking to it, soothingly, logically, as if she were speaking to something real.

"It was different when Mindy was a baby," she

said to the chair. "You could watch over her, and she wasn't afraid, But now she's bigger and having a . . . having a ghost in the house frightens her. Don't you see?" She held Mindy's hand as she spoke, feeling the small muscles gradually relax. Taking courage from that, she went on. "You're doing more harm than good," she said to the chair. "I know that isn't what you want. So I'm going to have to ask you to do something difficult. I have to ask you to go away."

Perhaps she imagined it, or perhaps there really was a charged pause in the room, as if the presence were weighing the information, deciding what to do. And perhaps it was only her imagination that the chair stopped rocking. But she was sure—absolutely sure—that the scent of violets suddenly left the room.

Mindy sighed.

"She's gone now," Susan said. Already Mindy's eyes were closing.

Susan covered her and sat for a moment on the bed. The baby-sitter was gone. And gone, too, Mindy's fears. Susan sighed with relief. Then a quick shiver went through her. Much as Susan had resented it, the ghost's protection had been reliable. What if something should happen? But tonight it was she who had seen to Mindy's welfare; tomorrow she would do the same. It was what she had always wanted. And, in the sharp, chilly air, it was not doubt but joy that rose within her.

༄

THIS APPEARED IN *MCCALL'S*, MARCH 1987

WATCHING FROM THE WINGS

My married sister, Lacey, seems all right when she gets off the plane. She seems all right when we pick up her luggage and even when we start off in Mama's car, which Lacey notices I drive very smoothly for someone who's had her permit only three months and officially isn't allowed to drive by herself at all. All this is a big relief. Before I came to the airport, Mama said: "Don't ask what's bringing Lacey all the way down here right after Christmas, you hear, Mary Beth? I will not trust you with this car if I have to worry about you saying something tactless, like is there trouble between Lacey and Brian." If you could see Brian, who married Lacey on the ninth of May, you would know why we don't want them having trouble.

Lacey still seems all right when we pull out of the parking lot where the attendant does a double take when he looks at her. Lacey has dark, thick lashes and enormous eyes, one of which happens to be brown and the other blue. This is because of Mama having German measles when she was pregnant. Brian says he could never decide if he liked brown-eyed girls or blue-eyed ones, "So I figured once I got both in the same woman, I'd better hang on."

Lacey nods at the parking lot attendant as if his staring is perfectly polite. She even has the good manners to comment on the crisp sunny weather, saying, "I haven't been this warm in months." So it takes me by surprise when we pass the "Welcome to North Carolina" sign and she says with an unmistakable catch in her voice: "I don't remember that."

"I think it's mainly for the film people," I tell her, being something of an expert on films. By the time you land in Wilmington you have flown over most of North Carolina practically to South Carolina, so you're kind of surprised to see a state welcome sign. But if you think of it as Southern hospitality for the actors and directors coming in from California . . . well, that makes a lot of sense. Mama says don't get started on the film people and especially not the movie I'm in, which was released three weeks ago and which I plan to take Lacey to see. But it's not my fault the welcome sign is there or that we have to pass the film studio on our way into town.

"We didn't shoot at the studio," I say to make conversation. "We shot on location the whole time, and to this day I have not seen the sound stages inside the studio itself." This is the type of thing you can say to a married sister who lives in West Lafayette, Indiana, where there is no film studio at all.

"Well, maybe next time," Lacey says. She understands that being an extra in one teen film is not going to be the end of it. By the time we reach the mall, where Mama manages The Boutique, I think after all Lacey has come home mainly because she's tired of cold weather (as she's said many times on the phone) and wants to visit while Purdue University, where Brian goes to school and Lacey works, is still on break.

A bunch of seagulls live in one corner of the mall parking lot. The ocean is just a few miles away, so the only reason I can figure them living here is that eating the leftover food people throw out is easier than catching fish. The birds flap up as we drive past, then settle down.

"Do you know how long it's been since I've seen seagulls?" Lacey sighs.

"Middle of May, I guess." Myself, I can't get too fired up about seagulls.

"Middle of May," Lacey says with that catch in her voice again, as if it were a million years ago.

Inside the mall, every girl between my age and Lacey's seems to be shopping at The Boutique's after-Christmas clearance. Mostly it is only cold enough for a few heavy sweaters, so it's nice if you can get them on sale. Mama had hoped to take off the rest of the day, but she says to Lacey: "Honey, there's no way I can get out of here with this crowd. How about if we meet at K&W for dinner? Then tomorrow I'll have the whole day."

Lacey looks a little disappointed, so I say, "After we eat, I'll take her to my movie."

"Now Mary Beth, I told you to let Lacey get settled first."

But Lacey says to Mama: "There's nothing I'd rather do tonight than see Mary Beth on film."

The next thing we do is drive home to let Lacey unpack. Between our house and the one next door is Mr. Williams' camellia hedge, the early-blooming kind with pink flowers that give off a sweet, spicy smell Mama says reminds her of winter holidays and the brief dimming of the Southern light. Mama is very poetic about flowers. When we were little, before Daddy died, Lacey and I used to judge how soon Christmas would be by Mr. Williams' camellias—sort of like an Advent calendar. They started blooming at Thanksgiving and were almost finished by Christmas—the way they are when we get out of the car with a few flowers still hanging on the bush but a lot of petals on the ground. Lacey takes one look at the hedge and begins to cry.

"I almost missed the camellias!" she sobs. This strikes me as odd because she and Brian deliberately spent the holidays with Brian's parents in Indiana in hopes of its being a white Christmas, which it was. Myself, I have never seen a white Christmas except on TV.

I go over and put my arm around her shoulder. "You had a fight with Brian, didn't you?"

"You know what grows in Indiana at this time of year?" she cries. "Nothing. Nothing!"

"You can tell me about it," I say. "I mean, everybody has fights."

She looks at me with her brown eye and her blue one, both of which are now bloodshot. Then she recovers herself. She takes a tissue from her pocket, blows her nose, and tries to smile. "I know you won't believe it, but this has nothing to do with Brian." I nod, but she is right that I don't believe her.

Later we are sitting in the K&W Cafeteria right across the street from the mall. Lacey used to make fun of K&W's country cooking but tonight, because Mama has only a few minutes to gulp her her food, Lacey doesn't complain. She eats no meat, just four different kinds of vegetables—okra, cabbage, black-eyed peas and turnip greens—which is odd for someone who never in her life ate a vegetable un-less Mama nagged her. I wonder if she and Brian have become vegetarians, which is a common thing for college students to do. Of course Lacey herself isn't a student, only married to one. She tells Mama about the professor she works for in the psychology department or about Christmas at Brian's parents' or the snow.

"It's just your typical teen movie," I tell Lacey when we get in the theater. I've seen it seven times, but I don't want to make it any big deal. "There're two scenes where you can see me real good."

What was Troy Wicket like?" She was a fan even before she met Brian.

"Pretty normal. I mean, after you shoot a scene to-gether twenty times, it's hard to be too puffed up."

I can tell Lacey wants to hear more, so I go on: "The first day this one extra said to him: 'Mr. Wicket, can I ask you something?' But he said right away, 'Not Mr. Wicket. Call me Troy. Don't make me feel like an old man.' After that we all called him Troy. I mean, he's only twenty-one."

"Is he as good-looking in person?"

The truth is, he isn't. He has pits in his skin you can't see on the screen. I don't want to admit this to Lacey. "Not as good looking as Brian," I say.

Her face loses all expression. I think: uh-oh, Mama is really going to let me have it now. But right then the lights go down. I sit back and wait for Lacey's reaction when she hears me say my line.

Lacey doesn't know I say a line in the movie. Mama and I agreed to let it be a surprise, because we didn't know until the movie was released whether the line had ended up on the screen or the editing room floor. Last spring when we filmed, Lacey was so caught up in getting married and going off to Indiana that she didn't pay much attention.

Everybody had said Lacey and Brian would turn out to be just a summer romance, him coming here to work at the beach two years ago and then going all the way back to Purdue . But he spent all winter calling and coming to see her. He sent her records like "Pretty Blue Eyes" and "Brown-Eyed Girl." When he finally proposed, Mama said jokingly, "I guess that's because he can't afford to keep up this courting anymore."

After that it was all Mama and Lacey could do to prepare for the wedding in May. There wasn't much money, so Mama baked the cake and Lacey sewed the dresses. There were hundreds of errands to run.

But since I didn't have my permit yet, I mostly got in the way. Finally my friend Marianne said, "Come on, go to the casting call with me, they don't really need you here." So I did. We filled out an application and attached our snapshot. A week later they called us, along with two hundred other high school kids who wanted to be extras.

The opening credits come on, superimposed over Troy Wicket riding his bike through an intersection when a car runs a light and hits him. He's not badly hurt except his leg. The rest of the movie is about Troy coming back to his high school and going out for track to build up his injured muscles. First you see him with a cast on, limping around school. Then the cast comes off, but he still limps. Then he tries running. I am in a classroom scene that was filmed the week before Lacey's wedding and a scene at the track filmed the week after. I don't tell her it took five whole days to make two scenes, or that most of the time was spent waiting around. I only tell her it was fun, which it was.

The director told us it cost twenty thousand dollars to shoot a minute of film. He said that's why "Quiet on the set" really meant it. There were dozens of tech people around. They had blackout screens made of wire and black velvet, that they put anyplace they thought there would be a shadow they didn't like. They shined lights into the windows to look like sun. They moved the booms and held light meters up to Troy's face, and they said things like: "We have sound," and "Rolling." One man even had a camera attached to him by straps and springs, so he could run beside Troy, bouncing up and down, and the camera would stay perfectly level. I have never seen anything like it in my life.

"That's you!" Lacey whispers when the track scene comes on.

"Just wait," I tell her. We are all sitting on the bleachers and Troy is running the four hundred. He is in the lead when suddenly his leg gives way. He limps off the track. The camera focuses on the bleachers again. A boy sitting behind me yells down to the coach: "That's what you get for running a cripple!" We girls look back at the boy. I stand up. My face is set and angry. I don't look ugly, I just look strong. "You better shut up," I tell the boy, "Or you're going to be the cripple." Later, of course, Troy will begin to win.

Lacey's mouth drops open. "You didn't tell me you spoke, Mary Beth."

"Didn't tell you I got paid almost four hundred dollars to say it, either!" I say.

"Ssshh," says someone in back of us.

On the way home, I tell her the rest. How the director decided there ought to be a little commotion in the stands. "You," he said, pointing to the boy behind me. "You're mad at the coach for letting Troy run. And you—" he pointed to me, "you're the one who's going to defend him." It wasn't even in the script!

Later the lady from the casting agency said to me: "There must have been something about you to make him notice you over the other girls, Mary

Beth." I hadn't thought about it before, but I guessed there was.

All spring I'd been feeling sort of invisible. There was Lacey, with Brian hanging around her. There was Mama so busy with the wedding. And me not even able to drive. Then at the wedding I was dressed up to be maid of honor but every eye was on Lacey in her drifts of white. All spring Lacey was like one of Mr. Williams' camellias, her life opening out like layers of petals, pink and perfumey. And me a tight little bud. It wasn't that I was jealous. Nobody loves Lacey more than I do. But I was tired of being invisible.

After the director chose me to say my line, I felt as much a part of the movie as those tech people doing lights and props and sound. I wasn't invisible anymore. The director had picked me. I could work summers as a production assistant. After high school I could study film. Become a film editor. A director. A star.

Instead of my thirty dollars for being an extra that day, I got a contract to be paid Screen Actors' Guild wage—more than four hundred dollars to say one line I'd have been glad to say for nothing. More money than I made all winter babysitting for the Moores across the street.

"Do you believe it, Lacey? I was rich."

Lacey is laughing, hearing all this. "I envy you, Mary Beth," she says.

"Are you kidding? That's when you were on your honeymoon with Brian."

43

Lacey sighs. "I wouldn't mind a chance to be in a movie."

It occurs to me for the first time that, in spite of being married to a hunk like Brian, Lacey is stuck working in the psychology department all day and here I am, in movies. Pretty as she is, with one blue eye and one brown eye, Lacey is probably too confusing-looking to be an extra.

The next day we all go to the store to buy chicken for supper. It's natural Lacey wants to look around, her being a married woman now, but she lingers at the produce section so long that I wonder again about her and Brian being vegetarians. Finally she picks up a bunch of collard greens and says: "I doubt half the population of Indiana even knows what greens look like—or fresh okra either."

I see then this is not about vegetables, this is about homesickness.

"I remember when I first came to Wilmington, I couldn't believe they didn't grow apples," Mama says to make her feel better. Mama was raised in the mountains where there are apple trees.

"Yes, but at least Wilmington isn't bleak," Lacey says. "I have never lived in such a bleak place in all my life."

"The only place you ever lived was here," Mama tells her.

"Yes, and last summer you said West Lafayette was the cutest little college town you ever saw," I add. "You said some parts of it were almost as pretty as Chapel Hill."

"That was before the winter," she says, looking at me fiercely.

By now we are in the checkout line. Lacey has a pouty look that stays even as we carry the groceries to the car. We drive down a street lined with live oaks so thick they blot out the sky. Lacey and I used to ride our bikes here, under the tunnel of branches hung with Spanish moss, and pretend it was the black hole of Calcutta.

Now Lacey says: "You're lucky to live someplace green in winter. In Indiana, everything is brown."

"One live oak is pretty," I say. "Twenty in a row are spooky." It's as if she doesn't remember the way things actually are. "Anyway, out there you have snow."

"Try driving in snow. Try having snow melt down the inside of your boots, Mary Beth."

I figure all this has something to do with Brian. I figure we will get to the real problem in a minute.

"You'll get used to snow," Mama says.

"No. I don't believe I ever will." But still we do not say anything about Brian.

Only two good things happen the rest of the day. First, Brian calls and Lacey talks to him as if they still like each other. Second, Mama makes the fried chicken and Lacey eats it, proving that she is not a vegetarian.

The next day is Lacey's last full day home before she's scheduled to fly back. Up 'til now the weather has been crisp, but in the morning when we wake up, it must be close to seventy degrees. It's the beginning of one of those balmy spells we get all through the winter.

Mama is due into work at eleven, but when Lacey oohs and ahs over the warm weather, Mama says without hesitation: "We'll spend the day at the beach."

Never in all the years she's been working has Mama called in sick when she wasn't. She says this is something you cannot do when you are supporting a family. But today she does. She calls even though the beach is fifteen minutes away and she could be back in plenty of time. She's acting almost as strange as Lacey.

The next thing I know we are walking on the sand, wrapped in sweaters against the wind. In spite of the warmth, the breeze is cold coming off the ocean. The water is green and foamy, and the sky is not sure if it wants to be gray or blue.

Bunches of seagulls gather on the beach and then take turns flying out over the water, searching for fish. They circle and dip, their wings broad and white. They look nicer here than they do in the mall parking lot. Lacey is so serious that I think she's going to get misty-eyed again. But when she finally speaks, it has nothing to do with birds.

She sits down on the sand and says, "I can't go back."

"Oh?" Mama sits down, too, in such a way that it's clear why she broke her rule and called in sick.

Right on cue, Lacey bursts into tears. "I just can't!" she sobs.

Mama scooches over on the sand and hugs her. "Well, let's have it," she says.

"Do you know what they did at Christmas, Mama?"

"What?"

"Here I was, so excited about a white Christmas and all . . ." She starts crying so hard that she can't even speak. I figure something terrible happened. Then she blubbers: "They opened their presents Christmas *Eve*."

Of course this doesn't have the first thing to do with snow or Indiana, much less with Brian, but since Lacey is crying her eyes out, we have to take it seriously. Finally I see the problem. All my life I have never opened a present Christmas Eve, only Christmas morning. And Lacey, either. Daddy used to read us "The Night Before Christmas" and we used to imagine Santa coming to our house while we slept, sneaking through the den inasmuch as we didn't have a chimney. But how can you tell a kid about Santa coming if you open your presents Christmas Eve?

Mama is wiping Lacey's tears away like she's still a little girl. "You and Brian won't always spend Christmas with his parents," she says. "You could open presents whenever you want to, when you have a family of your own."

"No, Mama. I mean, it wasn't just that. It was everything. The cold, the brown grass . . . and then on top of that"—she starts to sob again—"the idea of opening presents on Christmas Eve!"

Mama rubs Lacey's shoulder and says in a soft

voice: "And then you told him you needed a little time to think. Right?"

At this, Lacey begins to cry even harder. "I love Brian!" she sobs.

Right then Mama's attitude changes. She moves away, leaving Lacey by herself on the sand. "When I first came to Wilmington, I hated everything about it except the beach," she says. "I hated the flatness and the sandy soil and the fact that there was no fall. Where I grew up, the trees used to turn such beautiful colors."

Above us, the gulls have spotted something and start to get excited. "Now I've been here twenty five years, wife and widow," Mama says above the calling birds, "and the fall is still too warm and I still wish there were more trees that changed colors."

"Oh sure," Lacey wails. "That's easy to say. No snow all winter. Camellias. Sun."

"I hated the warm winter as much as you hate the cold. It didn't seem normal to me."

"Then why did you stay?"

"Because of your father, of course."

Mama lets that sink in. Then she waves her hand at the water. "The only thing I liked was coming to the beach. You know why? Because if you look at the ocean long enough, you see that it's more powerful than you are, and more lasting, and just keeps going about its business. Like you ought to be doing."

Mama's face is so stern that I almost think she's play-acting. Then I remember the year Daddy died, and how we came to the beach all the time. I thought it was because Daddy wasn't around and there was nothing else to do. But maybe it was to watch the ocean go about its business. It's surprising the things you don't know about your own mother.

The next day Lacey gets on her plane without even blubbering. I expect Mama to act relieved, but she doesn't. She lets me drive back into town, saying I can drop her off at work and keep the car if I'll pick her up later. She stares out the window.

"It really isn't just homesickness, it's more like culture shock," she tells me. "I don't think she ever thought about wearing heavy old wet boots to work in the snow."

"I guess."

"It's just . . . living there with him. The permanence."

I nod. I am still not sure what could be so terrible about living with Brian.

Mama opens the car window to let the warm breeze in.

We pass the film studio and she braces as if she's trying to keep from saying something that will just kill her. A TV miniseries is filming next month, using a lot of extras, and I want to ask about going to the casting call. But of course I keep my mouth shut.

Finally she says: "You know, when I was pregnant, everyone thought there would be something terribly wrong with Lacey, after my German measles. But it turned out there was just the eye color. We were really very lucky."

So why does she sound like she's about to cry? Getting out at the mall, she seems plumb out of ideas. She must expect Lacey to come running back home any day, this time for good, maybe ruining her entire life.

The seagulls in the parking lot are fighting over some stale rolls as I drive away. They look gray from exhaust fumes, permanently stained and nasty. I think maybe they've been here for generations, their ancestors coming because of the easy bread crusts, and now they've lost their way to the sea. It's like every choice you make cuts off another one, so your life gets narrower as you go along. Like Mama working so much she never gets to the beach, and Lacey loving Brian but wanting to live in Wilmington. I know when we passed the film studio Mama wanted to warn me I could be a director or an editor but probably not both at once. And probably not a star. It makes me mad to think about it. The gulls are all over each other, making a racket. "You're supposed to eat fish, not bread, idiots!" I yell out of the car. The ocean is only a few miles away, and if they really wanted to, the fool birds could get there.

It's funny how your body sometimes knows what to do before your mind ever thinks of it. After I take Mama to work I find myself heading for the grocery store, walking to the produce section. I rummage through the bins until I find a bunch of collard greens about twice as big as the others. I know exactly what I'm doing. All the time my hands are sunk deep in leaves and stalks, my mind is thinking it was no accident the director chose me to tell that guy in the movie he'd be a cripple if he didn't shut up. I am just the type to make it happen. I'm thinking how I'll direct my film and star in it both, maybe even do the editing. Lots of big stars do that. Mama will just have to see. Lacey will be all right, too. At home, I pack the collards in a box and take them to the post office. They don't weigh all that much, and the postage is less than I expect when I send them first class mail to Indiana.

⌇

THIS APPEARED IN *GOOD HOUSEKEEPING*,

JANUARY 2003

WHERE TENDERNESS BEGINS

By the time the baby was two weeks old, Sara realized that the flow of tender motherhood she had been anticipating was not coming. It had not come in the hospital, when she expected it to settle down on her like a cottony blue cloud, and it had not come later when she brought him home, nervous, wondering what on earth she would do with him now.

In the intervening weeks she had gotten up three times each night, howled into blurred consciousness by his hunger. She had ministered to him carefully, studiously, but without enjoyment. Tenderness eluded her. Her husband, Roger, slept through it all, pleading exhaustion after his piddling eight-hour day.

"You said you would help," she reminded him tartly.

"I will but I can't very well nurse him," he replied. "Do you want me to get up and hold your hand?" Though she resented him for that, and perhaps more particularly for the soft, even breathing coming from his side of the bed as she climbed back in during those nights, she had to admit Roger had a point.

And so it was that she sat next to him on a bright Saturday morning, the crystal-clear summer sky mocking her fog of exhaustion, sipping tea and eyeing Roger hatefully for his rested look. She reached into her robe to open the flaps on her nursing bra and let air flow over her nipples, which were now throbbing red points of pain. Roger didn't notice.

"You should have your tooth fixed," he muttered, his face buried in the real estate ads.

She realized she had been venting her frustration by sucking audibly on her broken tooth. It had fallen apart, a molar, all the enamel down to the huge fillings, the day she came home from the hospital. She suspected the birth had robbed her of some essential nutrient needed to keep it intact. Now it needed a crown. She could not envision taking the baby with her to the dentist—or worse, leaving him with a sitter.

"You probably need more calcium," Roger said, listening to her sucking. "You should eat more dairy products."

"I *am* a dairy product," Sara answered. She moved the robe away from her body, to keep it from sticking to the sore nipple.

"You're losing your sense of perspective," Roger said.

She stopped sucking the tooth, instead examining its jagged edges with her tongue. "You know, I don't even feel motherly," she told him. "I try, but I don't feel anything. I don't have a motherly temperament. Ironic that I should find out now."

Roger studied her. "I think you're just tired."

"I'm tired, I'm losing my sense of perspective, I

ought to get more calcium. I sound like a case."

"You always got eight hours of sleep before." He waited a decent interval, letting that sink in. "Maybe we ought to go somewhere. We could look at houses."

Sara put down her cup, remembering the time before she was pregnant when they had whiled away their weekends looking at development after development. They had agreed on just the sort of house they would buy someday, a two-story brick with a country kitchen and yard for the children they would have. But even their two salaries had seemed too meager to make house ownership a reality any time soon. And the idea of having a baby gradually became more important to them than having a house, the more immediate need, no matter where they had to live.

"Roger," she said slowly, "I'm in this apartment too much already. It would be one thing to look at houses if we could afford one, but to dangle them in front of me now . . ."

"Then let's go to the lake."

"With a two-week-old baby? Be serious."

"Two and a half weeks. Why not?"

"He'll fry."

"We'll rig something up."

"Oh sure," she said with the just the proper touch of bitterness. "Why not?"

The baby woke ravenous. Sara nursed him while Roger packed the car. Pins and needles shot through her as her milk let down, the baby frantic to fill his belly at once until—as usual—he choked. His throat closed, his little face turned purple. Sara sat him upright, her own breath stopping until his windpipe finally unlocked and let air rush in again. Then she returned him to her breast. This was perhaps the closest she came to feeling motherly: her brief, unthinking panic every time he choked.

Roger, organized as ever, took nearly an hour to get them out of the house. Into the trunk went the portable crib, along with two old sheets to shade it. "In case he sleeps," Roger said. "That way he'll be out of the sun but get plenty of fresh air."

In case he didn't sleep, there was the stroller which could be wheeled back and forth to comfort him. There were also diapers, several changes of clothes and a bottle of water to keep him from becoming dehydrated.

"But he won't take a bottle," protested Sara.

"There's always a first time," said Roger. "You never know."

Watching the mountains of equipment go into the car, Sara felt dejected. She knew now why she felt an unaccustomed numbness towards summer sunshine, why she had not been anxious to get out for walks. She thrived on spontaneity. There could be nothing impulsive about an outing with strollers and diaper bags and bottles. So much for her cherished independence.

The baby, somewhat less frantic now, sucked with a certain measured rhythm, his eyes half shut. Then some discordant inner music—a gas pain, perhaps—jerked him awake, and he pierced the air with short, staccato sobs. She chucked him over her shoulder and walked: living room, hallways, bedroom, back and forth over the worn sculptured rug, the route they trekked nightly until he settled into welcome limpness.

"All ready," smiled Roger. His toothy grin was clearly painted on for the occasion. Sara was not fooled. She saw her life spread out before her, chopped into little fragments of the baby's wakefulness. It was not a pleasant vision.

In the car he slept, as babies did, which indicated to her that he would wake up the instant they stopped and remain awake for hours. Roger, reading her thoughts, said, "It'll be fine. It won't be a disaster. Relax."

She didn't.

Later he said, "Your trouble is that for three weeks you haven't done anything normal."

She had to agree.

As they neared the lake he said, "You'll enjoy being on the water. You like to be near water."

Sara could never reconcile Roger's brisk logic with his feeling—erroneous—that he had a basic, intuitive understanding of her.

On the west bank of the lake, trees came down as far as the shore. A few bathers lay on the narrow strip of sand in front of them, lazy tanned figures with their eyes shut against the bright sky. Roger installed the baby in the shade in his portable crib. He woke up at once. Hiding behind a tree, nursing him with a receiving blanket thrown over her shoulder for modesty, she watched Roger plunge into the cool water. As a child she had suffered intensely on beach days until her mother released her into the waves. She hated waiting for blankets to be unfolded, sneakers tucked away. She was afflicted with a terrible water-yearning; she could hardly bear to watch it and not plunge in. And now, impatient as ever, she waited for the baby to release her. He pulled hard on a sore spot. She flinched and raised a hand to wipe sweat from her face.

At last he fell asleep. She placed him on his back in the crib. He began to scream.

"Let's try the stroller," said Roger. He had returned dripping wet, invigorated from his swim.

"You try it," said Sara.

He did. Up and down the weedy strip of grass he marched, the stroller in front of him. Sara watched sourly from beneath her shade tree, longing for sand and sun.

"Go on in," said Roger, gesturing toward the water. "I'll wheel him."

She went, glad for the chance but resentful at having to wait for his permission. She tested the water and quickly came out to check on them. That was the trouble, she thought. The baby wasn't something she could relinquish, even to Roger. There would always be this terrible sense of responsibility. For months—for years, maybe—she would not be able to walk around the block without a stroller and a diaper bag; she would not be able to have her teeth fixed at all. If only she could feel something more than heavy responsibility, she thought again, then maybe she wouldn't mind.

Roger was walking back and forth under the trees,

jiggling the stroller as he pushed it. The baby seemed to like being rocked in the dappled shade. She returned to the lake and, in the water, allowed her head to clear.

The sky was absolutely cloudless and hot. The water was cool. She watched it lap into wide circles around her, pools of gentle motion. Officially she was not permitted to swim for six weeks, but there was no resisting. She drifted on a cloud of green ripples, watching the world open out before her in the sunshine.

"You feel better, don't you? Admit it, you do." Roger was treading water beside her. "The baby's out cold. It must be the air."

"You just left him there?"

"Relax. You can see him perfectly well. Look."

She peered toward the shore and saw the stroller beneath the trees, a small bundle inside. "I do feel a little better," she admitted at last.

"See, I knew it." He splashed her, then dived under, yanking down on her foot to duck her. She splashed back. When she tired of the game she turned on her stomach and swam all the way into the shallows. For a moment her tongue fell across the jagged edge of her tooth, reminding her she would soon return to her long nights awake, in all their lurid detail. She turned on her back and found the pull of the sunlight stronger than her urge to sulk. She floated and basked—briefly, joyfully, irresponsibly.

Then through the mist of her headiness the scene of the beach began to register. Two slim figures, male and female, were leaning over the stroller, lifting the small bundle up and moving off, making their way deeper into the trees, carrying the baby with them. The baby. *Her* baby. And she neither remembered the moment when her giddiness drained nor heard herself screaming, "Roger! Someone's taking the baby!"

He started for the beach in a strong crawl, but she must have misjudged her own stamina, for she was already there several strokes ahead of him, splashing out of the water and running across the sand. Even from this distance she could hear the baby screaming. The woman was murmuring something, chucking him up and down in front of her, perhaps hurting him. The man beside her looked muscular. No matter, she was strong with rage. She sprang past the stroller and into the trees, reaching them on the end of a silent, anguished leap, and grabbed the woman's shoulder hard from behind. The woman wheeled around, startled, clutching the baby closer. Sara snatched him from her with a move so expert even she was astonished, cradling his head in one hand and his bottom in the other so that he could not have fallen if he'd tried.

"What do you think you're doing?" she demanded of the woman.

"We were looking for the mother," the woman said, obviously shaken. "The baby was crying."

Sara hugged him to her chest, still accusing and not thanking. "I thought you were taking him," she said.

"Of course not," the woman breathed.

"We didn't mean to frighten you," the man told her. And only then did she see that they had meant no harm, that the woman's eyes were clear and green as the water of the lake, and wide with surprise. Suddenly her strength was gone. She sagged, finding Roger solidly by her side, one hand thrust out to shake hands with the stranger while the other steadied her as her knees began to buckle.

"Thank you for trying to help," Roger said. As they turned to walk back, Sara discovered that her hands were trembling visibly. The baby, resting quietly in her arms, didn't seem to mind.

"I thought you didn't feel motherly," said Roger.

I didn't want anybody to *take* him," she snapped. But she could not seem to control her shaking, which had spread from her hands up and down, so that she trembled from head to toe.

By the time they had repacked and started on their way home, Sara had relaxed sufficiently to nurse the baby, who was hungry again. Surprisingly, her nipples didn't hurt as much when the baby sucked.

"The lake water must have hardened them," she said to Roger. "They say that happens."

"More likely you're just beginning to adjust," he replied with his accustomed bravado.

She considered this. Perhaps the kidnapping had snapped something back into place, she thought. She had acted quite like her old self; she had not been paralyzed. And yet she had been motherly.

She let herself dwell on the possibility that her life,

held temporarily in abeyance, might now resume. Perhaps she could leave the baby with a sitter while she went to the dentist; perhaps it was not so unthinkable. It was crazy to go on indefinitely with half a tooth.

He nursed with a slow, even rhythm, letting his eyes drift shut. He had not even choked. She was suddenly very tired. She leaned back against the headrest, not sure whether she was dreaming or whether a soft blue cloud of tenderness actually did waft into the car along with the breeze.

꒜

FROM *WOMAN'S WORLD*, JULY 28 1981

RASPBERRY SHERBET

The first thing I need to tell you is how Jeremy Taylor and I broke up. I picked him up from work because his car was in the shop, and he turned the radio to that Charlotte rock station he liked, where the music is so thick it makes me see an oatmealy gray mush in front of my eyes. Then suddenly the Emergency Broadcast System came on, and as always happens when I hear that high whining tone, everything in front of me turned such a bright orange that the road was barely visible. "Shut that off!" I yelled. "I can hardly see."

Jeremy did as I asked, but he also rolled his eyes.

"What does the radio have to do with what you can see? You sound about half crazy, Emily." He got such an annoyed look on his face that his dimples disappeared. But after four months of dating me, the man had a right to know what was really going on with me, I supposed. I made a U-turn and headed for Mama's.

Mama is probably the only woman in North Carolina still taking in boarders, a decision she made after Daddy died and left her alone in the rambling old house where I grew up. We found her in the kitchen making one of those Thanksgiving-style dinners she likes to serve her tenants.

"I came to show Jeremy those magazine articles," I said.

Mama raised her eyebrows but didn't say a word as she fetched her notebook of articles about synesthesia. It's a neurological condition that affects only one percent of the population. Those of us who have it can see things other people can't. But until Mama found that first article, when I was 16, we didn't know it had a name. We only knew that I saw glass columns when I tasted mint, and that Mama's roast beef made me see marble arches.

Mama's article collection saved my reputation in high school. One morning, Roy Wilson came up to me and for no good reason kissed me hard on the lips. I should have pushed him away. I meant to. I didn't even like Roy. But such a pretty raspberry sherbet color appeared in front of my eyes when I tasted his lips that I just stood there, liking it.

"Emily, anyone who sees raspberry sherbet at eight in the morning must be doing drugs," said my friend Betsy. Next thing I knew, she'd turned me in to the school's drug abuse program.

Mama had to bring in her stack of articles before I was released. "It's normal for synesthetes to hear and taste things in color," she informed the guidance counselor. "It's normal for them to see shapes in front of their eyes when they experience certain sounds and flavors and emotions." She frowned and took on the assured attitude that usually made people back down. "Compared to the rest of us," she said, "people with synesthesia have a whole extra set of senses."

After she got me sprung from the drug abuse program, Mama warned me to be careful about what I said to anyone. And for seven years, until that day with Jeremy Taylor, I'd taken her advice and kept my lips zipped.

Jeremy looked all wrung out when he finished flipping through the articles. "I think this . . . this synesthesia might be worse than crazy," he said, pronouncing the word as if it were an obscenity. "I mean, seeing things just because you hear a certain sound . . . " He shook his head. "It's weird."

"Weird!" I yelled. "Why, it's like finding out I'm the only one who sees colors and everyone else sees just black and white. It's a wonderful thing! A gift."

"Except when the Emergency Broadcast System comes on," Jeremy sneered. "Then you can hardly see to drive."

"You regard that as a problem?" I asked, then answered the question before he could speak. "Well, obviously you do. In that case, I suggest you start walking home. You've lost your ride."

That wasn't quite the end of it, but the upshot was, Jeremy did walk home that day. Mama asked me to stay to supper with her tenants, but I just couldn't. "People think I'm crazy," I sobbed. "Why don't they know about this?"

"They're starting to, honey," Mama assured me. "They can get books on synesthesia from the library now, or they can read about it on the Internet. Why, there was even that segment on *60 Minutes*."

But I could see she wasn't convinced. Another

thing some synesthetes see is pain, and right then I could see it very clearly in front of my eyes: a thin, metallic, vertical line.

A few weeks later, once I got tired of crying my eyes into red puffs every night, I realized I'd never liked Jeremy's oatmeal-mush rock music anyway. And his kisses had never brought raspberry sherbet to my eyes, only a mustardy fluff. I didn't need Jeremy, I decided, or any other man. I certainly didn't need any more mustard. I would devote myself to my career.

For a year I'd been assistant manager of Bonnie's Baskets, owned by Bonnie O'Dell, the best pastry chef in town. Bonnie created the cutest baskets of goodies for hospital patients, new mothers, and college kids away at school. When I wasn't shopping for supplies, I handled customers on the phone or thought up new themes for the baskets—like Back to the Beach, with sailboat-shaped cookies, or Raspberry Sherbet Kisses, a heart-shaped cake with raspberry icing and candy kisses.

"Why raspberry?" Bonnie wanted to know. "Why not strawberry or blueberry?" But I just shrugged, and the basket became more popular than she'd expected.

After my breakup with Jeremy, I decided to work harder than ever. When one of the part-timers quit, I began delivering all the local packages myself and mailing the out-of-town ones at the post office. Bonnie soon promoted me to manager. Mama said she was proud, but she didn't see why the job required me to give up my social life. I told her I didn't think work and play mixed if you expected to be a truly independent woman.

"I never heard such nonsense," she replied, which was not like her at all.

The next day, I was at the post office with a box to mail in one hand and a basket of iced petits fours slung over my arm, to be delivered to the hospital. I was afraid the icing would melt if I left them in the car.

When I got to the window, the clerk turned out to be Walker McKenzie. He was one of Mama's tenants, and though I'd noticed he was good looking, I'd been too wrapped up in Jeremy to pay much attention before.

"Well, if it isn't Little Red Riding Hood," Walker said, looking at the basket on my arm.

I know it's a cliché. But there was such a warm, rust-colored tone to his voice that I was flustered. All those times I'd mailed packages at his window, I'd barely seen him. But there I was, suddenly noting his blue eyes and dark hair and how his eyebrows stretched across his face in a single thick line.

Before I had time to think, I blurted out, "And I thought all I had to worry about was this icing melting, when here I am, face to face with the Big Bad Wolf."

Brilliant. I felt my face go red as food coloring. It was entirely to Walker's credit that his laugh came out sounding like silver sparkles, not at all gray and whiny. I had my work cut out to show him my comments were entirely unlike me, probably caused by the heat.

Ever since Daddy passed on, I'd always tended his flower garden, except, I'm sorry to say, during the months I was serious with Jeremy Taylor. Now seemed a good time to make amends.

The very next day, I began going to Mama's most evenings after work. I mulched, weeded, fertilized, and staked. Walker's room overlooked the yard, so if he happened to glance down while he was waiting for supper, he could see how responsible I was. He was gone a couple of nights a week, but whenever he was home, he'd play CDs that I could hear through his window. He favored sweet, clear electronic music that made me see pretty shapes.

Some nights, when Mama asked me, I'd shower and change and join the tenants for dinner. Then I'd listen to Walker talk about his hometown, his job at the post office, and how he'd requested a transfer here so he could take courses at the college, which is where he was on the nights he wasn't home. In return, I'd mention a few details about my work, making every effort to appear purely professional. I was cool and collected—and careful not to say anything that would reveal my secret.

One night in mid-July, I was having trouble balancing on the stepstool while trimming the tall bushes, and Walker came out to help. That's when I noticed how hard he looked at me, and I can't say it didn't shake me, having his blue eyes stare me up and down. For a second, all I could think was: Thank goodness my legs tan so well. Then I remembered who I was, an independent career woman, and I concentrated on thinking up ideas for baskets to sell at the upcoming concert in the park.

After that, I took pains to make even clearer to Walker how devoted I was to my career. How working at Bonnie's Baskets all day and helping with the garden in the evening took up all my energy. But in less than a week, I made a fool of myself.

Mama didn't have any air-conditioning, only window fans, and one night it was so hot that Walker brought his CD player out into the yard. Sitting on the patio, holding a textbook, he was listening to music and pretending to read. I knew he wasn't concentrating, because whenever I looked up, there he'd be, studying my outfit—a new shorts-and-top ensemble—instead of his book. Our eyes kept meeting. It was embarrassing. The third or fourth time it happened, Walker blurted out, "I hope the music's not bothering you."

"Oh, no, I like it." It was a lot better than Jeremy's hard rock. "I like the green pyramids floating."

True, at that moment the music was making green pyramids float in front of my eyes. But why had I opened my mouth? A surprised, quizzical look spread across Walker's face before he said, "Yes, I see what you mean," like someone trying to humor a crazy person.

Naturally, I couldn't face him after that. It was just luck that Bonnie got so busy I had an excuse to stay out of the garden. July slid into August, and we were getting ready for the concert. I worked late and went home so tired I didn't think about Walker or anything else. I paid a high school boy to take Bonnie's out-of-town packages to the post office, but that was only because I was too busy to do it myself

A week passed before Mama called me. "Emily," she said, "I never thought you'd be such a coward, avoiding your own house."

"I guess those weeds are starting up again," I said, ignoring the coward part.

"You know perfectly well I'm not talking about weeds. I'm talking about a certain young man who has classes every Tuesday and Thursday. I'm talking about the reason you only used to work in that garden Monday, Wednesday, and Friday. And now you're afraid to come at all."

It's always interesting how Mama picks up more of what's going on than you think she will.

"If you're referring to Walker, we're just friends."

"Anyone so afraid the truth will be discovered just because they got hurt by it once or twice is a coward in my book," she said.

"But you're the one who told me to keep my mouth shut!"

"I told you to be careful who you talked to! That's different!" Mama shouted.

"It is not!" I yelled back. Then Bonnie gave me such a look that I said I had to get off the phone.

The concert was that Saturday. Bonnie's dessert table at the park was so busy, I didn't notice how hot it was all afternoon or how hungry I was until suddenly this warm rust-colored voice said over my shoulder, "Don't you think it's time you took a break for supper?" And there was Walker, giving me his blue-eyed stare, looking so handsome I could hardly swallow.

My heart was beating fast. Still, I think I would have managed a polite refusal if Bonnie hadn't said, "Yes, Emily, business is slow right now; this would be a perfect time to eat."

Moments later Walker was leading me down to the food table, and soon we were sitting on the grass, holding plates of food, gazing into each other's eyes.

"Your mother said you helped Bonnie make all those desserts," Walker said.

"Six dozen cheesecake tarts alone. Each one individually packed in ice." I would have launched into my speech about working on my career except that I remembered Mama's phone call and decided: better a crazy person than a coward. So I took a deep breath and said, "Well, I guess that overtime paid off, because here we are together, and that suits me just fine."

"I'm glad to hear it," Walker said. "For a while I got the idea you weren't all that anxious to be with me."

"Because of my career, you mean?"

"I suspected more because of that Jeremy guy."

"Jeremy! I haven't thought about him in a month!"

Walker grinned. "In that case, I think you ought to let me take you to the band concert later." Then he bit into his chicken leg.

You would not believe the face he made!

"What's the matter?"

"The curlicues in this chicken need to be unwound," he said.

"What?" It's a good thing we were sitting, because I would have fallen over. Never in my life had I known anyone but me who could taste the curlicues in chicken. It didn't seem possible.

Then I knew. Mama had told him. She'd revealed my secret because she thought I was too cowardly to do it myself. She had stuck her nose in where she had no right to go. And Walker had mentioned the curlicues as a signal. I waited for anger to flare up in my stomach, but nothing happened. So what if he'd found out from Mama? At least he didn't think I was crazy.

''I'd love to go to the concert with you," I said.

Walker reached over and took my hand. Right then I knew how it would be. When the trumpets sounded, silver sparkles would dance in the air. The mint in our lemonade would appear as cool columns of glass. And later, when he kissed me, a wonderful raspberry sherbet would appear in front of my eyes. The real thing—and not some second-rate mustardy fluff.

ᘓ

THIS APPEARED IN *GOOD HOUSEKEEPING*,
SEPTEMBER 2002

THE PREGNANCY

Betsy's mother made her announcement at the breakfast table, on one of those balmy spring Saturdays that remind everyone of summer.

"I wish we could be at the beach," sighed Tish, the ten-year-old.

"Me too!" cried Julie, who was nine. "We'll go there again on vacation—won't we, Dad?"

"No trip this year, kids," their father said apologetically.

"Why?"

"Because I'm pregnant again," her mother told them almost shyly, looking from Tish to Julie. "I never feel well enough to travel when I'm first pregnant."

"A new baby! All right!" Tish yelled.

Their mother turned to say something to Betsy, but suddenly there was havoc. The little girls were clapping hands, dancing around, ready to let a January baby atone for the lost vacation. But Betsy, who was 16, felt as if she'd been hit in the throat. Her toast refused to go down, her breath had stopped. *Pregnant.* She rose and ran to her room.

"I didn't mean for it to come out quite like that," her mother told her, trailing her there a few minutes later. "I meant to break it gently."

For a long moment Betsy couldn't bring herself to speak, and there was an awkward silence. "I'm sorry, Mom," she managed finally. "I just can't imagine you pregnant again. I thought you were . . . I thought you were too old." That had come out wrong and she tried to correct herself. "I don't mean that you're *old* . . ."

Her mother smiled. "I know what you mean. Old enough to have teenagers and be finished with babies. But really I'm not that ancient."

"Still. Oh, Mom, I'm sorry. I didn't mean to run off. I just need some time to get used to it."

"Of course you do," her mother said, touching her shoulder. It was all Betsy could do not to pull away.

After that the two of them spoke to each other with an odd politeness, as if to temper their hurt. Other summers Betsy had taken care of Tish and Julie as a matter of course while her mother worked in their father's office. Betsy had enjoyed being the oldest, sharing a silent comradeship with her mother, taking responsibility for her sisters automatically. But this year her mother broached the subject of babysitting carefully because of the tension between them. "One more year, Betsy?" she asked tentatively. "Tish and Julie are still a little too young to fend for themselves without you." And Betsy, who had been toying with the idea of a regular job, muttered, "I don't mind," through her resentment. The pregnancy changed everything: It was a betrayal of the understanding she thought they had, that her mother was growing older and Betsy was growing up.

Afternoons Betsy lay on the deck of the neighborhood pool, watching Tish and Julie swim, feeling time spread before her like an empty gray tablet, dull as the concrete beneath her.

"It's just that I can't quite believe she's pregnant," she confided to her friend Joanne, who lay on the towel next to her, slathered with oil. "It doesn't seem —I don't know—*normal*."

"Yes . . . you get stuck with so much babysitting," Joanne said. "And then the way she'll look if she shows up for the Christmas band program. Big as a house."

Betsy shifted onto her stomach, squirming a little at the unflattering picture Joanne was drawing of her thoughts. But it was true: Parents had sex, of course, but by the time their kids were old enough to know what was going on, at least they could be discreet about it. Her mother's getting pregnant was like an advertisement.

The concrete was rough beneath Betsy's towel and the sun was too hot above. Nothing pleased her. She supposed that a year ago the pregnancy wouldn't have bothered her. She stretched her legs before her, aware that she'd been one of those girls who grow tall early and develop late. Long after some of her friends had started dating, she'd been happy just to play flute in the school marching band and then join Julie and Tish at home, practicing gymnastics to the blaring stereo, the three of them prancing like a litter of puppies on the rug. Childish pleasures. Weekends she'd spent with Joanne, whose mother took them to the beach even in the dead of winter, where they walked on the sand and let the wind fling their secrets back at them from a slate-gray sea. She'd been perfectly content . . . until last year when her shape and her interests had suddenly changed.

"I take it your mother's disgraceful condition is why you're hiding from Mike?" Joanne asked.

"Who said I'm hiding?" Betsy replied.

She was, of course. Mike had been the first boy to notice when Betsy's stringbean figure finally gave way to curves. He played trumpet in the marching band and regarded her with eyes of five different colors (brown, green, blue, gray and gold—she'd counted). He started taking her to school dances and the mall. She hovered at the far edge of childhood for months, not quite his friend, not quite his girl. At night she dreamed of what might happen—his touch, the excitement, the possibilities. Then spring came and one night she found herself clinging to him, kissing, ready for something more. It disturbed her so that she suddenly pulled away. Now they had a tacit agreement that their relationship would be "resolved" this summer, when they had more time to themselves. But that was before her mother had gotten pregnant, when her parents had seemed beyond that, safe in the calm gray mists of maturity.

Now she wasn't sure she could deal with Mike—not just because she was embarrassed, though that was part of it—but because every time she remembered what was happening between them, she got a picture in her mind of her mother, pregnant, and she felt a little sick.

"Oh, come off it," Joanne said. "Of course you're hiding from him. But you're not going to be able to do it forever."

Her mother came to the pool at last one evening in July, at the urging of Tish and Julie. She wore a bathing suit that graphically outlined the emerging pregnancy: a small round mound in a thin-limbed body, which had always been flat in the middle. *So soon.* Betsy's father seemed overly solicitous, as if her mother had an illness. Betsy averted her eyes and dived into the pool.

Suddenly Mike was standing at the shallow end, Adonis materializing from nowhere. Tan from construction work, so fine-looking she could hardly breathe. She pushed her hair back, rubbed water out of her eyes, and tried to react normally.

"Joanne said your mother's pregnant," Mike said. "Is that the big secret? Is that why you didn't want to talk to me?"

"She's been tired lately. I've been watching the kids."

"She seems all right enough to watch them now." He smiled at her. "Can you take a night off? Tell them I'll walk you home."

Later, when they reached her house, he pulled her close to him and stroked her bare arm. A familiar sweet ache ran through her. She wasn't sure she could stand it if they couldn't touch—or if she wouldn't *let* him touch her—just because her mother's pregnancy had left her confused. She kissed him —several times—and then made an excuse to get into the house.

Her mother stayed home from work some mornings, sleeping until nine or ten. She was pale-faced from lack of sun, slower than usual as she did the housework. Betsy helped her without being asked, trying to be cheerful because it was so obvious her mother wasn't feeling well. Sometimes her mother seemed grateful, at other times just grumpy at Betsy's show of good spirits, and Betsy found herself annoyed at this pregnancy that made her mother behave so oddly, that caused so much tension between them. They made a lot of irritable small talk, discussing Julie and Tish more than they had for years.

"You look so worried," Betsy said one day when the small talk threatened to choke her. Her mother was sitting on the floor of the hot family room with the laundry basket emptied before her, staring at the walls instead of sorting socks.

"I *am* worried," her mother said, sounding relieved that Betsy had brought it up. "I worry about something being wrong with the baby because of my age. I worry how I'd take care of three normal children and a defective one." She breathed deeply, as if it had cost her something to speak. "I worry about you, too," she whispered.

Betsy found herself staring awkwardly at the floor. "I thought you were going to have the test to show if there's anything wrong with the baby," she said.

"Amniocentesis? Yes, but not for a couple of weeks."

"And if there's a problem, you can always have an abortion."

"I know it seems simple, but it isn't really . . . to me, at least."

"Well, since you didn't plan to have this baby . . ."

"Just because you don't plan something doesn't mean you don't want it when it happens," her mother said. "Even if it's inconvenient." She smiled a little, as if absorbed in her thoughts. "I didn't plan to have you a week before I graduated, or to have Tish and Julie thirteen months apart . . . but I've never been sorry it worked out that way."

Betsy pulled some socks from the basket and clung to them, wondering. She had been born two weeks early, forcing her mother to take finals late and receive her college degree by mail. It was a funny story the family liked to hear—but now Betsy wondered if her mother hadn't resented having a baby just then, at such an inconvenient moment.

"You missed your graduation. Your big day," she said, staring down at the socks—white in one pile, colors in another.

"No. Having you *was* my big day." Her mother reached across the laundry basket and firmly lifted Betsy's chin. "I wouldn't have changed anything— really," she said softly, meeting Betsy's eyes. She sighed and smiled at Betsy. "Anyway, it's not as if this baby were out of the question. Dad and I will be less than sixty when the child is twenty. We can afford it—and we're healthy, you know."

"Oh, Mom, I didn't mean to start all this."

"I know you didn't, honey," said her mother. But her voice was weary, as if a great exhaustion had taken hold.

Mike began coming to the pool every day after work and tracking Betsy down at the mall whenever she was there with Joanne. But she felt compelled to say no when he asked her out—all the while resenting her mother for getting pregnant again, for relegating her, Betsy, back to childhood.

Band practice started in the worst of August's heat, every morning from nine to twelve. Round and round the playing field they marched, weighted down by instruments, their desire for excellence wilting. Mike marched across from her, the sweat on his face turning his skin so golden that the sight of him left Betsy close to tears. In a perverse way she enjoyed the heat. She was already suffering; the physical discomfort gave it an edge. When her mother picked her up afterward wearing maternity clothes, she suffered even more.

"Hey, Betsy, I see your mother's expecting," friends would say. "When?"

"January."

"Good planning. Football season'll be over and they'll have you home to babysit." Chuckle, chuckle.

The girls were kinder. "Another baby, how cute." No envy in their voices, only good manners.

"What do you care what they think?" Joanne asked. "It's not their kid."

But Betsy did care. Her mother had had the amniocentesis and they were waiting for the results. Betsy half hoped for a defect—or at least that the child would be a girl—so that maybe her mother, with three daughters already, would have no qualms about abortion. ("Oh, yes, she was pregnant, but she lost it," she would tell everyone. And then she would get on with her own life.) But her hands shook when she imagined that outcome, and she rushed downstairs to do penance—get breakfast for the girls, load the dishwasher, anything to drive the guilt away.

When the test results came back she was afraid to ask about them beyond the question "Is it a boy or a girl?" She knew the test would indicate the baby's sex.

"I asked them not to tell me," her mother said. "I wanted to preserve a little of the mystery. But whatever the baby is, the test came out fine, honey."

And now Betsy did not know what to feel.

School started and the fall routine began. Betsy sat with the girls on the buses to football games, Mike sat with the boys. At one of the first away games, the weather was so warm that after the band played her hair was drenched under her uniform cap. She shook it free and Mike lifted a strand of it, holding the wet hair in his hand for a moment before putting it down. When he held her close later at a dance, her whole body trembled. Then she remembered her mother and thought: I have no right to want this. And she pulled away.

Her mother seemed ill. She cut her workdays short, wandered through the house in bedroom slippers, and spent her afternoons cooking.

"Cabbage rolls? You haven't made them since I was a little girl," Betsy said.

"I always love cabbage when I'm pregnant. You really do get these cravings."

But only Tish and Julie seemed to eat, stuffing themselves with stews and soups. Betsy yearned for more than food to sustain her. And her mother, for all her cooking, only nibbled. Her father watched her, worried. "Do you feel all right?" he would ask. And she, trying to smile, would answer, "Yes, fine." Then her father would watch her picking at her food again and, in sympathy, would also stop eating.

One night, despite a chill in the kitchen, her mother stood at the sink in a sleeveless dress, white arms hanging limp at her sides, belly large, the fluorescent light illuminating lines of strain on her face— an incipient oldness Betsy had not seen before—and above her lip, tiny dots of sweat.

"You're always warm when you're pregnant," her mother explained. "Your internal heating system is so efficient." But Betsy watched the haggard face and thought: This is the price she's paying for this pregnancy. And a small beginning of fear iced itself around her heart.

On Mike's birthday the band gave him a party— music, pizza, videos. Afterward Betsy clung to him in a dark corner of his basement, letting him kiss her for a long time, kissing him back, pressing against him. Then, without really meaning to—without thinking—she sat up.

"Not again," Mike groaned. "I thought we went through all this last spring."

"I just can't," Betsy said. "Not now."

It almost hurt her to talk; her voice was hoarse and strained.

He turned and sat still for a time.

"Why not now? What's the matter with you? You can always get birth control."

"I'm just not ready for that yet," Betsy cut in, not daring to look at him. "And if you can't understand that, well then I'm sorry."

"Suit yourself," he said finally, coldly. At her house he left her off without a word. Had they been friends before? Now all he seemed to want was a physical relationship; she might have grown mute, mindless, for all he seemed to care. And he refused to understand why she couldn't respond right now, however much she wanted to—not as long as her mother was still having babies.

He stopped taking her out, but he called sometimes, and that made it worse. In early December Joanne's mother invited Betsy to the shore. She liked the idea of getting away, where she wouldn't think of him so much, where the cold salt spray would distract her. But something held her back. Her mother had only six weeks to go, and she was huge, too weak to watch the girls and also cook and clean. "I can't," Betsy said. "She might need me to babysit."

"Why not let Joanne stay here instead?" her mother suggested. Her mother was solicitous lately, since the trouble had started with Mike. "We'll go out to eat. We haven't done that for ages." So Joanne came.

They went to a Chinese restaurant, reconciled for the moment, sharing an uneasy peace. Her parents ordered huge platters of sweet-and-sour shrimp, chicken with almonds, fried rice. When they rose to leave, her mother turned a greenish pale and clutched the back of her chair. She folded slowly, knees buckling, until her father caught her and sat her on the floor. Other patrons clustered around them—including one or two that Betsy recognized. It was Saturday night, after all, and the place was popular.

"Give her some air," her father said. Her mother stirred, opened her mouth and heaved the meal onto the tiled floor. Betsy's concern for her mother was lost in her shame.

"Sorry," her mother said while being lifted shakily to her feet. "It must have been the shrimp." And later, when they were in the car: "I never should have had the shrimp."

"If your mother's sick, maybe I'd better not stay the night after all," Joanne said. "You could drop me at home on your way." Betsy's father, driving, did not argue.

In her room Betsy stripped off her clothes and flung them on the floor. She had never been so embarrassed in her life. But more than that—she wasn't only angry, she didn't only feel cheated of Joanne's company—she was afraid. Her mother had never vomited before, even in the early months. Her mother was so big. So pale.

That night she dreamed her mother died in childbirth. She was stunned by grief—she couldn't move. Then the dream shifted and her sadness was tangled with resentment for being left with the burden of caring for Julie and Tish, spun directly from adolescence into middle age. She woke astonished at her selfishness. Didn't she care anymore about her mother? Her sisters? About anyone?

"I think I'm going to cut back on holiday socializing this year, Betsy," her mother said when she got downstairs the next morning. "To avoid causing anyone further embarrassment."

"Oh, Mom."

"No, really, honey. I want everybody to get through the rest of this in one piece."

So it was true: Her mother was sicker than she let on; there was something to fear. The ice gripped tighter around Betsy's heart. She told Joanne, who comforted her, and Mike, the next time he called.

"Well, it could mean a problem," he said offhandedly. "You never know, really, until it's born."

"You don't understand. The test showed there was nothing wrong with the baby. It's her I'm worried about."

"Oh. *Her*."

And when her mother stayed home from the Christmas band program, pleading swollen feet, Betsy was not relieved that no one would see her so hugely pregnant—but terrified that she might die. Her flute solo sounded like a thin whine, though her father and Julie assured her it was wonderful. When they got home, her mother was already asleep. Betsy looked up everything she could find in the encyclopedia about complications of birth,

Her mother waddled through the holidays, fat and slow. "Believe it or not, I feel better," she said, laughing. Betsy wanted to believe her; she was ripe for a little joy. Then Mike showed up at the band's New Year's Eve party with another girl, and it was all she could do to get through the evening. New Year's Day began with a white sky and brown grass, confusion and hurt.

"What's wrong, Betsy?" her mother asked. "Is it Mike?" Betsy didn't say. If it hadn't been for this pregnancy, she might have set her own timetable for falling in love with hazel-eyed trumpet players, But her mother was so large, so swollen; Betsy couldn't bear to burden her with blame.

"Maybe a touch of flu," she said, And it might have been true, because her jealousy felt exactly like illness.

There was snow, then a thaw, but Mike didn't call. She spent the last two weeks of her mother's pregnancy huddled into herself, nursing her pain.

The baby was born at 6 A.M. on a Saturday morning. "A boy!" her father shouted, calling from the hospital and waking everyone up, "Aaron James!"

"Aaron James," Betsy repeated, The sound of the name stunned her, as if there were someone else involved in all this, not just Betsy and her parents and Mike. "How's Mom?" she whispered.

"She's fine!" The ice around her heart cracked slowly, began to melt.

"You can all come and see him later on," her father said. Tish and Julie cheered on the extension. Betsy was trembling with relief

Aaron James lay in a portable crib next to her

mother's hospital bed, "Oh, look, he's so tiny," Julie breathed.

"Can we hold him?" asked Tish excitedly,

"Not just yet, sweetheart," her father said,

Only Betsy was ignoring the baby, looking at her mother.

"You always look pregnant for a couple of weeks afterward," her mother said. "It takes a while for your stomach to go down," In fact Betsy was thinking her mother looked pretty good. Less than twenty-four hours after the birth, and the paleness was gone.

"Look at your brother," her mother prodded.

Betsy looked, A red wrinkled form, tiny hands. Sort of ugly. He began to howl. His face grew crimson, the demand higher-pitched,

Her mother lifted him into Betsy's arms and the howling stopped. He opened his eyes, a dim blue, and seemed to be looking at her. He was real. Sort of interesting. She hadn't anticipated that. Hadn't anticipated anything: not weight, not warmth . . . not, certainly, the tiny smile creeping across his face,

"A gas pain," her mother said. Betsy was stung. "You think so?" she asked. "I thought it was because he liked me." *He.* He had smiled at her. Her mother smiled at her now, then took Aaron and laid him in his crib.

"Has Mike called?"

"No," Betsy hadn't called Mike, either, though she might have, to tell him the news. Her throat was tight with the beginning of tears,

Her mother sighed. "I know it hurts," she said,

"But you're so grown up now. . . he wouldn't have been the last love in your life, there'd have been too many others pushing him out of the way. Of course I'm prejudiced . . ."

Betsy tried to smile, but she couldn't manage it, She blinked and looked away to keep from crying. Her gaze fell on the baby and it struck her that he, at least, had nothing to do with old hurts. He seemed suddenly. . . remarkably new.

He twitched and flung a scrawny arm outside the covers. His wrist was no thicker than her flute. She had never imagined him in there—a separate person; she'd only seen her mother's belly and felt hateful. She reached into the bassinet and touched his fingers, Her mother, watching, leaned back against the pillows . . . weary, Betsy supposed, but the color in her face was like spring, Maybe she and Mike would have broken up even if her mother hadn't been pregnant. She wondered . . . She let go of the baby's hand to pull the covers up over his shoulders, astonished at the translucence of his skin.

꒚

THIS APPEARED IN *YOUNG MISS*, JANUARY 1986

THE LUCKY ONE

Rhonda Fisher stands in front of the mirror, appraising herself as she might appraise a project report at the engineering firm where she works—26 years of effort, now about to undergo final inspection. From the neck up, she is thoroughly presentable—hair just out of electric rollers, a good forehead, large eyes, thick lashes. A great mouth, Mark says.

From the neck down she leaves something to be desired. The green dress is flattering (good with her pale skin), but it doesn't hide the 30 extra pounds. The bedroom door opens and Babs, her oldest friend and current roommate, emerges, a sleek five-foot-five, a hundred and ten.

"You look great, Rhonda."

"So do you," Rhonda says. Which is, after all, exactly the problem. Babs' hair is dark, and her golden eyes slant up at the edges. "You shouldn't live with a girl like Babs," Rhonda's mother has said repeatedly. "She's too much competition." But Rhonda has known Babs since she was six and believes some bonds are irreversible. Competition—until this moment—had never been the point.

"You know, you don't have to do this just because Les and I broke up," Babs says.

"Oh, no—I want you to meet Mark," Rhonda tells her. "Besides, I don't get that much chance to cook."

"Well, it's really nice of you," Babs says.

Rhonda looks at her reflection in the mirror. I must be nuts, she thinks.

Rhonda first discovered she was fat in third grade when, arriving home from school one day, her mother offered her an apple instead of the usual cookie.

"I'd rather have a cookie," Rhonda said.

"An apple is better for you. It has fewer calories," her mother insisted. "Listen, I've had a weight problem all my life. I don't want you to have one, too. It's time you started to watch your weight." And so, without enjoyment, Rhonda ate her apple.

After that Rhonda understood that she was different. She became aware of the forbidden chewiness of brownies, the sugary sweetness of candy corn, the creaminess of mint-chip cones. By 14 she was five feet two inches tall and weighed 135—not the fattest girl in school but not fashionable, either. At 16 she completed her upward growth—five four and a half. She weighed 153.

"You're not really fat , Rhonda," Babs would say. "Besides, if you wanted to, it's only a matter of taking off ten pounds." Babs looked at her slightly squint-eyed. "Maybe twenty."

"Thirty," Rhonda told her. Babs shrugged. After a time they stopped discussing weight entirely.

In her senior year Rhonda became infatuated with a boy named Joel Pitts. She never actually dated him, but at parties he often danced with her and held her close. Once, riding home from a party in Barry Greene's car, Joel put his arm around her and touched her ample breast, a gesture Rhonda rebuffed. Some perverse logic told her that to take such liberties he owed her at least a formal date, a movie perhaps. He never asked her to the movies. Rhonda came to understand that, while thin girls were the vogue—Babs, for example, was going out with Sammy Vance of the football team—there were many boys (later many men) who yearned for abundance, for the firm pillow of her flesh. It was just that they preferred not to date a fat girl.

"Listen, Babs, I've got to lose this weight," Rhonda said, driven to frenzy by Joel's scattered attentions. "You've got to stick close. Don't let me eat a thing."

Babs beamed. Sammy Vance had broken his leg the last week of football season, and she had looked after him for six solid weeks. Now he was recovered, and she needed another project. Babs was meant for caretaking. 'Sure, Rhonda," she said. "I know you can do it. They say that inside every fat person there's a thin one waiting to get out." Rhonda was not so sure. It seemed to her that 153 was her normal weight, the real Rhonda, no puffed-up shadow. What lurked within was not some thinner version but a fatter one yet, one that regarded 1,200 calories a day as a prison from which there was no parole.

But she was determined. Twenty pounds off by May, and maybe Joel Pitts would invite her to the prom. Babs followed her everywhere. Rhonda could not enjoy mint-chip cones at the corner deli because Babs handed her diet sodas before she ordered. Rhonda could not indulge in late-night ham-and-cheddar sandwiches because Babs invariably called just as she thought of them. Babs' efficiency was remarkable. Rhonda went down to 142, but then stopped losing.

"It's a plateau," Babs said. "Everyone reaches plateaus. Sooner or later it'll start coming off again."

Rhonda's mother was not so forgiving. "Diet isn't enough," she said. "You have to exercise." Rhonda exercised. She did sit-ups, she bought an aerobics tape, she walked home from school. She held at 140.

"Well, you've tightened up, Rhonda. You really look terrific," Babs said.

She did not feel terrific. She felt hungry. Discomfort gnawed at the pit of her stomach like sharp teeth. But Joel Pitts began to pay court. He would swing into step beside her as she and Babs were returning from lunch; he sometimes said a few words on the way home from school. One night at a party he plopped down on the couch beside Rhonda and told her about swim team for half an hour straight. Then he looked around the room and said, "Where's your friend Babs?"

"She had a date tonight," Rhonda told him.

"With Sammy Vance?"

"No, they broke up," Babs had lost interest in Sammy once his leg healed. She was out with a myopic honor student who helped her in math.

"So she's not going with anybody right now?" Joel

Pitts asked, staring at Rhonda with bright, expectant eyes.

Rhonda's stomach knotted. "No," she managed to say.

"I guess she's already got a date for the prom, though."

"No."

"No?"

"'Scuse me, Joel. I've got to say hello to somebody."

She avoided Babs for a week. She gained two and a half pounds. The truth was, she felt a little better once she started eating again, broken heart and all. Perhaps some people like herself needed a little extra nutrition. She pictured vitamins and minerals leaching out of her as she starved.

One day as she left the deli where she'd stopped for a mint-chip cone after school, Babs literally chased after her. "Hey, Rhonda, I never meant for that to happen," she called, trying to catch up. "I never did anything."

"He called you," Rhonda accused, walking faster.

"Listen, I put him off. I really did."

Rhonda stopped walking. "It wasn't your fault," she said finally. "I've started eating again. As you can see."

"How much have you gained?"

"Six."

"But you don't look it."

"My mother says I'm built like a walrus."

Babs laughed. "You know your mother would say that." Of all Rhonda's friends, only Babs understood

Mrs. Fisher. Rhonda was smiling, too.

"Yeah, think what she must have expected to give me this name. Rhonda. A tall, svelte movie star with long hair and rhinestones in her ears."

Babs' laugh was like a bell ringing. After that they saw each other every day. In June they graduated together. Rhonda was valedictorian of their class, weighing in at 153.

Babs went to nursing school; Rhonda went to the state university. She didn't gain and didn't lose. She didn't have many dates, but she became good friends with a boy named Ron.

Ron discovered her in chemistry class, the week her blue crystals crystalized and his didn't. He talked to her about his work-study program, about his family and his girlfriend Sarah back home. They saw the free flicks together every Friday night, deep foreign films with subtitles, after which they leaned against each other for emotional support. They did not, officially, "date."

Freshman year passed. Sophomore year Rhonda signed up for qualitative analysis. She understood solution problems intuitively, while Ron struggled with them. She tutored him night after night in her dorm room. He was in pre-med and had to do well.

Once, past midnight, he abandoned his chair for the bed where she was sitting. He unbuttoned her blouse and fondled her breasts. She put up no resistance. They lay there for some time, caressing, but later he talked to her about his problems with Sarah. A great sense of emptiness filled Rhonda. If she'd been thin, he would have spared her the girl-back-home routine. Were fat girls supposed to be protected from hurt by all their fleshy insulation?

"Ron, I'm sleepy," Rhonda said. "Go home." Ron went. She thought that was the end of him, but somehow they stayed friends.

She preregistered for organic chemistry and advanced physics. She had decided to be a chemical engineer, and after she graduated *cum laude*, an engineering firm hired her. She rented an apartment and went to graduate school at night. The second year Babs came to live with her, and Rhonda took her home for Thanksgiving.

"You know, I think Babs may be too much competition for you," Rhonda's mother said when they were alone in the kitchen. Rhonda remembered similar conversations from years before.

"What, do you mean?" Rhonda asked.

"Well, you know. She's so thin."

"Oh, Mother, you don't give up a friendship because of that," Rhonda said, feeling that her mother must be the jealous one, not she. Her mother had never accepted her weight as Rhonda had. Still, the observation made her uncomfortable. She remembered Joel Pitts well, and it was true that at parties it was Babs men gravitated to, not Rhonda—though of course Rhonda had her share. Rhonda tried to ignore her mother's remarks, but she did not bring Babs home again for the entire two years they roomed together before Babs moved in with an insurance salesman named Les.

Les was just Babs' type, Rhonda thought. He was handsome but slightly cross-eyed, and star-crossed as well. He had lost two successive jobs and fallen into despair. Babs was trying to pull him out. Much as Rhonda missed Babs, she was relieved not to have to introduce her to her male friends.

Rhonda finished her master's degree a semester early and threw herself into her job. She worked for a company that survived on contracts from the federal government. She was adept not only at the engineering end of her projects but at bringing in additional work as well.

For a while she went out with one of the vice-presidents of her firm, an engineer named Mel who had just separated from his wife. Mel dated Rhonda for more than two months without letting on to a single soul. Then Rhonda recalled Joel Pitts, who had also yearned for her in private.

"Enough;" she told Mel when it became apparent that he was Joel's successor.

"Enough?" Mel asked. He was incredulous; Rhonda was firm. She felt her once-thin emotional skin growing thicker than her waist; she refused to speak to him even on the phone.

One night at a party Rhonda was drawn into the back room by a handsome stockbroker who kissed her long and hard among the coats.

"What I don't understand," he said, finally drawing away, "is why a pretty girl like you lets herself get so heavy, Believe me, hon, you'd look a lot better if you knocked off fifteen pounds."

Rhonda felt her weight coalesce into a ball at the pit of her stomach. Hon? She stepped back to arm's length, took a deep breath and smacked the stock-broker in the face. She went home, showered and got into bed alone. To hell with men; she would soon be named partner in her firm. Her skin was as thick as elephant hide.

None of which prepared her for Mark, who stood across from the door at a company reception, drop-ping ice cubes into his drink and staring at her as if her beauty stunned him into speechlessness. Finally he pushed his glasses up on his nose, cleared his throat and introduced himself. He had a Ph.D. in physics and worked for a company similar to her own. His hair was almost black. His voice was ex-traordinary. So much for elephant hide.

They went to four movies, a basketball game and two plays. They ate at so many different restaurants that she lost count. She kept waiting for his reluc-tance to be seen with her in public, but after he took her to his office and introduced her around, she found it hard to doubt him. At long last, love.

Then Babs' friend Les took a job in southern Indi-ana and didn't invite Babs to join him. She promptly moved back in with Rhonda. Mrs. Fisher's jealous soul must have invaded Rhonda then because she was afraid to have Mark meet Babs. And Babs was so upset about Les that Rhonda was afraid to leave her alone.

"What do I want with Indiana anyway?" Babs would ask, sniffing.

"Beats me," Rhonda would say. "He was a little cross-eyed anyway." This was clearly the wrong approach.

Babs looked at Rhonda accusingly. "You're the one with all the luck. You had the sense to take up engineering while I became the caring nurse. So you're about to be made a partner while I'm getting paid peanuts and working nights. You have a million friends while I cut myself off for a burned-out insurance salesman. And now you have this Mark and I have no one."

"Listen, Babs," Rhonda consoled. "You better take a look at yourself in the mirror before you start jumping off bridges."

Babs only swept her hand across the air as if to toss such a remark away. "I have a few good looks. Ten years from now I'll have wrinkles. I have all my luck hanging on my chin. Yours is on the inside."

Rhonda sighed. Luck on the inside, and also her jealous heart. Once Babs began to recover, Rhonda started meeting Mark in the lobby. "With two of us living there, the apartment is too messy to describe," she lied. "I don't want to clean it up just so you can walk in the door."

She met Mark in the lobby for several weeks. They often cooked at his place, and Rhonda began to feel quite comfortable there. One night they were eating a broccoli salad, a diet dish that required a great deal of chewing, when Mark frowned and pushed his plate away.

"Listen, Rhond," he said his voice a little heavy.

"If your place is so crowded, you could move in here with me."

Rhonda's heart leaped, her blood began to rush wildly through her veins. But her mind was wrapped in remnants of her elephant skin, cool as the broccoli on her plate.

"Not yet," she said. "We haven't known each other that long."

"Then at least let's go skiing over Christmas. Or something." He seemed too eager. Rhonda was suspicious.

"I can't," she said. "I promised my folks I'd come home."

"Invite me, then."

Rhonda's throat seemed to be lined with fuzz, but she managed the invitation and Mark accepted.

Rhonda's father took to him at once; her mother wasn't so sure.

"Rhonda, has he asked you to marry him?"

"No, but he's suggested I move in." There was something comforting about using shock tactics against her mother. But her mother only sighed.

"If you weighed a hundred and twenty he'd be proposing marriage."

"Oh, Mother. Not everybody thinks that way." She might have mentioned that featherweight status hadn't united Babs in matrimony with Les, but she felt it inappropriate.

Mrs. Fisher looked at Rhonda as if somehow she had failed. "Just don't say I didn't warn you."

Rhonda turned away. Her mother made her feel as

if she were not quite entitled to a full life. Well, she would move in with Mark if she decided to. But then, the morning before they left, her mother cornered her in the kitchen and asked pointedly, "Rhonda, has he met Babs?" And Rhonda knew she had better not start thinking about the full life just yet.

So now Rhonda lets Babs help her set the table for the three of them. Babs, still recovering from Les, has lost a pound or two, and her cheekbones jut dramatically from beneath her slanted eyes. She has started seeing a diabetic computer technician. She doesn't know him well enough to invite him to share this meal. But she has a date with him after dinner. If anything, Babs looks even better than usual.

Mark looks good, too. He is wearing a blue shirt that makes him seem even darker than he is. He has brought a bottle of wine, and Rhonda has made broiled shrimp and a layered salad. Mark and Babs talk easily, as if they have known each other for years. Rhonda is too miserable to eat. She feels like a waitress, going in and out of the kitchen, serving them. She sees the light in Babs' slanted eyes and the laughter in Mark's face, and she recognizes that the two of them—Babs and Mark—are meant for each other while she, the unwitting matchmaker, plays the fool. She brings in the strawberry cheese pie she has made for dessert. Babs and Mark both eat a large slice, but the sight of it makes Rhonda sick.

At last Babs' friend arrives. He and Mark shake hands and Babs goes off. Now it begins, Rhonda thinks. Excuses. Questions. About Babs.

Instead, Mark sighs. "Duty done," he says, smiling.

"What's that supposed to mean?"

"Rhonda, Babs is a lovely girl—I'm glad you have such a good friend—but you know how I am at making small talk."

"I think you did very well indeed," Rhonda says sharply. Mark only shrugs.

Rhonda narrows her eyes. "She is lovely, isn't she?"

"I guess," Mark says, shrugging again. "She's a little scrawny. Her face is a little flat."

"Her face is flat?"

"Isn't it?"

Rhonda considers this.

"Now that we've been through all the amenities," Mark says, "I think we ought to get back to our basic situation. About your moving in . . ."

For a long time Rhonda doesn't speak. "Normally I'm five pounds heavier than this," she says finally. The turmoil of these past weeks has robbed her of her appetite.

"I don't like bony women," Mark tells her.

"I'm not going to take up bicycling or jogging, either. I'm an engineer, not an athlete."

"Part of the reason I can talk to you," says Mark, "is because you are an engineer."

"One fifty-three is my normal weight."

"Rhonda, I know," he says. "Okay. Forget moving in. We won't have a three-month trial. We'll just plunge into marriage. Is that what you want?"

Rhonda looks at him dumbfounded.

"Right away, before you change your mind."

"June," Rhonda manages. "I always wanted to get married in June."

"June. July. Whenever. Does this mean yes?"

Rhonda makes the plans herself She accepts the partnership in her firm on the condition that she can have time off for her honeymoon. Babs is going to be her maid of honor. By now Babs is going seriously with the diabetic computer technician; she already has arranged special food for him at the reception. Only Rhonda's mother is skeptical.

"The maid of honor is going to upstage the bride," she says to Rhonda over the phone. "Can't you do it without a bunch of attendants?"

"A big white wedding is what I've always wanted, and Babs has been my best friend since I was six."

"Yes, but the bride is supposed to be the star. Not her maid of honor."

Rhonda wants to say that Babs will probably spend her life fighting someone else's high blood sugar; life is not always lived more gracefully by the thin. But her mother has never learned to like herself, and Rhonda does not expect her to understand.

"It will be fine, Mother," Rhonda says with conviction. And she laughs, even if her mother doesn't, because she understands that her luck is not like Babs', hanging on her chin. Her luck is safely cushioned inside.

৵

THIS APPEARED IN *MCCALL'S*, JULY 1984

OTHER PEOPLE'S VOICES

All of a sudden, in the fall, Krista began to think she'd never get her pilot's license. She'd been doing so well—soloed at twelve hours when other students were taking 20 or 30 —and then one day she flew into a weather front and got so scared that she knew she'd never have the nerve to log the rest of her solo time or do her four-point cross-country flight.

"If you're going to take lessons from an old airport bum who chain smokes and can hardly zip her jeans, then you have to expect to get spooked sometimes," her husband Chuck said. It was true people made fun of Sadie, who at 60 had a gut the jeans didn't quite hold in and was given to hyperbole in her flying stories. But when it came to airplanes, Sadie knew what she was doing. Long before it ever happened, she'd warned Krista a pilot needed only about 90 seconds to get disoriented inside a cloud.

"You've got to rely on your instruments and not on your feelings," she'd rasped in a voice hardened by 40 years of unfiltered Camels. "And don't think it'll be easy, either. You have to check where you are and make sure you're right side up. You have to keep do-ing what those instruments say, even if you feel like you're falling—which you will. It's not like being in a car on the highway, where even if the fog's thick you can always see that white line on the road."

So when Krista took off into clear sunshine one Sunday, and five minutes later clouds moved in so thick she couldn't see the mountain in front of her, she checked her instruments as Sadie had instruct-ed, and checked and rechecked her maps—but all the time she was squinting like a blind idiot into the gray drift outside, as if squinting would make her see through it. Then panic set in: blood pounding in her temples, the certainty she was falling, or at least banking, a raw and unreasoning fear. The in-struments were faulty; she had to trust her instincts and shift the plane's position—anything to feel she was in control. She might have done it except that at that very moment the front cleared as quickly as it had come. The mountain shimmered before her in the distance, right where it had been all the time. The plane was level, exactly as her instruments said. And she felt like a damned fool.

Her hands trembled. She tried to calm herself, but Sadie's favorite flying story came back to her like a reprimand. "Weather's the worst thing that can hap-pen to you sometimes, honey, and I got a few psychic scars to prove it," Sadie had said from behind a haze of cigarette smoke. "Why, the scariest night of my life was trying to beat a weather front back from Ocean City, and the fog rolled in so thick I didn't know whether I was coming or going. I turned around, and all of a sudden not fifteen feet from the wing were a set of radio tower lights. Scared the pee-doolies out of me. Couldn't find any place to land until there was only twenty minutes of fuel left . . . and then it was just a little hole in that fog . . . just one little hole right over the airfield."

At the time, Krista had kept her eyes expressionless. "And did that cure you for a while of trying to outrun weather fronts?" she'd asked, Sadie had guffawed a great puff of smoke into Krista's face and said, "Oh yes, it certainly did."

Now Krista realized if she'd been the one coming home from the shore that time, she'd never have been able to put the plane down any more than she'd been able to stay cool in the clouds today. She didn't have Sadie's nerve. If the fog hadn't cleared, she'd have bounced around in it until she ran out of fuel; she'd have stopped trusting her instruments and spun into the mountain; she'd never have seen Chuck again, or the kids. And weeks from now, Sadie would have told some other student pilot about the accident, with the usual relish in her voice: "Poor girl, she was cut out more to decorate a two-seater than fly in it," That's what people always thought—and maybe, after all, it was true.

She didn't go up for two weeks after that. Chuck said everybody had lapses of confidence; it was just a stage she was going through. "I felt the same way when the lumber yard took us for all that money," he said. But Krista and Chuck had been running their remodeling firm together long enough for her to know he was always under control, even after the lumber incident. A salesman had given him a phone quote for some supplies and then sent a bill for almost twice as much. Chuck had argued with him, but it didn't do any good. In the end Chuck said to pay, even though they'd lose money on their job. They could never prove what he'd been told on the phone. Krista was in a red dither about it for a month, but Chuck was so calm, he seemed as confident as ever. All he said was: "Everybody has to eat it sometimes, and I guess that was our turkey dinner." Thinking back on that, Krista had to smile.

She flew again, partly because Chuck and Sadie both seemed to expect it—and partly because the weather was so nice. The first day she'd ever been in a small plane, everybody kept looking at her expecting her to throw up, what with the motors so loud and the ride so bumpy. But the Cessna didn't bother her. She'd looked down at the valley where she'd lived all her life and felt happier than she could remember. She wanted to fly the plane over the mountain herself. It would be a way of possessing all the land she crossed over; flying the plane, she would be in control, creating the trip, creating her life. It was a crazy notion, but there it was.

Now all that magic seemed ruined—though not completely. Somehow she kept going, and one day in October something special happened: there were deer on the runway. At first she hardly noticed the small forms moving across the tarmac because she had just come into the landing pattern and was concentrating on another plane in front of her. Maybe in the back of her mind she thought they were dogs or even people. She was preparing to turn from the downwind leg of the pattern to the base leg, when a man in the control tower told her to circle one more time. "We don't want venison for dinner down here," he said.

After that, the forms became clear to her—three deer, running across the blacktop with great graceful strides. Krista felt as if she were being given a glimpse into some elusive secret, something she would never have seen if she'd stayed on the ground. She felt that way a lot when she was flying. At those moments, she felt as she had as a teenager listening to music, when the sound was so sweet she thought any minute she'd burst out of herself. If she had to describe it, she would have said it was like orgasm, only more spiritual. That wasn't something she could explain to Chuck.

The deer leaped across the runway and disappeared into the surrounding trees. Then the controller came back on her radio, giving her the clearance to land, and she remembered how he had sounded before. He had been not pleasant but testy, schoolteachery—"We don't want venison for dinner down here." As if, without help, she would surely have smashed into the deer and destroyed them.

"You know what I think?" Chuck said. "I think you're letting other people do your thinking. It's one thing, being scared, but at least let it come from inside yourself." He even checked with Sadie, who said Krista was doing fine. That was like Chuck, to be concerned for her even though he had no interest in flying himself. They'd been married 16 years, and she still thought it was largely luck that she'd ended up with him.

Krista almost never told anyone she met Chuck when she was only twelve. For one thing, they almost never believed her, or else they behaved as if finding him so young meant her life had ended prematurely. They believed if she'd met her husband at twelve, then she'd never had a really independent life at all.

Usually she just said she'd met Chuck at the swimming pool in town and didn't say exactly when. She'd been a little wild that summer, having developed so early. She kept trying to hang around with the high school girls, but the only ones who would let her near them were Stacey Johnson's gang, three tough girls who lived in the projects. Stacey always teased Krista, asking her if she had a boyfriend yet, because she knew Krista didn't. Krista was still scared of boys, not really interested in them. "Well, you find anybody yet?" Stacey would ask every day, and one day Krista got tired of it and said in a haughty voice, "As a matter of fact I did. See that blond boy over there?" She pointed to a nice-looking high school boy she noticed at the diving board.

Stacey got a dark look on her face. "Cute, Krista," she said. "Chuck's my boyfriend. You fool with him, and I'll tear your eyes out."

Krista thought Stacey really would. She might

have attacked Krista right then, except that Chuck dived in and swam to their section of the pool.

"Hey, what's going on?"

"Nothing," Stacey said. "Keep away from her," she hissed to him, nodding Krista's way. Chuck looked at her with more interest than he probably would have otherwise, to see what he was supposed to avoid. Krista got a crampy feeling in the bottom of her stomach, in the same spot as menstrual cramps, only pleasant. She wasn't allowed to go out with him for two more years, but he started hanging around.

Once when she was in tenth grade, after she and Chuck had been going together for a while, Stacey Johnson came up to her in the hall. "You think just because you have a cute face and those big boobs, you can have anything you want, don't you? Well, someday it's all going to catch up with you." At the time Krista was surprised Stacey had held a grudge so long, and a little scared maybe she'd tear her eyes out after all. Chuck only laughed. He said he wasn't going to let that happen, and besides Stacey was full of hot air. Stacey left her alone after that, and Chuck married Krista the week she graduated from high school.

Last year they'd had their 15th wedding anniversary. She was so astonished at the idea of it that she drank too much and got sentimental. While they were getting ready for bed, she smiled at Chuck and said teasingly, 'Why have you stayed with me so long, anyway? It's because your office wouldn't run without me, or your house, either, isn't it?"

"It's because I like the way you look in a tight sweater and pants," he said, touching her.

She knew it wasn't true—they had such a thick braid of life together—yet there was an element of truth in it, which frightened her. She didn't like the idea that her future depended on her breasts and butt, which had both lost a little spring since she'd had the children. She had no control over that whatsoever—and now she was 32. Maybe Stacey Johnson was right; her bravado would catch up with her, her luck would run out.

Chuck took the kids hiking on Sundays so Krista could fly. She didn't ask him to do it; he just wanted to. Patti was eleven and still a tomboy. Scotty was eight. Sometimes Krista thought Chuck had been waiting years for the kids to get old enough to hike the way he liked to: cross-country, off the trails. Krista liked the safety of the paths herself.

The weather stayed warm into November, with fewer storms than usual. Krista caught herself scanning the sky nervously before she went up, listening to the weather reports a little afraid, but she hid her fear well enough even from Sadie. Then she got into the plane, partly because there was no point going home, with the rest of her family hiking. The odd thing was that she felt victorious whenever she landed and got her logbook signed. As if she had conquered something, or someone.

One Sunday she headed south, looking at the Blue Ridge mountains on her right, bathed in the amber sunlight that had shone for days. She passed

Martinsburg and should be over Winchester in a minute. Then she'd head southeast to land at Front Royal. A race course was below her. Maybe she hadn't studied her map closely enough—hadn't seen the race course. She spoke too soon—blurted things out, she always had: "I see a race course beside the airport," she said to a woman on the unicom frequency on her radio, "and I guess I must be over Winchester, but I didn't know you had a race course down there." Even as she spoke she knew how stupid she sounded, because it had to be Winchester below her, race course or no race course; that was the only town it could be.

"Are you lost, one two-seven November?" the woman asked.

"Negative, Winchester. I know that's got to be you down there. Just got my maps messed up here for a minute."

"You sure you're not lost?" The voice was slightly nasal, like someone with postnasal drip—and at the same time accusing, sarcastic. It reminded her of someone else's voice, she couldn't remember whose.

When you got lost, you were supposed to remember the three C's: confer, confess, and climb. She didn't want to climb; she knew where she was. She wanted to continue on to Front Royal and get her logbook signed.

"If you're lost, maybe you should turn back." She recognized the voice now; it reminded her of Ann Paxton, her obstetrician.

"I'm all right, really. I just missed the race course symbol on the map."

"You sure?"

"Absolutely."

The sky was clear and the sunlight amber, and the voice that sounded like Dr. Paxton's disappeared as she flew away.

Eight years ago, after she'd been in labor all night with Scotty, she'd asked Dr. Paxton—in what she thought was a pleasant tone considering the way she felt—"Why is it other women just breeze through having the babies and I have to lay here so long?"

Ann Paxton said in her nasal, sarcastic voice, "Other women don't eat everything in sight for nine months. If you wouldn't let yourself get fat as a pig every time, maybe it'd go quicker." Then the doctor felt Krista's belly as if she hadn't insulted her at all. She'd never warned her that weight might be a problem. Normally, Krista stayed on the skinny side. She'd gained 65 pounds when she was pregnant with Patti, but Dr. Paxton had never said to worry—and sure enough, the extra weight had gone away by itself. Krista was going to mention that when she had another pain. Someone told her to push. Things got busy, Scotty was born, and in the excitement of having a son, she forgot all about it.

The weight didn't disappear like it had the first time. Krista wore her bathrobe every day until the woman next door asked her, while they were hanging laundry up outside their apartment, "Aren't you ever going to start wearing clothes again?"

"I will if I can ever fit into them," she'd said. "I've been eating nothing but cottage cheese and tomatoes for two weeks now, and I still can't get into a thing."

To this day she couldn't eat cottage cheese or tomatoes without thinking about that time. She'd had 30 pounds to lose. She ate cottage cheese and tomatoes and drank gallons of diet soda. She was always hungry. "I look like a walrus," she told Chuck. She kept an image of herself as a walrus in her mind, so she wouldn't eat when she was hungry. During that time she felt funny if she went out anywhere. Maybe she just imagined it, but it seemed people didn't treat her the way they used to when she was skinny, the women as well as the men. It was as if they didn't notice she was there any more—as if she'd become invisible. She'd never understood it.

Her good friends didn't act that way, of course—and Chuck was the same as ever. When the weight started coming off, he even said he admired her discipline.

"It's not discipline, it's that picture I keep in mind of the walrus." He laughed and kissed her, and a long time later, when she was thin again, he bought her a poster with a picture of a walrus on it, which they kept on a wall of their office.

The map of Front Royal showed a factory on one side of the airport and a forest on the other. Krista had heard that deer got on the runway all the time because of those woods and because of the mountains being just at the edge of town. Deer were even more plentiful here than at the airfield at home. She made a mental note to keep a lookout. After her last experience, she wasn't running the chance of having people tease her about venison for dinner again.

She looked around for the airport, but found herself focusing on the forest, acres of bare trees with a lovely maroon cast to them in the sunshine. She thought about the deer that must be down there, and remembered how special she'd felt that other time, seeing them from above. Then she remembered the airport, and began to feel uneasy, seeing only the trees. She knew she must be getting close to the field. She picked up the unicorn frequency on her radio and asked where the airport was.

"Do you see the factory?" an edgy voice asked. It was a man this time.

Now she saw it—the flat top of the factory, and the forest, and the airport, of course.

"Roger, Front Royal. I see the airport now."

"Lady, are you sure you know what you're doing? Because if you don't, maybe you better go back where you came from, where you know the airport." Usually people called you by your numbers and used the standard radio-talk, but this man was talking like she was some dumb kid standing right there in front of him.

"Sure I know what I'm doing,'" she said. She'd done it again, opened her mouth too soon, she always did that. It was as if she had no control over her own voice.

"Runway nine is in use and there's no known traffic," the man on the unicorn was saying. If there was no traffic, why did he sound so nervous? He really didn't think she knew what she was doing. He made her nervous, too.

She had turned into her final approach, dropping low, over the threshold. Maybe she was too anxious to get in after all that, or maybe it was because of the fear in her, but she flared just a little too late. She hit the blacktop hard and bounced, jolted. Even without thinking she opened the throttle, closed the carburetor heat, did a touch-and-go, and climbed back up.

She would go around again; if the airport wasn't busy it never hurt, Sadie always said—never hurt anything but your pride. When you had to fly out of a bounce, you took a few deep breaths, thought a few cool thoughts, got your act together. Sadie had a lot of touch-and-go stories.

"Two seven November, did you do any damage?" the man on the unicom asked.

It had not occurred to her that she'd done any damage. Of course she hadn't done any damage; she'd hit harder than that before. But when her voice came it was smaller than she expected, a tiny chirp: "I don't think so," she said.

"Two seven November, maybe you better make a low pass over the field so we can take a look," he said.

Make a low pass over the field! But her voice had come out small and now all the rest of her was shrinking inside. "All right," she whispered. "Affirmative."

Her head pounded as she flew low over the runway. She expected to see one or two people below her, looking up at the belly of her plane—but when she passed there were not two, not three, but maybe a dozen. All of them stood below her with their

114

arms crossed, as if she'd interrupted a party. She broke into a sweat. They might have been watching her belly, not the plane's, giving her disapproving, judgmental looks, making sure there'd be hell to pay if they spotted some imperfection. Sweating, she pushed the throttle forward and climbed.

"Two seven November, no visible damage," the voice said. And then, apprehensive: "Lady, you can still go back where you came from if you want."

Anger started up in her then like a small blue flame. Her voice shook, but she got it out: "Two seven November is turning final for runway nine to land."

The man's voice grew cooler now, more official: "Everything's clear. You sure you want to try this again, lady?"

Her anger did not diminish; odd how it took hold sometimes. Once a customer had put off paying for months, and when her anger descended she'd said, "Listen, we can't wait forever, we don't have FDIC written on our window, we're not a bank." She hadn't known she'd say that until it actually came out. Then it got all over town that Chuck and Krista didn't have FDIC on their window, and everyone thought she was so clever and funny. Even the customer paid up, and Chuck said admiringly, "The anger serves you." So maybe it did. But today she'd kept her mouth shut when she should have said of course there wasn't any damage to the plane, and sounded like she meant it. If only Chuck or Sadie were here to reassure her, to say, "Look, those guys can be jerks too. Take it easy."

But she was on her own. She thought: this has got to be the best landing of my life.

Throttle back, a 70-knot glide, first flaps lowered, plane retrimmed. She made her mind go blank—pushed the unicom voice out of it, and everyone else's: the man who thought she'd smash a deer on the runway; Ann Paxton condescending to her when she was in labor; and anyone who thought she'd turn invisible when she got fat or get herself lost directly above Winchester. She was not lost.

She descended through 350 feet, coming in on final, feeling good. Came over the threshold, leveled out the glide. She controlled the rate of sink as if she'd been doing it all her life. Wings level. . . glide halted . . . just a few feet off the runway. Then the flareout: nose up just a little, power reduced. Main wheels down, nose wheel. Done. Rolling out.

She'd greased it in there. She really had.

The people at the airport were waiting on the tarmac, anxious to see who she was. She noticed that when she finally emerged their posture changed—it always did when they got a good look at her. The women pulled into themselves, and the men registered approval. The judgmental looks disappeared. One of the men even approached her.

"You know," he said, "There hasn't been a student pilot land here for two months. The last one who did went clear off the runway. Wasn't nearly as pretty as you, either."

Apologizing because she'd turned out to look the way she did? She didn't smile. Looks were luck, her landing wasn't. She'd bounced—hardly a graceful entry—but she'd known what to do. She was more like Sadie than she'd thought.

They kept staring at her. "All right ladies and gentlemen, the show's over, your families are probably waiting for you," she said, surprised to hear what came out. They were startled and began to move away, but she stopped them by speaking again, in a voice she finally recognized as her own: "Somebody sign my logbook first. I'm trying to get my license."

౨

THIS APPEARED IN *VIRGINIA COUNTRY*, AUGUST 1986

CUTTING WEIGHT

Our father had moved out over Labor Day, but by November it still wasn't official and we all pretended he was coming back. Every night at six-thirty I picked up my twin brother, Eric, at wrestling practice while Mom supposedly cooked dinner and the two younger kids set the table. Then one night Mom came rushing out as I was leaving, yelling, "I'll come with you, Adele, I need a few things at the store." Every time she went grocery shopping she forgot half her list. She was a mess. Before Dad left, she never let me or Eric drive if she was in the car. "Move over," she'd say. "You've had your license two months. I've had mine twenty-five years." But that night she slipped into the passenger seat without a word.

At school, Eric, who was trying to cut weight before the season began, was waiting in the dark outside the gym, hugging himself into his jacket.

"It's sixty degrees," Mom said. "Not exactly Arctic weather."

"When you starve yourself long enough, your metabolism slows down so much you never get warm. It practically stops." She claimed to know these things from her years as a nurse before we were born. I turned up the heat until Eric stopped shivering.

I was no longer sure who was in worse shape— Mom or Eric.

After Dad left and Mom went into her zombie mode, Eric decided to wrestle at 119. I'd been watching him for three years at the high school, so I understood that wrestlers liked to be as thin as possible, but this was ridiculous. Eric normally weighed 127, and even then he was skinny. That fall he was a stick.

He'd begun dieting in late October, eating only packaged foods with a calorie count on the label. Mom said twins like us were no more alike than any brother and sister, but Eric and I had always been pretty much the same, even-tempered and sensible. Then suddenly he was buying Lean Cuisines and cans of ravioli and macaroni and lining them up on the desk in his room—spaghetti with red labels, macaroni with yellow. "Just don't touch anything in here," he'd say menacingly.

One day Todd, who was ten, and Trudy, who was fourteen, were in the kitchen eating Spaghettios for lunch when Eric came in. He grabbed Todd by the collar and yelled, "You got those from my room, didn't you? Didn't you?"

Todd just sat there. "I didn't," he said.

"You better not."

"The Spaghettios came out of the pantry," I said to him. "I can't believe you're ready to break his nose over pasta." Eric let go. With Mom largely out of commission, I was the one who had to stay calm. It wasn't easy. Everyone knew we weren't really upset about spaghetti.

"We're stopping at the store," Mom said when Eric got into the car. "I'm running a little late with dinner."

Running was hardly the word. For three months Mom had been moving in slow motion. She acted like she'd gained all the weight Eric had lost—not on her body, because she was long and lanky, but inside her head, where it sat heavy, making her slow. Aside from forgetting food, she sometimes let the housework pile up until I washed the dishes and Trudy did the laundry.

At the supermarket Eric and I helped Mom find lettuce, cucumbers, and the low-calorie bread Eric ate. A man at the checkout stared as if Eric were a concentration camp survivor. Then we saw he was Ben Craig, Dad's insurance agent. The first thing he said was "Haven't seen Marshall around for months."

"He opened up a new office down in Wilmington," Mom replied. "He's been staying down there getting it going."

"Yes, I heard." He paused. "We've known each other a long time, Lorraine," he said. "If it's anything more than that, you can tell me."

Mom gave him one of her thousand-watt smiles, which I couldn't help but admire. She was slow lately, but the smile was a dazzler, aristocratic and withering. "Marshall'll be home for Thanksgiving, Ben," she said.

Back in the car, Eric cradled the grocery bag on his lap. "I was going to take that guy down with a single-leg," he told us, "but I was too hungry."

In spite of everything, Mom had been watching Eric wrestle ever since Dad left. This was a surprise because she'd objected to Eric's going out for the team when we were freshmen two years ago.

"I've watched them try to kill each other on TV," she'd said to Dad back then. "Don't ask me to watch my own son."

"It's nothing like professional wrestling," Dad insisted. "This is not the show, it's the sport." But Mom wouldn't budge.

I wasn't eager to see Eric wrestle myself, but back then I felt I ought to go to his first freshman match. Having made varsity because there was no other lightweight, Eric in his body-hugging singlet looked like a long, white pipe cleaner. "Not all wrestlers are the short, stocky type," Dad whispered, but anyone could see Eric was the only skeleton on the team; it did not look promising. Just watching him sit there made the tips of my fingers go numb.

The other team was a nasty, scarred-up gang who'd been talked into staying in school to wrestle. They called themselves The Lethal Weapon and had a reputation for forming a betting pool before each meet, which went to the guy who pinned his opponent most quickly. Eric said they always made their bets in front of rival teams at the weigh-in, as if there were no question of losing or winning by decision, but only of getting a fast pin.

Eric's opponent was a guy who'd spent time in a drug program, for which his eligibility had been extended. He was more man than boy—a short, fierce-looking guy who wore a screw, not an earring, in his pierced left ear. As soon as the whistle blew, he shot toward Eric's leg and took him down before I knew what happened. Eric struggled to get up from his stomach, but he couldn't move. I remember sitting on my hands until they began to get numb. Eric's nose was mashed into the mat, and the hoodlum was using his ankle as a lever to turn him over.

Eric was squirming like a trapped animal.

The other boy had him on his back. Right then The Lethal Weapon must have realized that if their man won quickly, they'd have to concede their betting pool early in the match, and it would take the fun out of the evening. So they began to root against their own lightweight, shouting advice instead to Eric.

"Bridge. Bridge!" they yelled. Though Eric later claimed he couldn't hear much with his headgear on, he suddenly did try to bridge—to arch his back and keep his shoulder blades off the floor. It didn't work. The referee slapped the mat and blew the whistle. Eric had gotten pinned in less than minute. He went back to the bench with mat burns on his cheek and tears in his eyes.

Going home in the car, he said, "God, I'm such a sorry wrestler I've even got the other team rooting for me." It was meant as casual sarcasm, but his voice cracked.

"They think they can psych you out with that betting pool," Dad said. "But you've got to learn to make them beat you on the mats and not in the locker room."

"I guess," Eric replied.

To me it seemed he'd be better off quitting, especially if he had to face ex-druggies with screws in their ears every week. But Eric and Dad seemed to regard this as an issue between just the two of them, so I kept my mouth shut.

Of course the news made Mom even more set against wrestling. "I will not watch my son starve himself for a month," she said, "to writhe around on the floor with some muscle-bound hoodlum."

After that, Dad and I went to all the meets without her. Eric won only twice freshman year, but as a sophomore he had a winning season. Mom still wouldn't go. Then Dad left, and she'd been to every pre-season scrimmage and early meet, even though Eric mostly lost. I put down the losses to his hunger strike.

Dad did come home for Thanksgiving. Mom had predicted it, but we kids were suspicious, what with his long absence. But he stuck to his story: As a mortgage banker, he'd been waiting years to expand. Now Wilmington was growing—a pretty coastal town, perfect for a branch office, three and a half hours away by car, forty minutes by plane. Why did he always miss the last flight home on Fridays? Because he worked so late—and worked on weekends, too.

Even Todd didn't believe this anymore.

"Parents of four kids don't get divorced, do they?" he'd ask. And Trudy would reply, "Don't be a dink."

So at Thanksgiving we expected . . . what? That Dad wouldn't look us in the eye, that we'd feel the tension between our parents, something. But there was nothing. Mom looked her usual self, aristocratic with her hair pulled back, lean in the tailored skirt she wore to serve the turkey. She didn't flirt with Dad but wasn't sarcastic, either. Everyone admired the meal; Eric nibbled sparingly. On Friday we had leftovers, and Dad and Eric practiced takedowns in the yard. Nothing remarkable. Saturday Dad said Mom had cooked enough, he was taking us out for lunch. Eric's weight was good; he would cheat a little on his diet. Dad winked. Mom laughed. We were lulled into a false sense of normalcy.

It was as if Dad had given Eric permission to eat. Steak, vegetables, little round potatoes. Finally he sat back, smiling. But then Dad announced he was leaving that afternoon instead of the next day. It was a three-and-a-half hour drive, after all; he had paperwork to do before Monday. Eric and I looked at each other, and each knew what the other was thinking: We'd been bought. Sunday we'd be home with Mom, and Dad would be sitting on the beach with his girlfriend.

Who was this woman? We weren't quite sure. We'd been to Wilmington only once, on Labor Day when Dad moved into his tiny apartment. We swam and met the two women in his office—Beth and Tina. It could have been either. Both women were younger than Mom, though not so pretty. Both had noticeable breasts.

After Dad left, as if to punish himself for thinking things were normal, Eric cut to 700 calories a day—mostly the cans of ravioli on his desk. Instead of eating, he read Mom's cookbooks, testing the sounds of ingredients on his tongue as if they could replace actual food: "Confetti pasta. Sounds good, doesn't it?" His face paled to the color of macaroni, but *The Joy of Cooking* lay open on the counter. For a guy who'd never cooked anything but scrambled eggs, it was bizarre. The holiday issue of *Southern Living* disappeared into his room, where he gazed at the pictures more diligently than he did *Playboy*.

"Did you ever make a souffle?" he asked Mom.

"Never."

"Mincemeat pie?"

"No."

"It's not normal, a wrestler reading recipes," I said. He rolled his eyes. Anyone who wrestled was macho. The more weight you cut, the more macho. Superman, completely in control. I felt deserted. When you're twins, you get the idea that there's somebody to sail along with no matter what happens, even if your father leaves. But there was Eric, drifting away. If he and Mom collapsed simultaneously—which seemed ever more likely—who'd run the house? Not Todd and Trudy. Me?

The next week Eric's nose started to bleed in the middle of a match. The referee blew the whistle so the coach could wipe Eric's face and the mat, but the bleeding wouldn't stop. After a discussion of making Eric forfeit, they finally let him go on. Blood ran down his lips, but he kept at it. My own mouth tasted of blood, and Eric's skin looked like wax. Then the other boy got the advantage and turned Eric over like a sack.

Mom didn't say a word until we got home. "You're

anemic, Eric. That's why your nose bled. There is absolutely no rationale for dieting so strenuously that you become anemic."

"Oh. come off it, Mom," he said.

"Red meat," she told him, ignoring his rudeness. "I don't care if you don't eat another thing. But I'm going to cook red meat every night, and I expect you to eat it."

Eric didn't reply. Why should he? It wasn't as if she could put food in his mouth. It wasn't as if she had power over any of us anymore.

"We won't put up the tree," she said the following week. "We'll wait for Dad to do that. But we can put out the rest of the things so the house will look festive." I was half surprised she really expected Dad to join us.

It was Saturday and Eric had an away meet, but the rest of us brought down the Christmas decorations from the attic. Usually the family sorted them together, but that day Mom began to go through the boxes herself. She examined each thing with terrible slowness. It was clear she didn't want help. She came to an oversize felt stocking with pockets for Christmas cards, which always hung in the den. She looked at it and replaced it in the box. Todd kept asking for a job. Finally Mom sent him outside to cut magnolia leaves for the mantel. Trudy called a friend. I flipped through the college brochures placed around the house. None of this felt normal.

"Don't ask," Eric said when he came in from his meet. "I got creamed. Pinned in the first period."

His face was pasty white.

"We put up the Christmas decorations," I said to distract him. "It looks nice, don't you think?"

"What decorations?" I thought he was kidding, but when I looked around, the den didn't seem very Christmasy without its usual felt stocking. Maybe it was because we'd always put up the tree along with the other stuff, but suddenly the whole house looked austere, even with its candles and magnolia leaves. Mom didn't believe in glitzy silver garlands or plastic.

She was in the kitchen, not even aware Eric had come in—moving slowly, weighted down, not paying us any attention. In her black turtleneck and jeans, she could have been some stranger with long arms and bony wrists jutting from her sleeves. They say a woman can't be too rich or too thin, but it wasn't true. Mom's body was as austere and ungenerous as the rooms. In Wilmington, Tina and Beth were softer.

Dad always called before dinner on Saturday. He said he worked all day but then started missing his family. We didn't believe this. We thought he phoned as a duty, before going out with his girlfriend. Upset as I was by the idea of what went on in Wilmington, sometimes I imagined Dad with his arm around Tina (or Beth, I was still not sure which), picturing them coolly, as if watching from a distance. Since there had been no official announcement, this seemed safe. But when evening came and the phone was silent, I wondered if we'd entered a new phase.

The phone didn't ring. Mom kept reading. I couldn't stand it.

I walked over to the couch. Eric looked so exhausted that I decided not to wake him, but suddenly he shouted, "No!" and startled from sleep into a sitting position.

"What?" I asked.

"Oh—I thought I was still at the match," he said sleepily.

I sat down next to him and patted his hand. "Can I get you something to eat?"

Eric slung his arm around my shoulder. "Yeah, what's for dinner?"

I shrugged. All week Mom had been making hamburgers and steaks, and Eric had been politely eating some. But now she was reading her magazine and no food had been taken from the freezer.

"After the season's over," he said to me, "I'm going to cook about three nights a week."

"Oh, sure, and I'm going to swim the English Channel." Even Todd was a better cook than Eric.

"I will," he said, squeezing my shoulder.

"I'll cook unless I have an exam, and sometimes we'll go out."

By now Todd and Trudy were listening. Todd nodded as if he believed Eric would take over the care of the family and everything would be all right. Fat chance. I shook Eric's arm off and moved away

"The first thing I'm going to make is a roast with mashed potatoes," he said, ignoring me. "And chocolate cake for dessert."

"You better do that on a weekend," said Trudy.

"You won't have time to do it after school."

"I'll make it on a Sunday. A Sunday dinner."

They all nodded as if this were perfectly reasonable. They acted as if this were about food and not about Dad. We all knew he wasn't going to call. "Sounds more like Christmas dinner," I said snidely.

"So?"

I was really getting angry. "Your Christmas dinner is right up there on your desk," I shouted. "You can have the Christmas dinner in the red can or the Christmas dinner in the yellow can. Only three hundred calories a hit."

"Adele, leave off," Trudy said.

"Dump it in a pan, turn the stove to high. About the limit of your culinary skills, too. Who do you think you're fooling?"

Mom came in from the kitchen. "What's the matter, Adele? Why are you yelling?"

"Me? Yelling?" I screamed. I was sick of being calm. Eric wasn't the twin I remembered, and Mom wasn't the mother. Why should I be calm for strangers?

Mom's eyes focused, but she was far away. She said, "Maybe we should send out for pizza."

After that I didn't care about either of them. Just didn't care. The next day Dad called and spoke only to Mom. Her face went completely blank. "He won't be home for Christmas," she said afterward. "In fact, we're thinking about a separation."

"A separation? I thought you were already having one," I said.

"Shut up, Adele," Eric said. I just stared him down.

Two days later Eric got up weighing 125. He'd have to lose six pounds before the meet that night, fasting and running. I figured it served him right.

Mom looked on the verge of tears, watching Eric starve and still gain weight. But she was distracted over Dad and didn't mention Eric's anemia or suggest he take a snack for after the weigh-in. No last pathetic attempts at motherhood.

That evening in the gym we watched Eric warm up with penetration drills. He was so pale he looked like he'd have trouble staying conscious all evening, much less wrestling. I bought popcorn and ate it with the box close to my face. I felt a little guilty but chewed on. At least I could smell salt and butter instead of gym shoes and sweat.

Mom clenched her fists when the meet started, but I kept eating. I was ice. When Eric came out for his match, I stuffed a whole handful of popcorn into my mouth and offered some to Trudy. Then I saw Eric's opponent: the guy who wore a screw in his ear. Tiny kernels stuck in my throat. I could hardly swallow.

Eric had wrestled the hoodlum only that once. Then the guy was in another weight class. But now there he was, his body a solid mass of muscle. There's no way, I thought. I put the popcorn on the floor.

Eric didn't pass out, and his nose didn't bleed. That was something. First period ended with Eric behind by two points, second period by five. At the beginning of the last period the hoodlum dropped Eric into a pinning combination. It would soon be over. Mom reached down and grabbed my hand. She was clinging to Trudy on the other side, and Trudy was holding onto Todd.

I didn't want to care. But it was as if they were depending on me, as if being twins were stronger than anything, as if I were the only one who could give Eric the strength he needed. I didn't think, I just started yelling: "Bridge, Eric, bridge!" Exactly the way The Lethal Weapon had yelled two years ago, only taunting wasn't on my mind. I could feel the fury gathering in Eric's chest, gathering in my own. He broke a hold, turned onto his stomach. Sweat, pallor, and concentration appeared equally on his face. A second later he was on his feet. He got the reversal, put the thug on his back. The guy grinned, as if to say, That's what you think, pal. I'll get out of this yet. But Eric was working so hard he wasn't there at all; he was only a weight on the other guy's chest. This was less about wrestling than about survival—about a kind of strength that had nothing to do with what you ate. Mom's nails were digging into my palms. The hoodlum tried to arch his back, but he was pinned. The whistle blew to end it.

The referee held up Eric's hand in victory.

Mom raised her own hand, still clutched into mine and Trudy's, and Trudy raised the hand she held with Todd. A chain. It lasted only a second, but Eric saw. He nodded up at us. And winked.

꒰ꇙ꒱

THIS APPEARED IN *SEVENTEEN*, MAY 1989

MISCARRIAGE

L u was lying on the operating table with her arms strapped to pads at right angles to her body, as if she were being crucified instead of anesthetized. The anesthetist had failed to find a vein in the left hand to start an IV, and had finally located one in the right after thumping it and finally dangling it to the floor to make the vessels pop up. Lu supposed she should be frightened rather than annoyed, but she could not count on her emotions. The anesthetist fumbled around behind her and eventually placed a black mask over her nose, which was something she thought he would avoid at least until she was unconscious from the pentothal. "Just a little oxygen," he told her.

"It doesn't smell like oxygen," she said. It smelled acrid, annoying, toxic. Later everyone would tell her: During that time you were not yourself. Not herself. But how could she be otherwise?

"Here, I'll flush it out a little," the anesthetist said, taking the mask away.

"It reminds me of getting ether when I was a kid with my tonsils," she said. She thought of her son

Teddy and his terror of people being in hospitals.

"We don't use ether anymore," the anesthetist said. "The smell's from the cleaning solution they use." He put it back over her face. "Is that better?"

"Not much."

"Big deep breaths. We're putting you to sleep now. Put your chin up while we're putting you to sleep." A nurse was rubbing her throat. "After you're asleep we're going to help you breathe."

She would not have imagined that one adult would actually say to another adult: we're going to help you breathe.

Bright lights, a waterfall. She woke up in the recovery room, coughing, unable to see because they had not let her bring her glasses.

"I hate not seeing," she said.

"Do you have any pain?"

"No." There had never been, she reminded herself, any significant pain.

*   *   *

She was 40 and had not wanted another baby. She'd spent ten years at home with Kent and Teddy—much of it, she'd often thought, simply waiting for them both to be in school. Now they were twelve and seven, safely started on their lives, and she'd gone back to work. She loved the barebones office of the little magazine, her meetings with writers, the hours going over copy. She felt fortunate to have gotten an editing job at all—lucky, after all that time, not to have been offered a slot in the data entry pool. A pregnancy was hardly on the agenda. She had nightmarish visions of herself dressed in a business suit, on her way out of town for a meeting, so nauseated that she had to stop the car at the side of the road for air. During the pregnancies with Kent and Teddy, she'd used most of her energy during the early months simply holding herself together.

Her husband, Evan, was more neutral. "We'll do whatever you think best," he said. She might have rushed off to the doctor as soon as she suspected, to have the blood test that determined pregnancy after only a few days, to take action. But she did not.

Partly it was because Evan, for all his professed neutrality, treated her gently, tentatively during that time as if, after 15 years of marriage, he believed anew in Lu's possibilities. "Anything?" he asked in the first days after she missed her period, when they believed it might be early menopause or a great mistake. She shook her head no, and invariably he touched her, as if to find out for himself. "Puffy," he'd say, exploring her breasts and her belly. That led to lovemaking, which she found herself wanting in a nervous, urgent way, perhaps for reassurance. But it happened so often she realized it was not reassurance that drove her, or even desire, but—in a surprising, 15-years-of-marriage way—love.

The pregnancy became their secret. She meant to get up at five to run the home pregnancy test and read the results before the boys got up. This was their plan. But both of them dozed fitfully all night, shifting position, trying to get comfortable, both of them restless, until finally they shaped themselves against each other and suddenly fell asleep. At that moment Teddy and Kent came bursting into the room, shouting, insisting they could find no clean socks. Lu stumbled out of bed to retrieve some from the laundry room, and Evan also rose—so smoothly that it was as if their moves had been planned—and quickly shut the door to the bathroom so the boys wouldn't see the small pregnancy kit sitting in readiness on the sink.

Later, when the boys had been sent downstairs for a forbidden treat of Cap'n Crunch, Lu crept into the bathroom, closed the door against another juvenile assault, ran the test, and opened the door to Evan, so the two of them could observe the perfect, pregnancy-confirming circle in the test-tube. They raised their eyebrows at each other, shook their heads in a worried way—and then, realizing that their sons were breakfasting on the sugary cereals they had always vowed not to feed them, and that they had locked themselves together into the smallest room in their house—laughed.

At work Lu was helping to plan the theme for an expanded anniversary issue of the magazine. She'd been so enthusiastic that she'd been put more or less in charge. But once her breasts swelled she began to feel waterlogged, distracted. She was sleepy; the meetings in the magazine's windowless conference room seemed endless, and she had to concentrate on staying awake. She yearned to be at home, where Evan catered to her lethargy cheerfully and continued to watch her with fascination. She could not deny that she liked it. One night they lay in bed not quite asleep, Evan's leg protectively against hers, and Lu was visited by an image she had not had for years—of the pig-tailed daughter she had once expected to bear, fair-haired and freckled like Evan. She had never thought it would happen.

Suddenly adrenaline coursed through her as if she had been struck. She didn't want another child, not really. She wanted the life she had now: days surrounded by other adults, wearing business suits instead of drip-dry cottons, coming home with a sense of accomplishment. Too late to go back. She was over forty. She should end the pregnancy. She should do it now.

She did nothing. She floated through her days, recalling how stifled she had felt when Teddy and Paul were small, how confined, how restless, and yet stunned, somehow, into inaction.

The doctor did not want to see her until she was six weeks along. The weekend before she was finally scheduled to visit, she began to spot. On the phone, the doctor said spotting was not uncommon; it might be nothing. Cramps gnawed at her, but the bleeding was slight. The weekend passed. On Monday morning she woke feeling lightheaded but not really ill. She got the boys off to school. Ten minutes later she passed a wad of tissue not much bigger than her thumb. The doctor called it a spontaneous abortion, complete and clean.

"If you'd been a few weeks further along, I'd want

you to go in for a D&C," he said. "But since it was so early it's really not necessary. Unless you have a lot of bleeding, which I don't think you will, this should be the end of it."

Lu was relieved. This would be the end of it. She would be careful not to let it happen again.

The recovery room lights came from all around her: harsh, fluorescent, glaring. The objects before her were clear, then fuzzy, not simply fuzzy at a distance, which could be accounted for by her near-sightedness, but indistinct even at close range. Objects focused before her and then went foggy again, as if her mind were stuffed with cotton.

"I wish somebody would bring my glasses up," she said.

"You'll be down in your room before long," the nurse told her. "As soon as you begin to feel more like yourself."

As soon as she began to feel like herself. That phrase again. As if she were some stranger, and the real Lu had gotten lost. She lay back against the pillow, watching the IV drip into her arm, trying to make the room focus properly, trying to shake the anesthesia from her brain. Trying to become herself.

Odd, how touchy she'd been after the miscarriage. She bled a little and had to wear a pad, but that wouldn't account for her irritability. Hormones, Evan said, her body trying to right itself. She did not remember feeling this way after the boys were born. For weeks the smallest things set her off—the boys' noise at the dinner table, their incessant rolling on the floor fighting, Kent's skateboard in the living room, his radio still blasting after he'd left for school. It was an unproductive irritation. Instead of insisting calmly that the mess be picked up, or suggesting some activity that would distract the boys from pounding on each other, she found herself yelling at them, "For heaven's sake, you two, get off each other, get out of here, shut up!"

Once Evan was late getting home from work, and the boys refused to settle down. Her heart beat fast in her throat, but her agitation only egged them on. A knot of pure anger settled in her chest. Why should her sons treat her this way? Why should Evan not be home to help? In a cool recess of her mind she understood that Evan, held up by a meeting, had no control over his absence, and the boys, overwrought, were not treating her any way, but only trying to kill each other. Yet still it was as if all of them had aimed their behavior at her—poisoned arrows—and she, already wounded, could offer no defense.

Being at work was better. Extra writers had been commissioned to provide copy for the expanded anniversary issue, and she was busy. Small, mechanical details suited her. Only when her colleagues, who did not know about her miscarriage, commented on her paleness, her absorption, did she become annoyed.

Teddy was to be in a choral show at school, which the whole family was to attend. In spite of everything, Lu found herself anticipating it with pleasure. The boys had inherited their singing voices from Evan, a relief since they had inherited so little else—her dark skin, her features, her build—but she had never been able to carry a tune. On the evening of the performance, Kent refused until the last minute to get dressed. "Why should I have to go see some second-grade production? Geez, I'm in middle school, I saw all that years ago, I have homework to do." Normally Lu would have ignored him, since he was grudgingly getting ready even as he complained. But though she said nothing, anger continued to well up in her even while they were driving to the school. She felt, as she had not since she had taken her job, powerless against her sons.

Finally, in the hushed and darkened auditorium, Kent sat quietly next to Evan and appeared as if he were going to behave. For the moment she could simply listen to the music. Teddy stood in the front row of the chorus with the other second graders, looking proud and a little silly in his button-down shirt and tie. A girl in an oversized dress stepped out to sing a solo. She was so tall and freckle-faced that she might have been the daughter Lu had once imagined. Her voice was perfectly pitched. Humming behind her, the chorus sounded surprisingly sweet. Lu's throat grew tight. Music had always had the power to. make her cry. But this was no sentimental moistening of the eyes. Suddenly tears were spilling from her eyes, down her cheeks. She rose, trying to hold great heaving sobs inside her chest. She could not. They burst from her even as she rushed into the lobby, unable to stifle the noise.

In the silent hallway, her weeping seemed to echo all about her, enormous and embarrassing. She couldn't stop. Then Evan was beside her. She expected him to be, had known he would come. She leaned into his shoulder, her sobs muffled by his sports coat, and let herself cry as if she would break.

"What's wrong?" he kept asking, thrusting wads of tissues into her hand. When she could finally speak, she blew her nose loudly and said, "I know you won't believe this, but nothing's wrong." And burst into tears again.

"Hormones," Evan said. The standard explanation. It seemed shallow and not entirely true. She blew her nose again, for lack of a more appropriate gesture, and composed herself to go back in.

Afterwards, on the way home, Kent said tentatively, "I guess it's your female problems again." Recently Evan had told the boys, in view of Lu's moodiness, that she was having some female problems and would soon be all right. A sexist, unsatisfactory explanation, but she had had no energy to offer a fuller one.

"I guess," she agreed.

"It's not so bad if you're just sitting there with the tears running down your cheeks," Kent said, in a voice that sounded at once patronizing and apologetic. "But when you really start to waah like that—geez, Mom."

"I think we'll send you down to your room now," the nurse said, though Lu wasn't at all sure she felt any better than she had before. Not that she had ever felt bad.

The ride on the stretcher through the hallways of the hospital was unsettling. Walls and ceilings flashed passed her, bright shapes blurred by her nearsighted haze, making her a little dizzy. Her room, by contrast, seemed grayish. She realized that most of the day had passed. It was late afternoon: the light outside was fading. A nurse came in and switched on a lamp above her bed, a pool of warmth against the shadows, Somehow she had expected Evan to be waiting for her, but the room was empty.

"Was my husband here?" she asked.

"He was, but he said he had to go, that he would come to get you later."

Of course. That had been their agreement. He would leave at 3:30 if she wasn't back in the room yet, and go home to reassure the boys when they came in from school, Later he would take them to dinner, then bring them to pick her up. That was important, given Teddy's views on hospitalization. He believed that once you went into a hospital, you never came out. That was what had happened to Lu's mother after her heart attack. He needed to see that it wasn't always so. Yet still, right now, fresh from surgery, she wanted Evan for herself.

"I guess you'll become a spirit now," Teddy had said when they told him Lu would have to go into the hospital for a minor operation. Three weeks had passed, and her bleeding hadn't stopped: it had even grown progressively heavier, though never alarmingly so. The doctor wanted her to have a D&C after all, in case a piece of tissue was still lodged in the uterus. "It's a very simple thing, nothing to worry about," Evan had explained to the boys. "She goes in the morning and comes out that same night."

"For her female problem," Kent guessed with some disgust.

"Yes."

"I suppose we're not going to get the lowdown on what this problem actually is."

"Right again," Lu had said.

"It means she'll become a spirit," Teddy added.

"Don't be ridiculous," they all told him, hoping to keep the mood light.

But two hours after his bedtime, Teddy had appeared in the master bedroom with a dead, false calm on his face, saying: "The old lady's in my mirror again."

He'd seen her before in the weeks after Lu's mother died—almost two years ago now. Night after night he'd woken with the same eerie calm, and come into the room to tell them. It wasn't Grandma, he said, but maybe it was her spirit. They tried to explain that he was seeing a reflection of the street lights outside, but Teddy was adamant. Then gradually the image had vanished, and Lu had all but forgotten it. She feared at first her moodiness had something to do with bringing it back, but decided not. Teddy was used to emotional upheaval; he had survived even Kent's prepubescent outbursts with relative equanimity. It was logical, from his limited point of view, to believe that entering a hospital presaged an ending. And in a way, Lu suspected it wasn't even that. He did not really behave as if he expected to lose her. It was more as if, subconsciously, the way children do, Teddy had somehow sensed a death—not Lu's death, but a real one, which he had not been told about but which, nevertheless, had occurred.

A death. She herself had not thought of losing the baby that way. Had thought, rather, in terms of inconvenience. But still . . .

They had come to remove the IV. "Some people, the IV bothers them more than anything else," the nurse said, working over her arm, applying a bandaid to the spot where the needle had been. It was a pleasure to have her arm free, to have complete range of motion. She bent her elbow, flexed a bicep. Small pleasures. She remembered other pleasures: Evan testing her breasts, stroking her belly during her brief pregnancy. As if they were celebrating something. Well, weren't they? It had been a way of rejoicing—hadn't it?—over the child she thought she didn't want.

"Need some help getting dressed?" the nurse asked.

"No, I think I can handle it." But her hands shook as she removed the hospital gown. Joy first, then sadness—not entirely hormones at all. Of course. Beneath reason, beneath consciousness, in the mysterious life of the cells, no child was really unwanted, even at 40-plus; and afterwards, despite the reasoned relief of the mind, still the body cried.

Now Evan was before her, tentative, coming into the room.

"You all right?"

"Getting there." They both smiled, awkwardly. Perhaps she also grieved for Evan, for his loving her so during those brief weeks of her pregnancy.

"I took the boys for pizza," he said. "Teddy's very nervous. He even combed his hair. He's pretty sure you're not really up here, that I'll come back down with some excuse."

"We're about to make his day," she said. Dressed, she sat in the required wheelchair for the ride down in the elevator. At the ground floor she said to the aide firmly, "From this point on, I walk."

Evan held her elbow as they emerged into the hallway, as if she were fragile, precious, even now. In the lobby, the boys were sitting on bright plastic chairs, looking, by contrast, serious and subdued. Kent waved casually when he spotted her, but Teddy's eyes widened with surprise.

"Are you a spirit now?" he asked. He studied her for a moment. "Or are you really you yourself?"

"Oh I'm really me myself," she told him, realizing, as she said it, that she was

❧

THIS APPEARED IN *VIRGINIA COUNTRY*, VOLUME XII, NUMBER 4, DECEMBER 1989

A KISS IN THE WILD

By the time Hollis reached the sign that announced a state campground at the next exit, she knew she'd never be able to make the last hour's drive to Ocean City and Aunt Rook's store without a break. Her head ached, her nose was stuffy and she was so exhausted from the long drive she was beginning to feel woozy.

It was not stopping to eat lunch, she decided, and pulled off the highway into the campground. There were still a few sandwiches in the cooler in the back of her car. Maybe if she ate she'd feel more able to cope with the last leg of the trip.

Except for the sign in the registration booth window announcing a ranger on duty, the whole park was deserted. It was still April, too early for people to want to sleep outside.

She dragged herself out of the car and shivered. Already the air had lost whatever warmth the sun had lent in the afternoon—or maybe it was just that she was beginning to feel feverish. She did a quick job of setting up her tent, then returned to the car for her sleeping bag.

A pickup truck rounded the curve of gravel road next to the campsites and ground to a stop. Her heart raced. She hadn't heard it approach. But it was just the ranger coming to check.

She went to the back of the car and bent down quickly to open the trunk and get the sleeping bag— *too* quickly. Her head swam and her feet felt unsteady. She staggered back and turned, heading for the tent, dazed but instinctively seeking shelter.

The ranger had climbed out of his truck and was regarding her steadily, disapprovingly she thought, from behind large, dark-lashed eyes. He was young, probably not yet thirty. Finally he walked up to her and asked, "You all right?"

"Yes, fine," she said quickly. He was frowning at her now. The disapproving eyes made her feel uneasy, even beyond the wooziness. It seemed to her she remembered that frown from the last weeks with Drew, when their money had all but run out.

"What's your name, Miss?" he asked.

"Hollis Witherspoon," she said.

His frown gave way to puzzled curiosity. "That sounds familiar."

She shrugged. Her name always seemed vaguely familiar to people, but most of them didn't make the connection, though it had been less than two years since "Sweet Baby Bumpkin" had been the number one rock tune in the country.

Those that did remember always stared at her as if they'd seen a ghost. "Hollis Witherspoon! Hollis and the Witherspoons! Of course!" Afterwards they dug at her for details of her downfall.

They'd tell her then about their own singing groups, how they'd almost made it themselves, how they still might. They'd sing lines from songs they'd written and ask her for advice.

When they found out the only contacts she had left in the entertainment business were owners of shabby taverns in little towns outside of Denver, Louisville and New Orleans—the last places she'd played before the split-up—they'd lose interest. Leeches, all of them, just like Drew. They strengthened her resolve, though. She would not depend on anyone again, ever.

The ranger was looking at her again with that expression of distrust and disbelief, studying her as if she were some unusual species he had come across in the woods. "Are you sure you're all right?" he asked.

"Oh, yes. I drove too long and I've got a little cold. That's all."

Then a wave of dizziness sent the gray sky whirling around her, taking with it the tops of the tall pines. Black dots sailed in front of her eyes like pieces of soot.

She woke up in a real bed, covered with a quilt. A cabin of sorts. The wall beside her was smooth polished wood, a window across the room looked out on trees. His voice reached her before she saw him standing there, and she started with fright. The disbelief had gone from the dark eyes, at least, and now they were full of concern.

"Feeling better?"

Her head still throbbed but she was not so dizzy.

Throat raw. Glands swollen and achy.

"Maybe the flu," she said.

"Yes. You have a fever." He sounded surprised.

"Did you expect something else? A drug problem, maybe?" It came out as a rasp, not very polite, but she was still too fuzzy for manners.

"We get a fair number of druggies in the summer. They come here because they can't afford a motel at the beach and they bring all their paraphernalia and whatever they've bought on the street—which isn't always what they think it is."

"I wouldn't drive twelve hundred miles on drugs," she said, insulted in spite of her bleariness. She tried to sit up but he pushed her gently on the shoulder and she sank into the pillow.

"I guess I fainted. I'm sorry."

"No need to be sorry. You're welcome to the bed as long as you need it."

The bed. As long as she needed it. "Where am I?" she asked suddenly.

"The bedroom. I thought it was obvious."

"I mean . . . yours?"

"It's part of the deal. A ranger gets a house. We're on the edge of the park, maybe two hundred yards from the campsite."

She felt immediately very safe, very cozy. "When I was twelve or thirteen I used to faint if I got a fever and didn't go to bed," she told him. "I haven't done it in years." Then, suddenly, without really meaning to, she felt too weary to do anything but close her eyes.

Later she couldn't count how many times she slept and woke. Sometimes he would be standing nearby, and she thought maybe his presence had stirred her. Other times the room was deserted. He brought her water and aspirin, later a cup of tea. Once he asked her where she was going.

"My aunt's," she said groggily, without elaborating.

"Do you want me to call her?"

"No. I'm not on a time schedule." She slept again, as if sleep were all she had ever really wanted from the world, after so many months without it.

Then it was morning—she wasn't sure which morning—and she woke with aching limbs and a clear head. He was sipping coffee when she caught sight of him in the doorway, dressed in his ranger's uniform, hair newly combed, eyes surprisingly gentle.

"I think I've been on a mammoth sleep-in," she said.

"I think you have," he said, smiling. "Coffee?"

"Please."

"I'm off to work for a while. Will you be okay?"

"Oh yes," she said, realizing now how much she had imposed on him. How much work had he missed because of her? "I think I'm almost cured."

"Good."

She crawled out of the bed when he left and examined the cabin. It was small but comfortable. The logs had been sheared off inside to make smooth, golden-hued walls. There was a tiny kitchen, a living room with a fireplace and the bedroom. She realized with chagrin that he must have been sleeping on the couch. For how long? Her tour of the place exhausted her. She was still dressed in the same clothes she'd been wearing for . . . how long? She meant to shower, to fix her hair, but she was suddenly too weak. She crawled back into the bed and slept.

He came home at lunchtime and fixed her a bowl of soup. "No more bedside service," he called. "You'll have to drag yourself to the table."

"You make me feel guilty," she said.

"Not your fault." He set soup before her and ladled out a bowl for himself. She knew how she must look, but she was suddenly ravenous. Besides, he made her feel so comfortable.

"I hate to ask you this," she said, "but how long have I been here?"

"Not so long. Two days."

"Two days!"

"And you don't even know my name," he said slyly. The absurdity of it—two days in his cabin and she didn't know his name—struck her as very funny. They were both laughing when he reached his arm across the table to her and shook her hand. "Pete Bowers," he said. "Nice to meet you."

"Likewise." Laughing, he looked entirely different, very handsome. She was once again aware of her state of disrepair.

As soon as he left she resolved to get herself cleaned up. But sleep overcame her once again, and when she woke it was late afternoon. She found her suitcase in the corner of the room, took out a clean out-fit and locked herself in the bathroom. She emerged feeling almost like her old, healthy self, hair still wet and tousled, but clean. She had walked halfway into the living room when she realized he was sitting on the couch, regarding her with a look she hadn't bargained for. Recognition in the dark eyes, and something like amusement.

"I should have known," he said.

"Known what?"

"I've figured it out."

"Figured out what?"

"Hollis and the Witherspoons," he said. "'Sweet Baby Bumpkin.' A couple of years ago. Am I right?" He was laughing at her now, laughing outright. She began to draw into herself. She didn't really know him, after all. The look on his face was so open and amused that she couldn't stay angry.

"I should have known it from the name," he said, "but you look so different that I didn't think. That wild haircut you had back then, sticking out like it is now."

She turned and caught a glimpse of herself in the bathroom mirror behind her. Her wet hair was sticking out just as he'd said. Yes, it did look like the way she'd worn it then.

"I must say the present hairdo is more becoming."

Suddenly she was laughing herself, laughing at Hollis of Hollis and the Witherspoons for the first time ever. She had worn her hair very short then. Every night before her show she had teased what there was of it out into a froth, so that she looked as if she had just been struck by lightning.

She went after him with the towel she had in her hand, flicking it out at him while he veered out of her way.

"It was a lot of trouble, that hairdo!" she cried through her laughter, chasing him. He stepped back and zigzagged.

"Is this what I get for my hospitality?" he roared. She struck at him again, but he was quicker than she. Then all at once her weakness caught up with her and it was all she could do to collapse untidily onto the couch. He sat beside her, still staring at her hair.

"So you were Hollis," he said.

"The lady herself."

"The big punk rock star. Imagine that. I may hold you for ransom after all." His voice was very gentle, and it surprised her. Usually their first reaction was shock and then curiosity. Never this, well, *wonder*.

"I wouldn't hold my breath waiting for ransom," she said wryly. "Star is past tense."

He seemed to consider this as if it had not occurred to him. "No, I guess not," he said finally. "There was 'Sweet Baby Bumpkin' and then—I don't remember any more."

"No more hits. No more good club billings. The usual story."

He stood, reacting to the tone of her voice. "You don't have to tell me about it if you don't want to. I'll still feed you. Hungry?"

"I'm afraid so. My appetite has apparently returned with my strength."

He took out a skillet and made hamburgers, not letting her help. Almost effortlessly, he turned the conversation away from the subject of her lost stardom, telling her about his work.

They did the dishes together and lit a fire in the fireplace. He brought her coffee as she sat on the rug in front of the hearth, then slid down beside her. They sipped the coffee slowly. He pushed at the fire now and then with a stick. They talked so easily she might have known him for years. He put his arm around her shoulders as they both leaned back against the couch behind them, warm and safe.

The next thing she knew he was kissing her, gently at first and then not so gently. So nice. She hadn't been kissed for a year. When she pulled herself free after a long time, reluctantly, he looked at her as if he didn't understand. But she sat up on the rug and pushed him away.

Did his mood change just then? Did all the gentleness drain away? Was there a trace of anger in his eyes?

"Don't worry," he said at last. "You're safe, if that's what you want. You won't have to barricade the bedroom door."

It was then that she realized he hadn't shown this kind of interest until he found out who she was: a star, however fallen. They were always drawn to something. With Drew it was the way he could shape her talent; with the others, it was her fame.

Now Pete was expecting payment. Two days of playing nursemaid . . . of course. You paid and paid and paid and when you stopped there was nothing left. The moment the money ran out Drew decided the backup singer Kendra had the better voice—a new chance, another talent to mold. They never wanted just her. She went into the bedroom and locked the door.

In the morning he was gone when she awoke. The clock read nine-thirty. She was half-relieved not to have to face him again, but she knew she should thank him in person and say goodbye. Instead she wrote a quick note and put it on the table, packed what few things she'd used and was loaded up by ten. Above the pine trees, the air was warm and golden, but her mood was bleak. At least she might have seen him.

Aunt Rook was in the store when she got there, making her way through piles of mess kits, Coleman lanterns, a tent display. The place was a shambles. The old woman looked up, pushed a strand of gray hair off her forehead with the back of her hand and said to Hollis, "About time. I thought you'd be here at the beginning of the week."

"I would have. I got slowed down by the flu."

"You look healthy enough," Rook said, peering down through half-glasses as if she expected Hollis to be covered with splotches.

"Well, yes, I'm recovered now."

"Good. Then you can go to work pricing these lanterns here." She stood to her full height and surveyed the mess. "I want to open at least two weeks before Memorial Day. You'd be surprised how many campers try to beat the season. And how many things they run out of."

By quitting time Hollis was exhausted. Rook showed her to her room in the little apartment above the store, and Hollis fell asleep without even unpacking. When she awoke Rook was standing over her in near-darkness, looking perplexed. "I didn't know whether to get you up to eat or not," she said. "I guess you really were sick."

Hollis sat up quickly and took stock of the situation. "Just a little tired yet," she said. "Aunt Rook, you've worked more hours than I have today. You should let me do the cooking."

"Of course I'll let you cook," Rook told her. "We'll work out a schedule and take alternate nights. Tonight absolutely not. On your first evening here you have to let me be the hostess."

Hollis sighed, slightly amused. She was sure Rook would be true to her word. They would divide up their duties just as she'd said. That was part of the reason she'd come. At least her aunt would treat her like an ordinary person, not a star.

During the next few days she settled in. "Ordinarily," Rook said, "I'd be all set up by now, but nowadays you can't keep help even with so many young people unemployed. Some of them are just so lazy."

Hollis took one look at the mess that remained even after three days of sorting out and she wondered. New stock arrived daily, but Rook seemed to have no system for handling it. She ran Hollis here and there and everywhere rather than giving her any clear responsibilities, so that neither of them accomplished as much as they might have. Rook wanted to be in charge of every detail. Hollis began to suspect that the resulting chaos, rather than the youthful laziness of her employees, was why Rook had trouble keeping help.

A beautiful, clear week melted into an equally lovely weekend. Rook announced on Friday morning that they would open the store on Monday, the disorder notwithstanding.

They piled unopened boxes hastily in the storeroom. A steady stream of customers kept them busy every minute, looking for disarranged stock. Obviously they would need more help—or better yet, a manager to see to day-to-day details while Rook supervised the overall operation. Considering the confusion, Hollis decided it was only Rook's location, on a busy street leading through the center of Ocean City, that kept her business thriving.

If there was a positive side to the chaos, it was that Hollis had absolutely no time for self-pity. The ache that had once threatened to consume her when she remembered Drew's infidelity had long ago dimmed to dullness. She slept well at night from her exhaustion and dreamed very little.

But Rook was really impossible. She simply wouldn't delegate responsibility, and finally Hollis bolstered her courage enough to say something about it. Rook only stiffened, peered down from her full height and said coldly, "Hollis, this is my shop and about all I have left in the world. I don't mean to let anyone else get their hands on it. I've survived ten years this way and I guess I can survive ten more if I have to."

"Oh, Aunt Rook, I don't understand you," Hollis said in desperation. For lack of anything better, she added, "I'm going out for a walk."

Rook only turned and lifted her half-glasses off her nose. "Suit yourself. It was my turn to cook anyway."

Hollis quickly made her way across the busy road that separated the shop from the oceanfront. The boardwalk was still relatively quiet this early in the season and she managed to ignore the T-shirt shops and amusement arcades, crossing instead to the steps that led down to the sand. With the roar of the surf in her ears and the vastness of the sea before her she immediately began to feel better. She'd been so preoccupied in the store that she'd nearly forgotten how much solace the ocean had always offered. After that night the walks down the beach became her regular routine.

One evening she left the store quickly after an especially frazzling day, only to be startled outside the shop by a familiar voice.

"Hello runaway."

She whirled around and stared into a pair of dark, amused eyes. "Pete!" Despite the awkwardness of their last evening together—and what she knew about him as a result—she couldn't help but be happy to see him. So long since she had talked to anyone but Rook and customers! His dark eyes held her with their warmth and she smiled back.

"I would have come looking for you sooner, but the good weather brought out the campers and I haven't had any time off."

"Neither have I!" Hollis said. Pete looked into the shop, at the array of tents, sleeping bags, lanterns and cook stoves on display in the window.

"Rock star sinks to shop clerk," Pete said. For a brief moment the bleak feeling settled on her again. Rock star. But when she looked up, his expression was as merry as it had been a moment ago.

"How about a bite to eat?" he said.

They ate rubbery hamburgers at one of the stands on the boardwalk that bravely opened before the summer tourists arrived en masse. After the tensions with Rook, even rubbery hamburgers tasted wonderful.

They went down the wooden steps to the beach, took off their shoes and waded in the chilly surf. How nice it was to be doing this with someone else instead of alone. Before long she found herself telling him all about the past weeks, talking as easily as if she'd known him all her life.

"Rook was my father's aunt but she was around all the time because she never married," Hollis explained. "She was always wonderful to us, but a character. And so stubborn. I mean, a woman nearly retirement age opening a camping equipment store. And that was ten years ago! You'd have to be stubborn, I guess."

Pete laughed, then his face turned serious. "Yes, but should you be involved with the shop even for the summer, Hollis? With your career, aren't there other things you should be doing?" For the moment, the anger gripped her again. He seemed to want so badly to imagine her as the rock star. She decided she'd better set the matter straight, once and for all.

"No. There's no career anymore," she said flatly. "I'm working for Rook because I need the money. I'm going to finish college. If I decide to sing again, I can do it afterward. Right now I want to be practical."

"That seems sensible," he said. She couldn't tell if he was pleased or disappointed. But he slipped his arm around her as they walked, as naturally as he had that night in his cabin, and she stopped thinking about it.

How easy it was to walk with him like this, not talking at all. With Drew she had always chattered incessantly, had always needed to prove herself. She let herself lean close to Pete and when he kissed her goodnight at the steps to Rook's apartment, she kissed him back willingly.

It might have been perfect except for the small smile he gave her when he turned to go, the light touch of his finger on the end of her nose, the whispered farewell: "Good night, rock star." Every muscle in her body tensed.

The summer season began in earnest. They were swamped with customers. Rook gave in and hired a teenaged boy part time, but still there was an awful lot to do. Almost clandestinely, Hollis found herself making a log of the merchandise coming in and creating a chart of the storeroom to let herself—and the part-time boy—know where everything was.

Rook was irritated when she discovered what Hollis had done.

"Listen, Hollis," she said curtly, "I don't mean to insult you, but I just can't have you running my store for me behind my back. Next year you'll be off somewhere and if I depend on you now, then where will I be? I'm an old woman, Hollis, and I mean to hang onto what little I have."

Anger welled up in Hollis's throat. She was ready to speak her mind once and for all, but Rook sat down unceremoniously, looking worn and rather pale, and added, "An old woman and just plain tired."

Hollis saw that despite her stony exterior, it was true. She swallowed the retort on the edge of her lips and announced instead what had become an old refrain: "I'm going for a walk."

She had to thread through the summer crowd to reach the boardwalk. The shops were so dazzlingly lit at this time of year that she could hardly forget where she was and just concentrate on the beach or the waves. Ocean City truly felt like a city. She longed for trees, for solitude . . . for Pete.

He had appeared three or four times, whenever he could wangle enough time off to make the trip, but she never knew when to expect him. She would unload her troubles with Rook on him, then listen increasingly wistfully to his accounts of life in the park, of winters nearly alone, of wildlife, of unmarked snows.

Yet each time she had been put off when he invariably referred to her as a rock star just when he was deciding to kiss her. Oh, he infuriated her! Now he was trying to talk her into coming up to the park when she had a couple of days off.

She would have loved the surroundings, but she knew what he must have in mind: another chance to extract payment for his hospitality when she was sick. As long as he kept calling her a rock star between embraces, what else could she think?

It was the next day that she heard the song. Kevin, the boy who worked part time, had switched his radio on during a quick break he took in the storeroom. Searching for a brand of sleeping bags Rook had ordered weeks ago, she froze at the very sound, then found herself listening intently.

When it was over the announcer said cheerfully, "That was Drew's Girl with our pick hit single of the week. In case you didn't know, folks, the lead singer on that is Kendra Gordon, who used to sing backup with Hollis and the Witherspoons a couple of years ago."

There was more, but she didn't want to hear it. A year since he'd taken off with Kendra and now this. Typical. He had named the group for himself this time. Now he wanted the fame as well as the money. *Men.* Oddly, the song hadn't been all that good and she was almost relieved to know she was out of it. Relieved, too, that the store was so busy she didn't have time to think it through.

When she walked out at closing time, there was Pete, waiting for her on the sidewalk. Oh, just what she needed tonight, another stagedoor Charlie who wanted to bleed her dry. Part of her was delighted to see him; another part was annoyed at her delight.

"At least you could let me know when you're coming," she said irritably. "Some nights I'm really beat, after a day of this."

His good nature annoyed her the more. "A little distraction is just what you need," he said, putting his arm around her as if he owned her, walking her down the street.

The evening was hot. Up on the boardwalk the tourists were everywhere. "Ah, the summer life," he said, his irritating cheerfulness unflagging. "For myself I prefer the uninhabited park lands. For you, milady, anything, even the thronging crowds at the beach."

"Oh Pete, stop it," she blurted out finally. "You think I like these mobs any better than you do?"

Suddenly his cheerful pose drained away. He dropped his hand from her shoulder and stepped back a bit to look at her. "Yes, I do," he said seriously. "I think you must like it very much. You've refused to come over to the park, so what else can I assume? You're used to stardom, you like being in the middle of excitement. I can understand how a sedate forest might bore you."

"Bore me!"

"Yes, exactly. Working in a camping store is one thing but to actually go out into the woods where no one would recognize you, where you'd be just like anybody else."

She realized people were watching them, but she screamed at him anyway. "It's you who is always making me into the rock star, Pete, not me who minds being like anybody else. Well, you might as well face it—there's no rock star anymore and there isn't likely to be, so if it's some celebrity you want to seduce out there in the woods, you better think again."

"Celebrity! Oh, right. I drive an hour here and an hour back after a day of work because you're such a celebrity. Do you really believe that?"

"Sure. Why not?" she yelled. "You took good care of me when I collapsed on you, then you found out who I was and since then it's one big come-on.

"Well, let me set you straight about something. I heard Drew's new group on the radio today and the first thing I thought was, I wouldn't even want it back if I could.

"You know who the star of the group was? Drew. Always Drew. A lot of kids can sing, but Drew was the showman. The clothes, the hair. He knew how to wrap an interesting package. First me, now Kendra. Well, I'm not interested in being just a package anymore."

Pete looked suddenly calm, suddenly quizzical, not a bit angry anymore. "You really mean that, don't you?" he asked.

"Yes. If what you're looking for is a star for a companion—"

"Hollis, I'm trying to tell you," he said so quietly that she could only just hear. "I never cared that you were a star."

His gentleness confused her. "Listen, Pete, don't say that to comfort me," she said. "I know it isn't true. You never made a pass at me till you figured out who I was. You were all brotherly and kind until I was Hollis and the Witherspoons. And then . . . boy!"

"Hollis, you were flat in bed with the flu before that day. I never ravish damsels in distress." His voice was warm and rich. Hollis realized with a start that he was telling the truth.

"I thought you wanted payment," she said flatly. "Drew always wanted payment. I depended on him too much. We used up my money, my talent. Not that there was so much talent. I didn't want to do that again, even for a little while. To depend . . ."

"It isn't always a matter of depending," Pete said softly. "Sometimes it's a matter of sharing. There's a difference. Look at Rook. She'll be able to hang onto her store till she's ready to retire, but she'll always have to work twice as hard as anybody else because she refuses to share the responsibility. Not give it up, not depend on anybody—just share."

Hollis looked into the warm brown eyes and saw no hint of deceit. Still, something held her back just a bit, some remnant of past hurts. "I'd really love to come to the park," she said slowly. "But I'm not sure I'm ready for the big seduction scene just yet."

"Then bring a tent," Pete said, smiling. "You can always escape to your tent." He put his arm around her again and began to walk. She thought how pleasant it might be, sleeping again under the quiet stars, not quite alone.

"It's a deal," she said. "I'll bring my tent."

༈

THIS APPEARED IN *WOMAN'S WORLD*,
FEBRUARY 1, 1983

CORKY

Ruth was fourteen when they told her she'd have to go to Camp Chesapeake again, not as a camper but as a counselor in training. She said wild horses couldn't drag her there, but it didn't do any good. The house was being sold, her brother was away, there was no place for her to stay in the city. Waiting for the bus that would take them to camp, she told everyone to call her by her nickname, Corky, which she'd made up on the spot. She pictured her father uncorking sparkling wine, the spray of bubbles, the possibilities. She'd always hated being called Ruth.

On the bus she was assigned to eight ten-year-old girls and a counselor named Darlene with Oriental-looking hair and nails the color of cinnamon. Darlene kept smiling as if Ruth were some unusual pet, and a boys' counselor kept smiling at Darlene. Someone started the campers singing "Ninety-nine bottles of beer on the wall." By 60 bottles of beer they were traveling through wooded countryside and Ruth was getting a headache.

"The singing keeps them from screaming," a boy across the aisle screamed when they got to 50 bottles of beer. He was older than Ruth, a junior counselor for a group of ten-year-old boys.

"I know about the singing. I was here last year," Ruth said.

"Yeah? What's your name?"

"Corky."

"I don't remember you."

"I was a camper last year."

"Now you're a zit." Counselors-in-training were called zits, a variation of c.i.t'.s

"I wouldn't make zit jokes if I were you." A row of pimples dotted the boy's forehead, but he wasn't insulted. He laughed.

"I'm Danny Gordon," he said. He had a narrow face, high cheekbones, a high-bridged nose. Ruth had seen a thousand versions of this particular face, male and female. Darlene the counselor had it, very delicate, and Eli Omer, who owned the camp, had an ugly version, with sharp cheekbones and the nose hooked and sour. But Danny's nose was straight and his cheekbones muted, his skin tan except for the pink pimples. Ruth envied the tan. She'd told her mother redheads didn't belong at camp where they were in the sun seven or eight hours a day. "Twenty years from now I'll have skin cancer—wait and see."

"Use sun block," her mother said. Her mother was too busy divorcing her father to dote on her. While Ruth was away their house would be turned over to new owners and her mother would move their things into an apartment. Ruth had spent two weeks destroying diaries, notes, most of the hard drive on her computer, anything her mother might construe as evidence of a private existence. Now she wasn't Ruth anymore. She was Corky.

Camp Chesapeake sat on a treeless bluff over-looking the Chesapeake Bay. Two hours after they arrived, they were shoving suitcases under their cots and getting ready for the first of two swims required every day. Eli Omer believed swimming kept the campers from heatstroke, given that all other ac-tivities took place in relentless sun. Even the bunks offered little respite—wooden boxes with unfinished walls and no insulation or air-conditioning. The windows were small screened holes in the wood, with flaps that could be closed to shut out the rain. Electrical wires snaked up the bare plywood to un-shaded ceiling bulbs. Daddy long-legs spiders lived in the wooden toilet stalls.

"I'm surprised these buildings met code," her fa-ther had said last year when he toured the place, but he'd sent her there again anyway.

In the bunk, Corky's cot was among the ten-year-olds', though Darlene the counselor had hers behind a wooden barrier. The little girls eyed each other as they changed into bathing suits, paying special attention to a girl named Abigail who wore a train-ing bra and undressed facing the wall. Corky plucked her suit from her belongings and went into the toilet to change. A Daddy long-legs inched its way across her foot as she stood there, regretting her refusal of the can of Raid her mother had offered.

The beach was a narrow strip of sand dumped

at the bottom of the bluff; the water was silty, slow-moving, brownish. There was no swimming pool, so all water activities took place in the bay. A net for keeping jellyfish out of the swimming area was torn. Crackerjack Bunk, as the girls had named it (each bunk had to have a name) was the first into the water. Sheila and Jessica, the two prettiest ten-year-olds, chose each other as buddies. Everything was done on the buddy system. At regular intervals Bruno, the swim director, blew his whistle and yelled, "Buddies!" All the sets of buddies would raise joined hands to show they were still alive. Sheila and Jessica walked down the dock and jumped in. Seconds later they came up festooned with jellyfish—draped across their shoulders, their bathing suits, their arms. They began to scream. Darlene put her polished fingers to her mouth. Corky did nothing. Ruth would have done nothing. Bruno blew his whistle.

Now everyone from Crackerjack Bunk was screaming. Other children began to arrive on the beach. "All campers out of the water!" Sheila and Jessica pulled jellyfish from their bodies, flung them into the bay. Bruno scooped them out with a net on a pole and dumped them onto the sand. Campers found sticks to poke into their melting, gelatinous tentacles.

"Okay, everybody back in," Bruno yelled. The braver children started wading into the bay. No one from Crackerjack Bunk moved. "All right, girls," Darlene said. The fingers with which she motioned toward the water were long, delicate, without authority. The girls stood their ground.

"Rebellion on your hands?" asked Danny Gordon, who had come down with his ten-year-old boys.

"This is just how I remember it from last year," Corky said.

* * *

Four days later, Corky's skin was burned raw. "On visiting day you'll recognize me as the bright scarlet one," she wrote her mother on a piece of lined notebook paper. Everyone had to write home, at least a full page. "I'm the only counselor-in-training who wears a man's undershirt over her bathing suit," she reported. Mention of her father's underwear should gall her mother, and reference to the sunburn call up guilt. She shed the shirt reluctantly—100 percent cotton, kind to the skin—and dressed in Friday Night whites: scratchy shorts, T-top that rubbed. The little girls were also in white, and Darlene had zipped herself into a tight white jumpsuit before ducking behind her wooden barrier to curl her Oriental hair.

Corky combed her own carrot bangs over a magenta forehead. She smoothed on beige foundation that made her look like a geisha, then washed it off. She'd ached and run a slight fever all day, swallowed Excedrin every four hours, played volleyball in the undershirt, helped supervise a nature hike in the woods. Newly scrubbed but still aching, she herded the little girls toward the dining hall.

Nausea hit her as soon as she smelled food—another symptom of sun poisoning. At the long table Sheila pinched Jessica on the butt, which was something Corky thought only boys did, and Jessica pinched back. Corky positioned herself between them, though she'd hoped for an end seat where her shoulders would be free to the air. A girl from the oldest bunk started saying grace, and the girls settled down. Then waiters were bringing out trays of chicken and mashed potatoes, the smell of grease mingling with the smell of unfinished pine walls. Abigail of the blue eyes, the plump thighs and the training bra, who no more belonged at Camp Chesapeake than Ruth did before she became Corky, turned a waxy shade of white.

"I think I've got to go back to the bunk," she whispered to Corky. The girls had taken to confiding in Corky, not Darlene, because Corky slept among them and had given up changing clothes in the bathroom—or more precisely, didn't sleep, what with the sunburn, and knew Abigail and a few others didn't sleep either.

"Your allergies again?" Abigail had a perpetual stuffy nose and sneezing spells. Seven pairs of eyes stared them down.

"Could we just go?"

"I'll take her," Corky said, too nauseated to eat.

The problem turned out to be not Abigail's allergies but the arrival of her period. Abigail had turned ten last December and had had her periods since March.

"What a rotten break for you."

"At least I don't have to go swimming," Abigail said.

Abigail complained of cramps and in truth looked so pale that Corky let her lie down for a while. When Corky said she'd gotten her periods young, too, Abigail seemed comforted. The bunk was close and hot. After a while Corky said, "We ought to go down to the rec hall. It'll be better than lying in bed. All you have to do is sit." Abigail looked skeptical, but she went.

They crept into the rec hall and sat at the back, among a sea of campers looking civilized in their whites. In front of them, Danny Gordon sat with his ten-year-old boys. "Nice sunburn," he said.

"Shhh," Corky turned away from him and tossed her hair. A senior counselor was making a few announcements. Danny leaned back and whispered, "Meet me outside during the movie." Corky nodded.

Junior counselors and c.i.t.s were allowed to go outside during the Friday night movie, as long as they stayed on the wooden patio that surrounded the rec hall. If they were found wandering off, they'd be confined to their bunks or even sent home. Eli was very strict about social behavior.

Danny took Corky's hand and led her to an empty picnic table at the edge of the patio. They talked for a long time. He told her about school—he was 16, a junior—and after a lengthy recital of his interests in sports (baseball) and academic subjects (any kind of science), he asked her where she lived. Corky said, "Nowhere right now. My mother's in the process of moving us to an apartment."

"You mean you're going home to another house

after you leave here? What a crock."

He started to put his arm around her. She pulled up her sleeve to reveal the water blisters on her shoulder. "Nothing personal, but if you touch me I may pass out from pain."

"I thought I'd heard everything," he said, backing off.

"Be thankful for your Mediterranean skin."

He lifted a lock of her hair off her neck. "I like red-heads," he said.

* * *

"Most of your real life," her father had told her, "is lived inside your head." He tapped his graying temple. "That isn't going to change whether you're here or at Camp Chesapeake or anyplace else." This discussion had taken place after he'd told her she was going back to camp as a counselor-in-training. She'd been too upset at the time to think of a clever reply.

She lay behind the wooden barrier on Darlene's cot, with Darlene's reading lamp shining down on her stationery, writing a letter to her father. It was Saturday night. Darlene's curfew wasn't until one. She had gone off on a date with Bruno. The ten-year-old girls all had crushes on Bruno.

Corky wrote about her sunburn. She told her father she'd run a fever of 102 for two days, which was a lie. She told him she remembered what he'd said about living in your thoughts. Then she wrote, "Maybe if you'd lived a little more in your head, all this wouldn't have happened."

Her father had moved in at first with his mistress, Carol. Corky's brother had said at the time, "He's thinking with his dick instead of his brains." Now Carol had moved out but the divorce was still in the works because, as Corky's mother said, "The damage has been done."

On the other side of the barrier, Abigail was getting up. Corky knew it was Abigail because she heard her rummaging in her footlocker and then walking to the bathroom with her heavy step. Abigail changed pads at least ten times a day; she must have come to camp with half a footlocker of sanitary pads. When Abigail came back to her cot, she started crying softly. Some of the other girls had also cried at first, but now only Abigail did.

Corky turned the reading light off and went into the camper's section of the bunk. "Abigail," she whispered. Abigail held her breath so Corky wouldn't hear her crying.

"Come on outside for a couple of minutes. It'll be cooler."

Abigail followed Corky outside. The sky was gray-black, hazed over, no stars. It wasn't cool. Corky sat on the top step and Abigail below, with her chubby arms and legs sticking out of pale shorty pajamas.

"Homesick?" Corky asked. "I get homesick too."

"You're just saying that."

"No. Really."

"I'm not that homesick. I just wish I didn't have this—you know." None of the other campers had their periods yet.

"It won't last forever," Corky said.

"I hate it here."

"Hate's a strong word." Corky had not said hate. She had said to her mother, "Wild horses couldn't drag me there."

"I hate swimming. I hate volleyball. I hate everything but drama and arts and crafts."

"You'll hate the prune whip," Corky said, naming the camp's least-favorite dessert, trying for humor.

Abigail ignored her. "I can't sleep without air-conditioning," she said. "My head gets all stopped up."

"I can't sleep when I'm sunburned." Corky's shoulders itched. The water bubbles were bursting. A bright red wounded skin was emerging underneath, which had to be covered with her father's cotton undershirts.

"I never get sunburned," Abigail told her. "See?"

"I feel rotten outside of air-conditioning."

"When we have the overnighter at Locust Point, it won't be so hot," Corky said. Last year when she'd still been Ruth, she'd been bitten on the lip by a spider while they slept on the Locust Point beach. She woke up with her lower lip swollen to twice its size, but she'd still had a good time. "You'll like the overnighter," Corky said.

"What I'd really like," Abigail said, "is to go home."

"I know. But you'll feel better when your period's over. Wait and see." She was tired of feeling sorry for Abigail.

Back in the bunk, Abigail fell asleep right away.

Corky wrote to her father, "At Camp Chesapeake most of my life is lived not in my head but in the open air with campers like Abigail, and on my sunburned surface, which itches. That's not my fault. When you moved in with Carol, you had no such excuse."

She thought she wouldn't have the nerve to mail the letter, but she did.

* * *

Danny had been kissing her for a long time outside the rec hall while a rerun of "The Outsiders" played inside. Every once in a while Eli Omer walked around the building to check who was there. Danny let go of her then and pretended they were talking. A whole week had passed and the sunburn was better. She was being more diligent with sunblock, though it didn't protect her entirely. "Your skin's getting some color," Danny said.

"I'm not getting tan."

"You're getting beige. Most people get a tan. You get a beige."

Her stomach was aching in a pleasant way. She hadn't made out with anyone before, at least not for very long, though she'd had ample opportunities. Each time she'd pulled away in disgust, repelled by a memory of her father and Carol kissing in the hallway of his new apartment when she'd arrived for a visit—obviously a scene she wasn't supposed to see. She hadn't thought of that at all tonight. Quite the opposite. When the movie ended, she didn't want to let go of Danny. He made himself pull away first.

"Your parents coming Sunday?" he asked. Sunday was visiting day.

"My mother," she said. He was making her think of everyday things and she didn't want to do that yet. She wanted him to . . . what? Kiss her again. Exhibit a little wildness. But now he was straightening his clothes. She did the same. What had she been thinking? While they'd been kissing, her life had been lived in her stomach, not on the inside of her head.

* * *

The campers' families came after lunch on visiting day. There was a free social hour and then a mini-day at camp, during which the campers demonstrated their daily schedule.

Corky's mother was late. Corky finally recognized her by the baggy capris she always wore, which she thought were fashionable. What Corky didn't recognize was the man her mother was holding onto. He was dark but not particularly handsome, with his shirt open to show the hair on his chest. Her father would have said the man was wearing a chest wig. He said hairy men were more closely related to monkeys than smooth-chested men; it was a known fact that mammals lost their bodily hair as they climbed the scale of evolution.

"Ruth, I want you to meet Raoul," her mother said. "Raoul, this is my daughter Ruth."

"Everybody here calls me Corky."

"Corky?" Her mother sounded more incredulous and laughed more brightly than she would have if Raoul hadn't been along.

"Nice to meet you, Corky." Raoul extended his hand. Corky expected an accent, but he didn't have one.

"So how is it?" her mother asked. "Not as bad as you thought, is it? You don't look as sunburned as I expected."

"How about if we go up to the dining hall? They have refreshments up there."

In the dining hall Corky gave Raoul a glass of iced tea and some cookies, and excused herself and her mother.

"Rah-ool?" she asked.

"Sweet, isn't he? He's a neighbor in the new apartment building. He's been helping me carry things in little by little."

"Is Raoul the reason I was shipped off to camp this summer?"

"Don't be paranoid, Ruth. I just met him two weeks ago."

"You didn't mention Raoul in your letters."

"There was nothing to mention. He's helping me unpack. He's taken me to dinner a couple of times."

"Those pants make you look fat, Mother."

"What?" Her mother put her hands to her hips.

"I can't believe you'd bring him out here today," Corky said.

"It was very decent of him to drive me out here. You know I hate to drive all the way out here myself."

"First Daddy and now you. I'd think you'd at least have the decency to wait until you'd moved out of the house."

"I have everything almost moved out, Ruth."

"My name is Corky."

"Corky is a ridiculous name."

"Ruth was a ridiculous name."

"Would you have been upset if I'd brought Aunt Helen or some woman friend? If I nobly went everywhere alone? Raoul hasn't done anything to hurt you. He's trying to help me out."

"Screw Raoul," Corky said. "But then, I guess you are."

Her mother almost hit her. She could see the way her arm started to come up and then stopped. Her mother had noticed the crush of people around them, and checked herself.

"I have to help with the program," Corky said, and left.

Her mother and Raoul followed her to the mini-day activities. Corky helped with a basketball game and a tour of the beach. No one actually swam. Eli Omer had planned it that way. He had taken to sending counselors into the water before each swim period to scoop up whatever jellyfish floated through the net. Most days this didn't help. The campers kept to the shallow water where only their legs could get stung. Eli didn't want anyone whining about jellyfish with the parents there.

"I guess we'll take off," her mother said after the beach tour, kissing Corky on the cheek. "We've seen everything. We want to stop for crabs before we head back to town."

Corky cut arts-and-crafts and went back to the bunk so she could be alone. She kept thinking about the feeling she'd had in her stomach when Danny kissed her, and applying that feeling to her mother and Raoul, which made her a little sick. She lay down on her cot and fell into a dead sleep. The next thing she knew Abigail was sobbing into her face. "I asked them to take me home with them but they said no, being out of doors agreed with me."

Abigail blew her nose into a tissue. Being out of doors did not agree with her. Her eyes were swollen and she sneezed a lot. Her jellyfish stings didn't disappear like everyone else's, but rose into puffy red marks that lasted for hours. She made up excuses not to swim and carried books to read. She belonged in a nice air-conditioned apartment in the city, where she could develop according to her own tastes

"Think of it this way: camp's half over," Corky said.

"Two more weeks." Abigail began to cry in earnest. Corky put her arm around her. "I used to hate camp as much as you. It passes. It's really not so bad."

Abigail continued to cry. Corky started thinking Ruth would have been more grateful and less teary, had someone comforted her this way last year.

The town of Locust Point was actually only a post office and a convenience store next to the bay—no houses. Crackerjack Bunk hiked forty minutes up the beach from camp after dinner, singing "Ninety-nine bottles of beer." Their sleeping bags were brought in Eli Omer's pickup truck by one of the boys' counselors. The beach was wide here because the bay washed more sand up onto the point each year. Stands of locust trees sheltered it almost down to the water. The girls spread their sleeping bags. Corky unloaded marshmallows, graham crackers and Hershey bars for s'mores. The truck left. In the morning someone would bring it back for the sleeping bags while the girls hiked to camp for breakfast.

All the campers except Abigail were excited. They spread into the trees to gather wood for the fire. Abigail hung back and rubbed her right leg, which looked sunburned but wasn't. It was only more red and swollen than usual from jellyfish stings. The walk up the beach had aggravated it.

"Come on, Abigail, the stings always clear up after a while," Darlene said, motioning for the girl to gather kindling. Darlene brushed sand from the bright red shorts she was wearing, and smoothed down her hair. To Corky she whispered, "Bruno has the night off. I think Danny does, too."

They lit the fire, which made the beach seem darker than it was, the wind louder in the trees, the lapping of the bay more ominous. "Let's tell ghost stories," Jessica said when the s'mores were gone. "Darlene first."

"Did you ever hear the one about the ghost with the bloody finger?" Darlene positioned herself so her hair wouldn't blow. The campers shook their heads.

"There was an old inn. Whenever it was full, the innkeeper offered to let visitors sleep in the attic, but he warned them the attic was haunted. Sure enough, late in the night the visitor would see an eerie light, and a voice would say, 'I am the ghost with the bloody finnger'"—Darlene was making her voice as deep and quavery as possible—"and the visitor would be so frightened that he would run out of the inn as fast as he could and never be seen again."

A moaning came from the trees.

"What's that?"

"Nothing. Just the wind."

"Anyway, the next night another visitor came, and the innkeeper told him he'd have to sleep in the attic if he wanted to stay."

The trees rustled, and there was a murmuring as if of intruders.

"It's somebody."

"Did you hear anything, Corky?"

"No."

"And the visitor said, okay he'd stay in the attic. But in the middle of the night an eerie light appeared . . ."

An eerie light appeared from the trees. A flashlight shone between the leaves. The girls screamed.

"It's nothing."

"It's prowlers!"

The girls hugged themselves, hugged each other, pulled their sleeping bags close.

"And a sound came, saying . . . "

An echo, a groaning, from the trees.

"It's boys," Jessica said. "I bet it's boys."

"I am the ghost with the bloody finnger!" Darlene intoned. "But this visitor was braver, and he ignored it. And then after a while the sound came again . . . "

More moans from the trees. Boys! Giggles. "And

the visitor said, 'Oh for heaven's sake, get a bandaid out of the medicine chest and let me go to sleep!'"

Outright laughter. "Oh Darlene!" Silence from the trees.

"That was stupid," Abigail said.

"Jeez, Abigail, you don't like anything."

A dark wind blew across the beach, making the fire flutter.

"Are those boys still there?"

"No, I don't think so. I think they just wanted to scare us and now they're on their way back to camp."

The girls hugged themselves closer and, very soon, slept, even Abigail.

Danny and Bruno ran out of the trees, across the beach.

"Shh, you'll wake everybody. What're you doing here anyway?" Darlene moved so the firelight caught the gloss of her hair.

"Come on." Danny pulled Corky into the woods. They could see the campers from there, and the fire, but not Darlene and Bruno. Corky wondered how Danny had gotten a night off during the week. It was impossible. She liked that.

They kissed for a long time, lying on the sand under the trees. Her heart beat so fast she knew he could feel it, and her stomach ached the way it had the other time, only stronger. Then an odd thing happened. She was still kissing him, but she began to feel as if she were far away. She felt as if she were looking down at herself from a distance—at herself and at Danny kissing her—watching very objectively as if she might write an essay about it. She wondered if that was the way her mother kissed Raoul or her father kissed Carol, and she felt a little sick again the way she had on visitation day in her bunk.

"What's the matter?" Danny asked.

"Nothing. How'd you get off on a weeknight?"

"Shh." He put his hand over her mouth so she'd stop talking, and then he kissed her again, but she felt outside of it. The aching in her stomach had stopped. She noticed that Danny was cupping her breasts exactly the way her mother showed her to feel grapefruits, to see if they were ripe. She knew she had noticed that on purpose, so that she could live not in her stomach but on the inside of her head. Danny moved away from her.

"You're turned off, aren't you?"

"It's not you. I was thinking."

"Oh great. I'm trying to seduce her and she's thinking."

He rolled over and lay next to her, touching her shoulder very lightly. She had made him do that— move away, but not too far. There were no street lights in Locust Point, and the fire was almost out; except for its glow, everything was dark. There was no curfew. Up in the sky the Big Dipper sat in a vastness of stars, but she didn't feel small. The lapping of the bay made her think how big the ocean was, how big everything was—and yet how just by thinking she had made her stomach stop churning, and Danny stop kissing her—how she could do anything.

In the morning Abigail's leg was purple. The other

girls rolled up their sleeping bags, but Abigail said she couldn't move.

"Oh come on, Abigail, all you ever do is complain," Jessica said.

"It's an allergy," Abigail told Corky. "I'll bet you anything. To the jellyfish stings."

The campers twittered. "It always went away before."

"Now, girls," said Darlene.

Corky touched Abigail's leg, which felt hard and slightly hot. Ruth's spider bite last year had been swollen like that, but she hadn't made such a production of it. It had gone down in a day. Abigail sat on the sand, purple-legged and about to cry. Corky thought she should feel sorry for her but she didn't, not really. She only felt responsible, and a little embarrassed.

Eli Omer's pickup truck pulled off onto the shoulder of the road and Danny got out. He smiled at Corky.

"They let you drive?"

"Sure. Why not? I have my license."

"Then I guess you didn't get caught for sneaking out last night."

"Okay girls, after you roll up your sleeping bags, put them in the truck," Darlene said.

"I can't move," Abigail wailed.

"We're going to have to take her back to camp in the truck," Corky told Darlene. "She's not going to be able to hike all the way up that beach."

"Oh great."

"I'll ride with her," Corky said. She didn't want to hike forty minutes up the beach. She wanted to be with Danny. "Get in the truck, you'll feel better inside," she told Abigail. She said it so the other girls wouldn't tease. Soon the sleeping bags were loaded and Darlene was marching the girls toward camp.

"If you really want to do me a favor," Abigail said as Danny and Corky got into the truck on either side of her, "don't take me back to camp, take me home."

"Let's take her home," Corky said. She felt a little giddy.

"Yeah, sure," Danny said.

"Let's. Otherwise they'll put her in the infirmary and she won't be able to do anything, anyway. She might as well be home."

"If they think she's really sick, they'll call her parents."

"They won't. The leg'll go down. Her parents won't come. They think it's good for her to be outside."

"I hate it here," Abigail said.

"If we take her home, they'll have to let her stay." She sounded crazy, but it didn't matter. She kept thinking about champagne uncorking, all the power it had, pushing the cork up and up, the spray of bubbles, the power she had—she could make herself do anything, and Danny, too—and she didn't care that there was no place to go home to in the city, didn't care at all.

"You want them to arrest us for stealing the truck?"

"They won't. We'll call. We'll say she was inconsolable."

"We'll get fired."

"So?" Corky looked at him. She dared him to. If he had any wildness in him. She saw them going down the highway at 65, sleeping bags flopping around in the back, hot wind coming in the windows, rock music blasting from the radio, or classical, or country, anything but "Ninety-nine bottles of beer."

⤳

THIS APPEARED IN *VIRGINIA COUNTRY* SEPT/OCT 1985

PHO

I had a small victory at the music festival in New Orleans, a first place win for my top piano student. I stayed for the awards ceremony, then drove my rental car to Biloxi to see the Nguyens before flying home to Maryland. It was late April, already oppressively hot in the muggy lowlands of Louisiana, the air so thick and weighty that my euphoria soon drained. My fingers ached, especially in the bad right hand. I struggled to grip the wheel. It was one of those days when I could hardly make a fist.

It had been a tense, competitive trip. At home there loomed recitals, papers, the hubbub of wrapping up the season. I thought again of retirement, a favorite theme lately. The Old Goat had left a little money; I could happily live out my days without giving another lesson. Why not?

Along the bayous, a fine mist rose from the wet ground, clouding the landscape like fatigue. I told myself no, no, I must not consider retirement yet, not until summer. Only a month and a half. Then I would be free to read books, tend my garden. Collect my thoughts.

Nga had given me directions to her store. Her new

house was across the bridge in a residential suburb, but the store was in the center of Biloxi, not far from the casinos. When the family had first left Maryland, they'd bought a boat and started a shrimping business which never really took off. Biloxi was a squat, squalid town then, unremarkable except for the elegant estates along the waterfront. The Old Goat and I visited once, not long before his final illness. The Trans lived in a shabby apartment then with their first son, Paul, who was in elementary school. The younger children didn't come along until later.

Then Tran's boat was destroyed by a fire just as Biloxi was beginning to transform itself into the Riviera of the South, and he had the good sense to use the insurance money to go into real estate. Where before there had been a rundown waterfront, now rows of tall, glitzy hotels were attached by ramps to casinos which sat a few yards out into the Gulf because by law a casino had to be on the water.

Following Nga's directions, I turned inland away from the hotel strip and discovered that not all of the decaying houses or weedy vacant lots had disappeared. Nga's shop was a decrepit convenience store on a dusty corner where tough looking men, Vietnamese and Hispanic and black, loitered in the street.

"Ah, Sheila!" Nga's voice cried out as I opened the door. We hadn't visited for several years, and the sight of her was a shock. Nineteen when she arrived in this country, she had been tall for a Vietnamese woman, reed slim, her hair shoulder length and shiny black. A beautiful girl with an ugly name: Naahh, like an animal braying. Now she was forty five and chubby, her waist thick, her hips wide, even her pretty face round and moon-like, as if layers of fat had been injected between her skin and her high cheekbones.

She rushed toward me, her smile wide on cherry colored lips. "Ah, Sheila! So nice you come. You look very good!"

"Well, so do you! So do you!" After my long week, I looked like hell. Was I supposed to hug her? Hold out my hand? "So nice to be here!" I shouted, falsely cheerful.

Nga grasped my hand, pumped it until the swollen joints screamed (I, on the other hand, had long ago schooled myself not to scream), and in the space of the handshake, pushed the awkward moment aside. Ever the diplomat, she possessed social graces I'd never mastered, qualities that at once soothed me and made me feel small. "You sit," she said as she rushed to retrieve a cane backed chair from behind the counter. "You tire? Sit."

I laughed. "I've been sitting all day."

"Oh, yes." She fluttered her hands. "You want something to drink?" Without waiting for an answer, she hastened back to the refrigerated case, plucked out a bottle of tropical fruit punch. "This very good. Very good."

I unscrewed the cap, took a long swig, studied the store. It was awful. Brown paneling peeled from the walls, an ancient air conditioner churned and dripped. The shelves were so sparsely lined with goods as to be embarrassing: a few cans of green beans, a single package of toilet paper. Only the refrigerated case with beer and soft drinks, and a shelf of cigarettes above the cash register, were fully stocked.

"You give concert in New Orleans?" Nga rippled her fingers as if along a keyboard.

"Oh, no. Not for years." I held up my hands. They looked even worse than they felt. "My students played. It was a competition."

"They win?"

"One did."

"Anne Marie play piano," she said, pointing to a photo of her daughter taped to the paneling behind the counter. "Only eleven year old and she play very good."

The door jangled open. A scruffy Hispanic man headed to the back for a six pack of beer. In quick succession half a dozen others followed, working men with blackened fingernails and soiled shirts, paying for their beer with grease stained fingers. Nga waited on them, pleasant but reserved. Pearl among swine.

I wandered the store, let her work. The supply of foodstuffs was meager, but there was a nice selection of combs and barrettes in the corner, and a surprising display of picture frames, which made me smile. Twenty six years before, the week after Nga and Tran arrived in Maryland, Nga had plucked a white fili-gree frame off a shelf in the supermarket where her church sponsors were buying supplies, and thrust it at the volunteer in charge. "I need," she said.

"Well, nobody needs a picture frame," the volunteer told the Women's Auxiliary later. "Certainly not a refugee who's arrived with only a few clothes and a box of photos from home."

"And all those Vietnamese music tapes!" another woman clucked. "They must have thought when they got here, a tape deck was the first thing somebody would give them."

More out of rebellion than sympathy, I had been tempted to rush to Nga's defense. After all, the photos of family members they might never see again were practically all they had. But as something of an outcast myself, I judged I could only aggravate the assault and kept quiet.

"I told her we were spending the church's money to buy essentials, not picture frames," the volunteer concluded. "First things first."

Now I fingered one of the frames on the shelf and thought, well, there is more than one way to thumb your nose at somebody, even twenty six years later.

I sipped my drink and watched Nga make change for a thin, wiry man whose baggy trousers seemed about to lose their tenuous hold on his hips. Would the haughty churchwomen feel vindicated now, seeing Nga cater to the downtrodden? Would they think: well, that's exactly what she deserves, after being such a leech herself? A few would, I knew.

The fruit punch was so wickedly sweet that I began to wake up. Between customers, Nga asked about my trip to New Orleans and gushed over my award. "Ah, you must be very good teacher!"

"I've been doing it a long time." Long enough to grow bored. Long enough to grow old.

"You teach in summer?"

"No. Summers I have off."

"Ah."

"And what about you?"

"Me too doing same thing for long time." Despite her thick accent, Nga's English was easy to understand, while her husband's was still a mystery. "I have store since Zachary a baby. Eight year. I still here all the time." She smiled to show it was all right. "Me and Tran have houses, too. Many houses now."

They'd bought their first slum house before the first casino arrived—"Very cheap then. Not so cheap now."—and renovated it and rented it out. When the gambling business boomed, so did real estate.

"You probably don't need this store anymore," I suggested. Surely Nga knew she didn't belong here, in this dangerous neighborhood, selling beer to workmen off the street.

"Sometimes I think we sell, but then I think, no, not yet." She pointed vaguely out the window. "Soon they build a casino on the water over there." There was a small lagoon a block away. "Then they buy this for a parking lot, we get good price."

Several times the phone jangled and Nga spoke to the caller in rapid Vietnamese. Once a bewhiskered, white haired man shuffled in and announced that he needed a cigarette, and for the first time Nga dropped her guard and spoke easily. "You buy a whole pack today?"

"No, just one." The man turned sheepish and doubtful. "Okay?"

Nga handed him a single cigarette from an open pack under the counter. The man counted out some change.

"For weeks he ask me to sell one cigarette," Nga explained when he'd gone. "I say no, you have to buy whole pack. But he ask and ask and finally I do." She laughed. "I sell anything to make money."

"Nga!"

She shrugged. "I send money to my country, help my family. We go to Vietnam two year ago—remember I tell you? People there very poor. Also, Paul in medical school now. He study for doctor."

Well, of course! Paul! He'd been born in Maryland, where Nga had given him his American name, fed him meat every day from the time he was old enough to chew, and insisted protein would make him grow. Now Paul was six feet tall and in medical school. Good for him. Good for her!

The door opened again and Tran entered, his face brightening at the sight of me. "Sheila! So glad you come!" His voice, oddly high pitched, oddly twangy and sing song, reminded me of some exotic Oriental musical instrument.

Like Nga, Tran had filled out, lost the girlish slenderness most of the Vietnamese men had when they arrived in the '70s. His hair, streaked now with gray, was slicked back so it no longer flopped onto his forehead, a formal style that made him look like the property owner he had become. I was impressed.

Until then I'd always thought him lesser than Nga—a rough country boy where Nga had come from Saigon, a city girl, polished.

On Tran's heels came a natty looking Vietnamese man in dark trousers and a crisp white shirt, following him so closely that I thought they were together. But Tran focused his attention on me while the other man turned earnestly to Nga.

"Last month I buy one house," Tran told me after we'd exchanged greetings. "The house, it sit where they want to build casino. Not cost much, only fifteen hundred. But to move it to another lot—Thirteen thousand. *Whoo! Too much!*"

I smiled because I remembered whoo! too much! from a quarter century ago, and the good-natured way Tran delivered it, like the chorus of a comic song.

At the cash register, the Vietnamese man pulled a heavy gold watch off his wrist. Nga turned it over in her fingers.

"We got twelve houses now," Tran said, speaking faster as he warmed to his topic. "Some just me and Nga. Some we partners with family in California." His voice rose and fell, tonal and often incomprehensible. I nodded and tried to follow. "Last year I finish new house for my family. Wait, you see. Four bedroom. All winter Nga's brother family stay with us. Anh. You remember Anh?" I nodded. "But they move out now. We got plenty room for you. Happy you visit."

A few feet away, Nga set her customer's watch under the counter, then opened the cash register, handed the man some bills. From his pocket he retrieved a few slips of paper, coupons of some kind, and placed them in Nga's hand. The transaction looked sinister.

"Tonight, my family, we take you out to eat," Tran said. "Nga, she like to cook you something but she in the store all the time, no food at the house. She don't close till seven."

I was disappointed. Nga's tasty spring rolls were legendary, better than those in any restaurant. I had been looking forward to bowls of rice and pork and vegetables, to puffy shrimp chips in pastel colors. But especially to spring rolls. "That's fine," I said too loudly. "Going out will be fun!"

Tran's look of relief was all too familiar. Twenty five years ago he'd called the church every morning to say Nga had the flu, a headache, sinus problems, and couldn't come to work at the day care center where the sponsors had gotten her a job. When asked if she'd be at work tomorrow he'd say yes. It would be impolite to say no. No one knew yet that Nga was pregnant with Paul, plagued by morning sickness. The sponsors had gotten a translator to tell her about birth control, and she'd been afraid to admit she was already pregnant.

"Tomorrow we take you to special Vietnamese restaurant," Tran went on. "Pho. Noodle soup. You remember?"

"Of course! But I have to drive back to New Orleans to catch my plane."

"What time you go?"

"Ten thirty. Eleven at the latest."

"Plenty of time," he said. Then he asked again, "You remember pho?"

"Oh, yes, very well. How could I forget?" Once, after they'd moved to Mississippi, Nga and Tran had come north for a visit and taken me and the Old Goat to a pho restaurant where different kinds of soup were the only items on the menu. They ordered for all of us and showed us which condiments to add to our bowls from the lazy Susan in the middle of the table. The Old Goat and I were the only non Vietnamese in the place. It was a wonderful meal. Tran insisted on paying the check, which he could ill afford. The Old Goat protested, but Tran was adamant. "Nga and me, we like to thank you for all you do for my family when we live in Maryland," he'd said.

At the front, the Vietnamese man with the coupons took his money and left, and Nga retrieved his watch and examined it again.

"You run a pawn shop," I said, realizing.

"Just with some. I don't have license. Just with Vietnamese or Thai." She gestured toward the door. "He a casino boss. You work for casino, make good money. But if you start to gamble—oh." She shook her head. "Seventy five percent who work for the casinos, they gamble." Before I could reply, she changed the subject. "Now I show you my house. We take your car. Tran stay here till we come back. The children, they like to see you." She grabbed her purse.

A black man in paint splattered clothes lumbered

in as we headed for the door. "Eight hours today," he told Tran, who was now behind the counter.

Tran frowned. "Eight hour? I no think so. You take one hour for lunch."

"No, man. Just a half hour. Half hour tops." The man jiggled his right leg as if it had fallen asleep. "This afternoon I finished painting the whole kitchen and the back door."

Thoughtfully, Tran opened the cash register and lifted out some bills. The painter stuffed them into his pocket without counting them. As Nga and I went out to my car, I felt foolish for misunderstanding. No wonder Nga didn't want to sell the store. No wonder she allowed it to look so seedy. It was a perfect front for the pawn shop, the remodeling business, any other enterprises they might be running off the books. The IRS was not going to think such a place was making money. I had forgotten how much Nga liked to cajole and finagle, wheel and deal. It was a game. Nga was having fun.

* * *

The Nguyen's house was a two story Colonial much like all the others on the block except for its bright red front door. "The children wait for you," Nga said as I pulled into her driveway. "They very excited." I smiled, but I was thinking: Why would they care?

"Before we move here, I no leave the children home alone in the afternoon. They have to come to the store. Now, they fine. They do homework. Not babies now." She surveyed the manicured yards, the two little girls roller blading down the sidewalk. "Very safe here." She sounded doubtful.

Nga insisted on lifting my bag out of the trunk. "Anne Marie, she very smart. Zachary the only one not good student. Paul and Anne Marie, yes. But not Zachary."

Inside, air conditioning purred, and everything seemed unnaturally tidy. A white tiled entryway gave way to white carpets and pristine white walls decorated with Oriental prints. To our right was a dining room furnished with a black lacquered table and chairs, a matching china closet. Across the hall, a baby grand piano, also of black lacquer, dominated the living room. The couch and chairs were scarlet.

Anne Marie bounded down the stairs in front of us, a replica of Nga but even chubbier, with her mother's same wide smile. "Hi, Sheila!"

"Anne Marie, how are you?" I had met the girl a few times on her visits to Maryland. Her long hair was caught up in a ponytail, not as shiny as her mother's. "You've grown!" Well, of course she had. But what else was there to say?

"Here, I made you this." Anne Marie thrust a small package in my direction. It was a pin cushion, two pieces of bright pink felt stuffed with cotton and roughly sewn together.

"Why, Anne Marie! How sweet."

Nga ushered me into the den. On yet another red couch, Zachary was curled into a fetal position, watching cartoons. Small for an eight year old, he lay with his matchstick legs tucked into his chest, his forgotten school books fanned out on the couch beside him. Animated creatures in bright colors ran across a ridiculously huge screen, more like a movie screen, something I'd seen before only in bars and restaurants. I glanced toward Nga, but she wouldn't meet my eye.

We both knew how she'd longed for color TV all those years ago. How she'd wanted it more than anything. Wanted it to the point of embarrassment. This was in 1975, not long after they arrived, when not everyone had a color set and those who did paid dearly for it. Someone from the church gave them an old black and white model, but Nga wasn't satisfied. Smiling winningly, speaking in a soft beggar voice that set my teeth on edge, she asked everyone she saw, "You have old color TV you give me? I like to have color."

In the end I said, "Don't, Nga, this is not something you can ask for. It costs a lot. People don't have extra color TVs lying around. You have to save money and buy one for yourself." What Nga appreciated about me, I thought, was that I was straight with her when everyone else smiled and stayed silent and soon deserted her.

"No TV till after homework," she told Zachary now. "How many times I tell you?" She picked up the remote and switched it off.

Anne Marie crossed her fleshy arms in front of her chest. "Zachary slept through science again today," she reported.

Nga regarded him sharply. "Did you?"

Zachary shrugged. He looked lost in his oversize

T-shirt, his arms like pipe cleaners jutting from the sleeves.

"Don't you like school?" I asked. He turned to me, his face brightening as he opened his mouth to speak.

"He doesn't like anything but math," Anne Marie cut in. "We Vietnamese seem to be good in math."

Zachary sat chastened and mute. Why don't you let your brother do his own talking? I thought. Anne Marie flashed a smile. "You want me to play something for you? Mama says you teach piano. I started taking last year."

"Sure, I'd love to hear you," I said.

We sat on the couch in the living room while Anne Marie settled herself on the piano bench and lifted her fingers to the keyboard. She began with "Morning Mood" from the Peer Gynt Suite, a pretty piece. I was glad her teacher had chosen something tuneful. Beneath the careful playing lay a certain soulfulness I wouldn't have expected, after her rudeness to her brother.

She played several more pieces. She was good, as Nga had said. Not a prodigy but certainly a talent. She got up and curtsied when she finished. We applauded.

"Now," said Nga, "we go eat."

Zachary went over to his sister and whispered in her ear.

"He wants to ask you something," Anne Marie told me.

"What?"

Zachary grinned but shook his head no.

"He's afraid it isn't polite."

"Not polite, don't ask," Nga said, her expression darkening.

"I'm sure it's all right," I said.

Zachary shook his head harder, his shiny black bangs flopping against his high forehead.

"What he wants to know," Anne Marie said, glancing at the floor so as not to be blamed, "is did you really have a husband named The Old Goat."

"Zachary!" Nga admonished, though only Anne Marie had spoken.

"Yes. They called him that because of his goatee. A kind of beard." I stroked my chin to demonstrate and smiled maniacally to show I wasn't angry.

Zachary laughed and pointed to his mother with glee. "See?"

I didn't tell them the rest. That such a nickname sounded derogatory but hadn't started out that way. That he was a gifted historian and a warm, generous man. That his students used the name with affection.

I didn't say he was fifty-one years old when we met, or that many people disapproved of us. At the church they began to use the term to refer to his sexual prowess. They believed I'd taken him away from his wife. To ease the sting, he began referring to himself in the third person: "The Old Goat doesn't think so." "You know what The Old Goat would like for dinner? A juicy, high fat steak."

We used the name proudly, in jest at first and then out of habit. It didn't entirely ward off disgrace.

Once, an elder in the church approached me. "Look at the two of you," he said. "An older man, a younger woman. The commonest, basest kind of affair."

We went to church every week, a matter of principle. It had been our church—mine and also his—before we ever got together. In the end, his detractors had the satisfaction of watching his decline. His diabetes grew worse. There were complications. Before it was over, he gave up a leg and most of his eyesight. I gave up performing and only taught. He would have lost the other leg if he hadn't died when he did.

* * *

We picked up Tran in Nga's minivan that had been in the garage. As the two of them closed the store, the children grabbed candies from the shelves and stuffed them in their pockets.

"We no like to bring them here because they eat, eat, eat!" Nga said. "Get as fat as me." To the children she called: "Not too much!"

Nga motioned me to sit in front with her while she drove. Tran climbed into the back with the children. He had never liked to drive. That first year in Maryland, two different men had given up in frustration over trying to teach him. He hadn't learned until later, after Paul was born and Nga's brother Anh arrived and the sponsors stopped offering rides.

"I show you some of our houses before we eat," Nga said. "While still light."

We took a lengthy tour. There was a row of duplexes in a little court, with a few chickens roaming in the street. Several tiny ranchers in what must have been the shabbiest section of town. And finally the building they'd moved from the casino site, small, with just two bedrooms, yet sitting now on a deep lot with attractive homes on either side. Proudly, Tran and Nga insisted we go in. It had been completely gutted and redone, the walls now white and clean smelling.

"Who will rent this?"

"Casino boss, maybe."

"Ah."

"And do people bring their rent to you at the store?"

"No, I have to collect." Tran made a motion as if knocking on a door. "Oh, very hard!"

A filmy dusk had gathered, but Nga drove the whole periphery of the waterfront to show where the newer "boats" had gone up—though the casinos weren't really boats, only immovable concrete barges set out on the water to meet the law. In the backseat, Anne Marie and Zachary sucked on fruit flavored candies whose scent filled the car.

"See that?" Nga pointed to an unsightly warehouse. "I was offered that for seventy five thousand, but at that time I said no, too much. Then they build Boomtown across the street and now they offer the owners six hundred thousand because it too ugly and they want to tear it down."

"Whoo. Too much!" Tran said.

"But the people say no, not enough. Now I wish I buy it."

She said "I" whenever she spoke of money, not

"we." We drove past all the various properties she'd been offered, the possible casino sites, the lots that might have potential.

"When you finally became a capitalist," I told her. "You did it with a vengeance."

A look of pleasure spread across her face. "Yes," she beamed.

* * *

By the time we parked at one of the casinos and walked through a long red carpeted hallway toward the huge cafeteria, I was faint with hunger and my hands had begun to ache as they often did at the end of the day.

"Sometimes we eat here too much," Tran said. "Children get tire of it. But Nga, she busy in the store. Hard to go home and cook."

"I like the Casino Grand better," Anne Marie piped up. "The food there is glorious."

Glorious?

"And you?" I asked Zachary. "What's your favorite?" Zachary shrugged.

From her purse, Nga pulled some pieces of paper I recognized as the coupons she'd gotten from the man with the watch. She handed them to the cashier at the entrance to the cafeteria. They were tickets for free meals, I realized, relieved they were nothing illegal.

"Casino bosses get these to give to big gamblers," Nga explained as we got our trays and silverware. "They come to my shop, give to me."

The line moved slowly. Zachary leaned sleepily against Tran. It was after nine o'clock. If I had had children, they would have eaten at six, been in bed by now, asleep.

"Seventy six items." Tran pointed to the food in front of us. Along with the usual chicken and roast beef were zucchini casseroles, seafood gumbo, a huge vat of King Crab legs.

"This what Vietnamese like most," Nga said, piling crab legs onto a plate.

Once we sat down with our food, a steady stream of Vietnamese diners came up to greet us. They seemed more deferential to Nga than to Tran. Had they all, at some time or another, had something to pawn?

Anne Marie ate ravenously. "The barbecued ribs are delicious."

"They are," I agreed.

"Scrumptious," she said. "Superb."

Zachary pushed his food around on his plate. He had nearly fallen asleep by the time Anne Marie nudged him and asked if he wanted to go back for second helpings.

"No eat too much," Nga cautioned her.

"I won't." She skipped off toward the buffet.

"She just like me," Nga murmured. "Sometimes I cannot stop eating. But Anne Marie, she too young to get fat."

"She's just chubby. She'll grow. Maybe she needs some exercise."

Nga watched her daughter in the food line. "She like to play basketball at school, but I scare. If she play basketball, she look like a boy."

"That would take an awful lot of basketball!"

"Sometime I think I send her to ballet, but her feet will get very ugly."

"Oh, Nga."

"That why I send her to piano. She practice, give her something to do." Cracking a crab leg with her fingers, Nga pulled a long strand of meat from the shell.

"But playing piano doesn't use up calories."

Nga bit into the white meat, slid it between her teeth. "Summers here very hot," she said. "Zachary play outside anyway, but Anne Marie, no." She picked up another claw, offered it to me. I shook my head.

"From Maryland and don't like crab!" Tran said.

"Now and then I do." I could get crab any time. What I really wanted was one of Nga's spring rolls. They were part of the reason I had come.

"Back in Maryland, not so hot," Nga told me. "If Anne Marie in Maryland, she play with her friends, lose weight. Maybe study piano, too. She like to go to Maryland this summer. Maybe I send her, who knows?"

"Mmmn." Back in Maryland, the Vietnamese had formed a tight community. Nga and Tran still had many friends there. But I was a bit surprised by her misplaced concern for her daughter. If either child needed special attention, surely it was Zachary. Was Nga so busy she didn't see? Like many refugee women, she'd had her first baby right away, just as the Holocaust survivors had done a generation before, to show they were unvanquished. But after Paul was born, while most of her friends were having two or three more, Nga had saved money, come to Biloxi, supported relatives, waited to have another child for nearly fourteen years. Even then, it had been a leap of faith. But at forty five, running two or three businesses, maybe she found her son's distress more than she could admit.

Anne Marie and Zachary returned with their desserts. A teenaged boy who'd come over with his family to greet Nga clapped his hands on Anne Marie's shoulders, leaned over, and said cheerfully, "Mmmn, a hot fudge sundae, my favorite. Can I have a bite?" For the briefest second, Anne Marie stiffened. She shuddered almost imperceptibly. Then she recovered and laughed. "Get your own sundae, Tuan." She sounded so merry that I thought I'd seen wrong. At fifteen or sixteen, the boy was just flattering her, teasing her, meaning no harm.

After dinner we walked next door to the Casino Grand, where Tran gave the children a few dollars to spend in the video arcade while we explored the casino. Decadently elegant, with crimson tinted lighting, it was a monument to video poker and video blackjack, where overweight retirees in polyester slacks fed hungry machines from large plastic cups of change. At the live game tables, the dealers were mostly Vietnamese, young men and women in white shirts and black bowties, dealing cards with swift, deft fingers.

"You remember my brother Anh?" Nga asked as we stopped beside a craps table, a game I'd never understood. "He here now, in Biloxi. He married. Got two babies."

"Yes. Tran mentioned him," I said, though a grown-up Anh was hard to imagine. And with a family! He'd arrived in Maryland a year after Nga and Tran did, a willful, skinny boy who proved too much for the church sponsors. I was the one who registered Anh for school. I was the one who bought him his first hard shoes because his accustomed open sandals were not allowed. When he whined that the new shoes pinched, I ignored him. I hadn't wanted to help Nga just then. Like the church sponsors, I was tired of her. I didn't care that she was busy with the infant Paul or that she couldn't drive. I had no sympathy for the fact that she had now taken in another charge, a half grown boy not much younger than she was. I did a few grudging tasks because I had once been a victim of the same sidelong glances from the people of the church, the same disapproving whispers. I wanted them to see that I was a better person than they were. I did it for revenge.

Anh stayed with Nga and Tran two years. Even as a young teen, he was restless, troublesome, shifty eyed. When Nga's father arrived and settled in California, Anh went to join him. By the time the Nguyens moved to Biloxi, I had lost track of him entirely.

"Anh come to Biloxi last year," Nga said. "He stay with me long time. Just move out last month."

"Ah." It was ten thirty. I was very tired. My hands were sore and swollen. Tomorrow was a school day for the children.

Nga looked troubled. "I give Anh money to take

class for casino dealer. He say he get certificate, but I don't know. I in store, I cannot tell what he do.

"His wife, I no think she good for him. If he want to go out, she say okay. He want to spend money, she say okay. If the woman has no control, not good."

We finished our tour of the casino, came out into the hallway where the light was not so dissolute and red.

"Anh stay with me seven months, and then I say, you cannot stay anymore."

"Well, of course. You couldn't support him forever."

"Now he in public housing. He drink beer all the time, not work."

"It's not your fault, Nga."

"I know it not my fault. But still it bother me. He my brother."

In the video arcade, Zachary had run out of money. Half asleep, he sat on the floor next to Anne Marie, who was driving a race car down a treacherous cartoon track, hurdling all obstacles in her way. She was very good.

* * *

Back at the house, Tran carried my bag upstairs. Zachary had fallen asleep on the way home. Nga tucked him into his bed. Anne Marie was still chattering.

On the upper floor, everything was as messy as it had been tidy below. Baskets of dirty laundry littered the hallway. Anne Marie's bedroom was full of French provincial furniture covered with clothes, as if she'd been selecting and discarding outfits for days. The guest room was jammed with wall-to-wall beds.

"This is where my uncle Anh stayed," the girl explained. "Mother and father and two little kids. Before that, we sponsored another Vietnamese family. We haven't had time to rearrange it."

"Last year, we have twenty people here," Tran laughed. "Too much people. Whoo!"

Nga came in with a pile of sheets. "Yes. Sometime house very full." She turned to Anne Marie. "Go to bed now. Tomorrow, school."

After Anne Marie and Tran left the room, I took a corner of the sheet Nga had selected, and helped her make the bed. Exhaustion had settled over me like a glaze. It took an act of will to make my fingers obey.

"In my country now, you want to leave, you have to come to Vietnamese relatives," Nga said. "That why the house so full."

"All these people are your relatives?"

"Some, yes. Others no, but government think so."

We talked a few minutes longer. I opened my suitcase and discovered the forgotten gifts I'd brought for the children, white cotton T-shirts with big red crabs in the middle, reading, "Maryland is for Crabs."

"I'll give them these tomorrow," I said.

"Children get up early. Have to go to school," Nga told me. "You tire, you no have to get up."

"Oh, I can't help it," I said. "When you get old, you get up.

* * *

That night I dreamed the Old Goat and I were arguing. This was odd because in real life we almost never fought. I said I wanted to quit teaching. The Old Goat objected. Teaching piano was not that strenuous. Each life had a path. You followed it until you couldn't. I had given concerts until my fingers had stopped working properly, and now it was natural that I should pass on my skills. He himself hadn't stopped teaching history until they amputated his leg. "Not everyone is like you," I protested. Even in the dream, I could feel how tired I was, how powerful the aching in my fingers. In the morning, I awakened late and groggy. When I came downstairs Nga was gone and the children were about to go out to the bus. I gave them the shirts.

"I love it!" Anne Marie exclaimed. "It's . . . ethnic!"

"Well, not exactly."

Zachary held his shirt up to his chest and made a comic face. Anne Marie tugged at the tight, stretchy fabric of her shorts that squeezed her thighs and made a lump of fat pouf out beneath the hem. I wished earnestly that Nga were here to make her daughter change.

"Come back soon," Anne Marie said.

"I will. And I'll remember you every time I use your pin cushion."

The girl hugged me awkwardly, as if it were a gesture she had rehearsed.

After the children rushed out I opened the refrigerator, looking for juice. It was nearly empty. A few bottles of soy sauce and ketchup, nothing else. Not even milk.

Tran came into the kitchen. "Nga go in to open store," he explained. "We meet her there, then go have pho."

"Who'll watch the store for her?"

"Oh, she close for a while. Don't get busy until later."

* * *

The pho restaurant was just a diner, but the staff was solicitous and the soup even more delicious than I remembered. Nga fished noodles out of her broth with her chopsticks, so gracefully that I wished my fingers were lithe enough to do the same.

"Tran mother sick now, we like to go back to Vietnam to see her," she said between bites. "But very expensive. Last time we spend twenty thousand dollars."

"Twenty thousand dollars!"

"Everyone expect you to give them money," Tran said. "Relative come from everywhere. Some you never know before, but don't leave 'til you give money. Whoo! Too much!" He plucked a soaked green vegetable from his soup and lifted it to his mouth.

"My aunt, I give her a hundred dollars and she complain to my mother, I should give three hundred," Nga said, laughing.

"Your mother. I thought she was going to come here."

"No. She old now. She no want to leave her friends. We help her. Send her money every month."

"Oh." Years before, Nga had confessed that her father also had a second wife, the one who'd come with him to California.

A young man approached from across the room to offer the standard respectful greeting. His wife, still seated at their table, waved to us warmly. Nga nodded with royal aplomb. Then she introduced me. "Sheila my sponsor from when we first come here," she said. "From when we live in Maryland." This was not precisely true since the church had been the sponsor, but the man seemed impressed.

"Very happy to meet you. Nga, she help me get work here. Before, I live in Florida, no good jobs. She tell me come to Biloxi, she help me."

"He live in one house I buy," Tran said.

"They very big help," the young man said. "Help me very much."

After he left, Nga put down her chopsticks and said to me dreamily, as if the thought had just flitted through her mind, "Anne Marie— I worry now that summer so close. I no like her be in the house too much this summer. Zachary okay, play with friends. But Anne Marie—"

After last night, I wasn't sure why we were discussing this again. "You think she'll sit around inside and eat?" What she would eat from Nga's empty refrigerator I couldn't guess.

"Last year and year before, we have many Vietnamese family in house. Anne Marie help take care of babies, have a lot to do. This year, house empty."

"But like you said, the neighborhood is safe."

Nga frowned. She took a deep breath. "You remember I tell you about Anh?"

"Sure." We had had discussed her brother only the night before.

"Anh no live with me now, but sometime he drink too much, come over to see her."

I was horrified. Everything I knew about the Vietnamese, which wasn't much, had never suggested—

"You mean—"

"Nothing happen yet, he don't touch her, but I see him look at her. Not right. She too young, she don't know. But I worry. I scare."

"Nga, that's terrible." It was sharply clear to me that Nga was wrong about Anne Marie not being aware of her uncle's impropriety. Anne Marie did know. Her involuntary shudder last night at dinner, when the teenaged boy had touched her shoulders, must have reminded her of some other touch, Anh's touch, unsavory and unwanted. No wonder Nga was worried! "Well, you're absolutely right. She needs to go to camp this summer. Even if it's just day camp. She needs to be out of the house when you're not there. Or like you said, you might send her to Maryland. To your friends in Maryland."

"I no send her to friends." Nga shook her head. "But you, maybe. You alone now. Maybe she come and—"

I was utterly taken off guard. Vietnamese families did not send their children off with aging American widows, even harmless ones. Were they too embarrassed to confide their fears about Anh to other members of their family? To their close Vietnamese friends? There must be many other places Anne Marie could go. I didn't understand. I suspected I never would. In any case, with Nga it was important to speak quickly and plainly, as I'd done so many times before. "Oh, no, Nga. It's out of the question. I like Anne Marie very much, you know I do. But I've never had children, I wouldn't know—"

"She like music. You teach her piano. She keep you company. Help you out."

I shook my head vigorously. "If you want to send her to friends, or send her to camp, that's different. I could help. I have a little money."

Tran put up a hand to fend me off. "We no take your money."

"You have to send your own money to Vietnam, you said so yourself. And I'm alone. I don't have that many expenses, I don't really need—"

A waitress came up and pointed across the room to the young man and his wife, who were standing up to leave. "He pay your bill," she announced.

Nga lifted an arm to the young man to acknowledge his generosity. "Thank you. Thank you very much." The young man grinned and waved back.

I felt abashed. I had thought the least I could do was redeem myself by paying for our meal.

We had left my car back at the store, where I meant to make a quick get away to New Orleans. But a real estate agent was waiting for Nga in the parking lot, a tanned, blond, thirtyish man in a golf shirt and khakis, who flashed a wide all-American smile and followed us into the store. I disliked him at once.

"This Johnny," Nga told me. "Sometime he find houses for us."

"Building lots, too. We deal in lots of lots." Winking at his own cleverness, Johnny produced a business card hidden in the palm of his hand, a magic trick.

"Sheila not buy house," Nga said. "She live in Maryland. She my sponsor from twenty-six year ago. Long time."

"Oh, your sponsor." Seeing I wasn't a customer, he segued from ingratiating to patronizing. "Then you must be very proud of them." The way his voice dripped, I half expected him to pat Nga or Tran approvingly on the head, a Vietnamese no no.

"You make them sound like children," I said.

"I mean—To go from nothing to owning all this property." His handsome features sought the proper expression to direct at me, wavered, hung in unattractive limbo.

"Well of course I'm proud of them. They're like family to me." I used my old dowager voice, a full octave lower than normal, that I'd cultivated to deal with difficult parents. "I always expected Nga and Tran to do well. It doesn't surprise me." I raked him up and down with my eyes. "Follow their example and maybe someday your own parents will have reason to be proud."

Even Nga had trouble suppressing a smile at this. Who did Johnny think he was? Didn't he see Nga's peers pay their respects as if to a Mafia don? If I was proud of her for anything, maybe I was proud of that.

Undone by my displeasure, Johnny busied himself showing Tran and Nga a packet of real estate information. Nga nodded and asked questions, but she seemed distracted. What a strain it must be, operating on the seamy edge of the law, no matter that the law was stupid. At least she was getting away with it. Sending money to Vietnam, sponsoring relatives who weren't related. Why should the tax man have her money?

"Well, I'll let you take this and look it over," Johnny said, giving me a last furtive glance as he handed over the papers and beat a hasty retreat. Except for the three of us, the store was empty. Tran and Nga and I stood across from each other in the dimness, among the half stocked shelves.

"Your plane—" Nga began.

An image came to me of Anne Marie, her tight shorts hugging the ample flesh of her thighs as she faced a drunken Anh among the sea of beds in the guest room. I imagined the smell of beer on his breath, though what I smelled was only the beer in the cooler.

What Tran and Nga was doing was very hard, I thought, harder than anything I had ever done, even when The Old Goat was dying.

Then I reminded myself what Nga had asked of me, and how uncharacteristic it was, and how little I understood it. I cautioned myself to keep quiet.

"Oh! I forget!" Nga exclaimed, and rushed to a small refrigerator behind the counter. She extracted a paper bag, slightly stained with grease. "This spring rolls I make this morning. I no have time last night, but not busy when I first open store. Take with you. They very good." She smiled with what looked like genuine delight.

"Nga, thank you! You remembered how much I like them!" I took the bag and said goodbye. I didn't offer to take Anne Marie. Nga smiled and waved and didn't judge me.

In the car on the way to the airport, it was as muggy as it had been the day before, but the air no longer weighed me down. Although not considering it seriously, I rolled the idea of Anne Marie around in my mind. She was an annoying child, no question. Yet she had made me that silly pin cushion. Really rather sweet. Away from Zachary, maybe she wouldn't be so bad. And Zachary could certainly use the reprieve. I could teach her piano, send her to the girls' basketball camp at the Y. She could run upstairs for my laundry, help me weed the garden. Sometimes she'd visit Vietnamese friends. She wouldn't have to be my whole life.

The lovely aroma of spring rolls rose up from the bag on the seat. I remembered our delicious breakfast. I told myself again that Nga was the supreme con woman. The idea actually made me laugh. For the first time in weeks I didn't feel tired. I felt energized.

Even my hands didn't hurt. It must have been the soup.

THIS APPEARED IN THE *CHICAGO TRIBUNE*,

NOVEMBER 11, 2001

NELSON ALGREN AWARD RUNNER-UP

NEWLYWED

One Saturday morning during their first year together, Joshua looked up from beneath the fat quilt he had wrapped around him like a cocoon, watching Jenny step into her jogging gear.

"I wish you'd stay in bed," he told her.

"I couldn't," Jenny said. "I'd feel awful. I've got to move around."

"Not healthy to move around so early," he mumbled.

"Oh, Joshua!" She tied her shoe, let herself out the back door of the apartment and ran down the hill past the swimming pool. She always wished he would come with her, but never asked.

Low-slung houses blinked by, squat patches of stucco surrounded by lawn and junipers. When her lungs had worked beyond their initial sluggishness to open and let the morning in, she felt that if she stopped moving she would simply fold into herself and shrivel. She'd tried to explain that to Joshua, but he smiled as if she were clever and inscrutable. His own life churned away deep under the surface, leaving him no need for muscles moving beneath skin to prove himself alive. But yet she wished he would run with her.

He was sitting on the couch in his bathrobe when she returned, head bent to the morning paper, eyes still misted with sleep. His hair fell untamed across his forehead, giving him an unlined look that always swept her through with tenderness, before his face became entangled with thought.

"How about pancakes?" she asked.

"Sounds good."

She fixed a whole wheat batter with wheat germ and eggs and skim milk. At least she could save him from fatty meats and a life of sedentary sloth. Sometimes, thinking of the difference between them, she was afraid that was all she could do. He was a lawyer, he was brilliant; she was a mediocre student who had yet to decide on a major. Even their marriage, which she had wanted so much, left her feeling undefined except in his shadow.

"Let's go somewhere today," she suggested. "At least let's go for a walk."

"I've got to work," he said. "I wish I didn't." She pictured him sitting in the extra bedroom, locked behind a law book, and the brightness of her morning dimmed.

"A short walk," she said. "Half an hour."

He pinched her forearm gently, scientifically. "I think you've got jumping beans under your skin," he said. "Tomorrow we'll go. Tomorrow I promise."

During the week, while he worked, she went to the university. She'd met him there a year ago, while he was still in law school and she was a freshman. He'd taken her for coffee on the pretext of helping her choose appropriate courses. "Take basic sciences," he'd said solicitously. "At least until you decide what you want to do. Then you'll have the background for anything."

At his suggestion, she'd signed up for chemistry and zoology the second semester, though her best grades continued to be in dance. She'd hated the long science labs. Their appeal consisted entirely of his presence in the hallway afterwards, waiting to see how she'd done. Still, this year she'd taken more zoology.

Twice a week, her comparative anatomy lab lasted until four. Her carpool left without her. Jenny didn't mind. She walked the two miles downtown to Joshua's office, shaking off the sharp smell of formaldehyde in the open air. She waited for him in his armchair, pretending to study as she watched him rummage through the books that lined his shelves, noticing the way he wrinkled the skin over his nose until his two thick black eyebrows became a single line across his face. She thought him particularly handsome. Looking up from the textbooks that never quite engrossed her, she'd find him smiling at her and decided her reward for science classes was—still—Joshua's presence.

Other times, his research consumed him. She felt him edge off far into the distance, losing himself in thought. At those moments she would be struck with her own lack of definition against his clarity.

Why should he want someone as amorphous as she? She wanted to rush down to the street below, to run against the crowd until she lost herself in the workings of her own strong limbs. Instead she tried to return to her books, be as brilliant as he, but there was no reaching him in things of the mind. She was caught by the idea that finding him, just what she needed, had left her somehow smaller, diminished.

* * *

When she returned from school early, she changed clothes and jogged around the swimming pool to loosen up before she started dinner. Sometimes on the lawn outside, two little girls from upstairs played with a toy crane and trucks. They liked to see her come out, to claim her, an adult, as their friend

One day they waved and smiled as Jenny headed downhill, the early September sun warm against her shoulder. Inside the pool area, the concrete deck was stripped of chairs and the water was dark green from chemicals. Already there was some suggestion of autumn in the air, some chill beneath the surface. She imagined being shut up for weeks in the cold, cloistered between buildings and cars and the apartment. Joshua laughed at her: the winter was nurturing, he said, cozy. But she thought of snow, shuddered, and picked up her pace.

"You run good," the girl named Betsy said when she came back up the hill. "Better than a lot of ladies."

"Well, thanks."

"Will you race us to the fence?"

"Sure. Why not?"

The girls got up, abandoning their crane on the grass, setting their feet at an imaginary starting line.

"Ready?" the one called Linda yelled. "Set. . .go!"

The two of them sped down the hill while Jenny loped behind. At the bottom, by the pool fence, they dropped into a heap on the soft grass, giggling.

"You didn't try!" Linda accused.

"I'll beat you next time."

Up the hill in the parking lot a car pulled in. For a moment she thought it was Joshua's. She did not want him to see her here, racing with children, did not want him to think her foolish. Then she saw that the car was a deeper blue, a newer model. Along with her relief came the sudden need to be inside, putting on brown rice to cook, getting about the serious business of life.

"I've got to go now," she said.

"Oh, don't." But without really hearing them, she took long strides back up the hill and disappeared into the patio door.

* * *

When Joshua worked especially hard, he came home with blinding headaches. Loose from running, her limbs flowing over the contours of the armchair, she felt guilty that he, not she, should suffer. One night he dropped his briefcase at the door, pulled the knot out of his tie and slumped down onto the couch.

"I'd better lie down," he said.

"Isn't there anything I can do? Aren't you going to eat?"

"Maybe something light later." He closed his eyes; his face crumpled with pain. He flung a tired arm over his brow.

Setting a bowl of soup before him, she said, "I hate to see you like this. I've never had headaches. I wish I could help."

"It's not your fault." He touched her hair and worked himself into a sitting position to eat. She willed herself to melt into him, to offer comfort. Then she remembered how it was in there, where thought was so heavy that it caused pain. She saddened and turned away.

She got a D on her first zoology lab exam: a shock. And Joshua was upset. "It's because you've never really learned to study," he said. "You have to go over and over the connections of those muscles. Get a picture of them in your mind."

Actually she had tried to do that, to imagine the pale bones of the cat she was dissecting and each thin thread of muscle: origin here, insertion there. But the vision blurred in her mind and the Latin names of the muscles ran together. She found herself stretching her legs for diversion, moving her arms in small circles (good for her triceps), anything to escape.

"Jenny, for God's sake," he would say. But she couldn't help it. One night a whole dance formed in her mind, her project for advanced jazz, while she struggled over cat muscles.

"You'll never learn anything jittering around like that," he said. "It's clear you aren't concentrating." The music in her head shut off as if by a switch; the dance steps fell away.

"I'm telling you, you've got to home in," he said. "Block out everything else."

"Weren't you ever bored?"

"Of course I was bored. But I didn't do the jitter-bug."

She closed her book and started for the bedroom, hurt. And angry, too: that he should still her music with his words.

"I'm not *you*, Joshua," she said.

* * *

In early October, as if from the effort of trying to be more worthy of him, she was suddenly sick her-self. She woke in the darkness, with the room spin-ning and her stomach knotted against the motion, aching in all her bones. Long streaks of pain shot through her chest, into her back, leaving her drained. Joshua lay beside her in a deep sleep. She thought to wake him. Then a bitterness seized her—borne of her pain, she supposed—and she hated him, hated him, for his easy rest. She turned away, floating free of him, so fuzzy against her dizziness that she felt suspended. A brief dozing, then consciousness, ex-haustion. Sleep did not seem to touch it. She began to be afraid. Putting her hand to her ribs, she felt for the beating of her heart. It didn't reassure her. The weariness returned again and again, compelling, until she slept, waking to fever and pain.

After two days, Joshua wrapped her in her robe and took her to the doctor. She was too off-balance to dress.

* * *

"You probably feel worse than you are," the doctor said, taking blood tests. "It looks like a virus, a mononucleosis-type thing." He patted her arm. She stared up at the fluorescent lights set into the ceiling of his office and wondered if she would faint. She told herself that if she fainted the doctor would know what to do. Then she let her dizziness claim her, spin her away.

At home Joshua gave her more aspirin; she slept again. When she woke, he brought her white toast and tea with white sugar. She wondered how he had found them. She always hid the white bread and sugar in the far corner of a cabinet, so he could have them if he asked but would not find them right off.

"I don't eat white flour," she said.

"You don't?" He looked surprised.

"I never have."

The illness hung on. She planned to study at home, but cat muscles held no attraction for her. After a few minutes, she would look up from her books to find the room spinning. She sank back against her pillows and closed her eyes.

Sometimes she stared up through the half-opened blinds that hung against their window and tried to place herself in time. The bright weeks of October slid past, liquid and unfocused against a blue sky. Joshua took care of her. He came home to make lunch, rushed back to work, returned early in the evening. A mechanical caring, she thought, but she was too weary to dwell on it. Sometimes she wondered if he would find her frivolous now that she could do nothing for him; if, discovering her to be a burden, he would discard her. But even her worry had the quality of distance, of love stripped bare by needs of her own.

She began to dream of running. In the dream her legs were weightless, cotton. She sped past the junipers like a seed pod on a puff of wind. Silently, fast and light she moved through the streets, legs never quite touching the pavement, no rush of air in her lungs. She was frightened because there was no life in the dream. When she woke she was feverish, her arm falling asleep from leaning on it. She wondered if she might be dying.

"There's a long convalescence from these things sometimes," the doctor said when Joshua took her again. Jenny was not reassured. She wanted health at once, this moment; her every thought had turned inward. If Joshua was cold to her those days, she hardly noticed.

One night after dinner he tucked her in on the couch before he went to work in the armchair, a gesture he didn't have to make. The room was filled with soft yellow light, but his face was clouded as he bent to his books, wrestling with whatever he was reading, and his eyes were opaque with concentration. She would never be able to study like that. He looked up to smile at her—with pleasure, with approval—and she was comforted.

The fever subsided little by little. In time she decided to drive to a night class, resting at home first all day.

"I'll take you," Joshua said. He packed his briefcase and pretended he had work to do in the library. During the lecture her hands were too numb to take notes. When the class was over he met her at the door. He was a softness against her pain.

She dreamed about running again that night, but the floating sensation was gone. She felt the watery feeling her legs had before she got her second wind, felt her body vibrate with each thud on the pavement. The hard hot road steamed beneath her, and perspiration beaded under her arms. She woke in a sweat, no longer frightened. Her strength would return in time; she was not to die.

In the mornings the apartment began to be cold. Outside color was fading from the trees. She lay back in their thick cocoon of a quilt, wondering if she wanted to get into her robe, to fix Joshua whole wheat toast with his tea. Sometimes she did . . . and sometimes she let him cook for her, curling into herself as she watched, harvesting her energy for the day. Never had she protected herself so; never had he. He came home with sacks of granola under his arms, packets of tofu and sprouts. She ceased to be astonished.

The two little girls from upstairs came to visit her, bringing chocolate chip cookies their mother had made.

"We're sorry you're sick," they said. "We liked when you used to run in the afternoon."

"I'm glad," she said from the distance of her tiredness. "I'm going to teach people to run someday. And dance and do exercises."

She had not said that before, though she'd understood it for some time. She did not think Joshua would find her frivolous; at any rate that was no longer the point. Her appetite for half-truths had vanished with the illness: the pretense, which had diminished her so, that she would willingly live her life as an addendum.

She remembered to offer the children their cookies, which she suspected were made with white sugar, bleached flour and artificially colored margarine. But recalling the isolation of the past weeks, knowing the girls were watching, she bit into one anyway. It tasted better than she expected.

One night she played the record she had chosen for her dance project, while Joshua worked in the den. She found a notebook in her desk and began to map out the steps on paper. She played the music until the dance took shape before her eyes. When she looked up, Joshua was standing in the hallway staring at her.

"My dance," she told him.

"You were very absorbed," he said.

"You used to worry that I couldn't concentrate."

"Not anymore."

"I've been thinking about majoring in phys ed, with a minor in dance," she told him. That way I can teach school. Or aerobics. Or whatever."

He smiled. "And abandon your career in zoology."

"Well—that, too."

"Jenny's School of the Dance," he read, as if off an imaginary tableau.

"It does have a certain ring," she agreed.

By Halloween, she was going to her classes every day, though when she came home she sat exhausted, waiting for her body to tap its reserves. She dropped zoology and struggled with her other courses. She had permission to make up the dance classes later.

One evening she rested at the window in the warmth of the late afternoon sun, watching the two little girls play tag on the lawn outside. They ran and fell down and ran again. Bits of crushed brown leaves clung to their coats. They pretended to be worn out, but Jenny knew better. Soon one leaped up and tackled the other with a great burst of energy, laughing at the joke. Jenny could not remember the last time she had felt that way.

Light began to drain from the sky in the west; dark was coming early. The two girls circled a last time and with a whoop disappeared around the corner to their door. In the parking lot the old blue sedan slid into its appointed place. Getting out, Joshua waved to her in the window. She did not worry about him anymore. Sometimes the darkness in his gaze reminded her of the place where they were separate, but then she closed her eyes and imagined herself running, dancing, moving, as if doing it inside her head would keep her body from forgetting. She smiled and opened the patio door to let him in.

ᴕ

THIS APPEARED IN *VIRGINIA COUNTRY*, VOL. XIII, NO. 3, OCTOBER 1990

RUNNING FROM LOVE

Probably I am the only woman waiting for the bell at Fairview Junior High School with the arch supports for a pair of running shoes in her hand. This is because Eddie Rudisill, my charge, always forgets. He is 14, a string bean of a boy, who needs to be picked up each day and driven to the high school for cross-country practice or (today) a race.

"Hey, Wheels," Eddie greets me, emerging from the flow of students. He slings his backpack over one shoulder. Every boy at Fairview carries a backpack in this exact manner—one strap slung over a shoulder and the other dangling. To wear a backpack over both shoulders would be uncool.

"Did you bring your running uniform?" I ask. He nods, patting his backpack. "And your arch supports?"

Eddie clunks the heel of his hand on his forehead. Without the arch supports, his knees will begin to hurt after a few miles. "Damn," he says.

"Watch your language." Benevolently, I open my palm to reveal two spongy blue wedges. Presto chango, Eddie smiles. We have only 20 minutes before the race. Technically, Eddie is a freshman and allowed to run with the high school team, but most ninth graders wait until they're out of junior high. Eddie was too impatient. His only concern is that he is shorter than the rest of the boys, and, as he mentions repeatedly, "My voice hasn't really changed yet, has it? Tell the truth."

"It's getting there," I say. You would think that a 14-year-old boy would not want to discuss this with an unrelated woman twice his age, but Eddie doesn't mind. I was 14 myself when he was born, and Eddie has known me all his life. As a teenager, I baby-sat for him, and when he was old enough to go to summer camp, I took care of his hamster. Growing up with workaholic parents who spent 12-hour days in their offices (largely, I suspect, because they didn't like each other), I was grateful even for the company of a rodent. Now I am on my own, and my parents have divorced, but I continue to live here in Fairview, working as a technical editor and, as fate would have it, Eddie's chauffeur.

This is because Eddie's household has lacked a second driver since his mother died eight years ago. Eddie's grandmother, Lil, lives there but never learned to drive. His father, Peter, a research biologist, is at the lab all day. Lil used to take Eddie by cab wherever he needed to go, but recently he announced that cabs were uncool. When he insisted that he would walk everywhere (or run) rather than go by taxi, I was called in to help.

Peter knew that my hours were flexible, and he

offered me free room and board in exchange for doing some driving. Frankly, I was delighted. My boyfriend, Greg Richards, is in England on an assign-
ment that will keep him away for several months, a
stretch that promised to be a long, lonely time. When
he comes back, we will have to decide if we're going
to go on living together—or get married. Meanwhile,
by moving in with the Rudisills, I could sublet my
apartment and save some money. The only down
side to this arrangement is that Eddie hasn't once
called me Teresa since I moved in. I have become,
simply, Wheels.

Eddie and I arrive at the high school's three rolling
acres, and he goes off to the locker room. Waiting for
the race to begin, I stand with a group of spectators.
I feel a little out of place. The parents are older than
I am; the students, younger. It's a relief when I hear
Peter's voice saying, "How did he seem?"

"Nervous," I say. "But no worse than usual." Peter nods. He too looks nervous. Except for the worry lines around his mouth, he looks a lot like Eddie.
They're both dark and intense—even handsome, I
suppose. Eddie has that adolescent unfinished look,
but Peter is really very attractive, which comes as a
surprise to me. I am still getting used to the idea that
he is younger than I believed him to be when I was a
teenager calling him Mr. Rudisill. He is 14 years older than I am, just as I am 14 years older than Eddie.
And, while I know that Eddie considers me pretty
ancient, I am beginning to realize that Peter—at 42—
is not ancient at all.

The runners are off, and eventually we see that Eddie has gotten into a good position. Peter actually sighs. He does this a lot lately. He sighed when his firm was awarded a new contract; he sighed when Lil's doctor said her arthritis was no worse. In the Rudisill household, things seem to happen every day that call for worry or sighs of relief. My own rather solitary background didn't prepare me for this. So I guess that's why I came here—not just to be Eddie's wheels but to see what it's like to be responsible for a family.

Lately, this issue of family is very important to me. Greg wants us to get married. In fact, he wanted me to marry him and go to England—but he feels we should put off having children. His company has promoted him quickly, and we will have to travel and entertain. Greg believes children will tie us down. Rationally, I accept most of this—and the idea of living all over Europe excites me—but I dislike putting motherhood on hold. And sometimes I fear that Greg might put off having children indefinitely. So I want to find out if the strains of family life are really what he says they are.

The runners emerge from some trees, and Eddie finishes in a strong sprint. In a burst of enthusiasm, Peter claps me on the back. "All right!" he shouts. His gesture makes me feel oddly happy. Then Eddie approaches, looking at me awkwardly, and I realize he wants me to leave so he can go home in his father's car.

"Lil wants me to stop at the store on the way

home," I announce quickly, feeling suddenly deflated. I remind myself that I am an outsider, after all, and I beat a hasty retreat.

Driving home, I suddenly remember that this is the day Greg usually calls. I am surprised that I could have become so wrapped up in the doings of a 14-year-old that I would forget. Still, my heart begins to pound in anticipation.

The Rudisills and I are eating one of Lil's wonderful dinners when the phone rings. I jump as if I've been scalded. Sometimes the long-distance connections are static-filled, but tonight Greg sounds as if he were calling from next door. I immediately want to touch him. He always affects me this way. The first time Greg kissed me, I thought I would be perfectly happy pressed against the bulk of his body forever. My reasons for staying behind seem suddenly unimportant.

"You can still change your mind, you know," Greg tells me. "We could get married over here."

"Not without settling this business about a family," I say. But, even as I speak, I am wondering: What is wrong with me? Why don't I tell him yes?

On Saturday, Peter invites Lil and me to ride along with him to a nearby town where Eddie is running in a regional meet. At the park where the race is to be held, we marvel at the scenery. The trees are at the height of their fall splendor, a picture-postcard vision of burgundy, amber and orange.

Eddie is standing with a pack of boys, all wearing identical running uniforms. Usually he ignores us when his teammates are nearby, but today he jogs over. "You won't believe this," he says to me, and I know why he's so friendly.

"I thought I reminded you," I say. An expression of worry begins to spread across his face. Peter and Lil both look puzzled. Eddie's worry slowly turns to panic. Then, as discreetly as possible, I pull the blue arch supports out of my pocket and slide them into Eddie's palm.

He sighs with relief. "Thanks, Wheels." Then he trots off to join his team.

Peter laughs. "Did I include that in your job description?" he whispers in my ear.

"Well, you should have," I say. The place where Peter's breath has warmed my ear feels red, sensitive. It reminds me of Greg whispering to me through the long-distance lines.

At the end of the race, the runners come into view from behind a hill and sprint toward the finish line. Lil remains in the lawn chair we have brought for her, but Peter and I position ourselves to watch the finish. To our astonishment, Eddie appears many places ahead of where we thought he'd be. In his excitement, Peter puts his arm around me and hugs me close. For the moment, I forget about Eddie. Peter's chest is broader than it looks. He smells of spicy aftershave, vaguely familiar but one I can't identify. The skin on his face is smooth and masculine. Absurdly, my knees go weak, and I feel myself relaxing against Peter's chest. My heart begins to pound.

"Under eighteen minutes," Peter says, still holding me but looking at his watch as Eddie comes in. "Terrific!" Then, as if he has just realized his arm is around me, he quickly releases it. He gazes into my eyes for a long moment before both of us awkwardly look away. I realize that Peter's eyelashes are the thickest, longest lashes I've ever seen on a man.

The next day, the weather turns chilly and gray. Eddie trades his colorful shorts for sweatshirts and jeans. Peter leaves for work early on the theory that it takes his car extra time to warm up. I know he's avoiding me. He never intended to touch me like that, and I never intended to react as I did.

A cold gray rain begins, accentuating my misery. It's still raining on the day of Eddie's next race—a foggy drizzle that soaks the ground and sends up a chill that cuts through my clothes as I wait for the race to begin. As I expect, Peter fails to show up. He'd rather miss his son's race than risk standing here with me.

When Eddie and I arrive home, Peter is lying on the couch with an unsightly gash on his forehead. My heart takes a giant leap into my throat. He raises his hand as if he fears I'll rush to his side and wants to ward me off. "It's nothing. It looks worse than it is," he says, before I realize that he is talking not to me but to Eddie, who is standing in the hallway. "I had a little fender bender."

"You'll have a headache for a week," says Lil as she examines his injury.

"I left late for the race and skidded on a wet road,"

Peter explains. "My car will have to be in the shop for a few days," he says to me. "You think you could drive me to work if we feed you more?"

I start to agree, grateful he's making a joke out of it when the last thing either of us wants is to share a car twice a day—but I sneeze instead. Eddie sneezes with me. By the next morning, both of us have full-fledged colds.

As Lil predicted, Peter cannot get rid of his headache. Eddie and I cannot get rid of our colds. The damp weather continues.

Peter and I drive to work pretending to be absorbed in our separate thoughts, letting the car radio fill the silence. Through my stopped-up nose I think I can smell Peter's familiar aftershave. This is probably my imagination.

Coming home one night, we find Lil stirring an enormous pot of chicken soup. Just as we sit down to eat it, the phone rings. Eddie's coach has been calling to check on his cold, but, when Eddie answers, he turns to me. "For you, Wheels. Your Big Wheel in England."

"I'm sorry I missed you last night," Greg says. "I had to fly over to Paris for a meeting." The connection is weak, and for a moment I don't know what he's talking about. Then it dawns on me that last night was his night to call, and I didn't even realize he hadn't.

"Listen," he's saying, "I can't stand this anymore. There I was, in a restaurant right near the Eiffel

Tower, eating great Continental cuisine, and I thought how insane it was, you being there and me here. Teresa, I've been thinking . . . maybe one child right away wouldn't get in the way after all."

I should be elated, but for some reason, I'm not.

"I have a few days off next month," he is saying. "I want us to spend them together in Paris. I've sent you a plane ticket." A wave of emotion sweeps through me. It must be relief. Greg and I will see each other again. I will remember how I feel. "When?" I ask.

"The weekend of the twentieth."

"Oh."

"What's the matter? You sound disappointed. You sound different."

"Just my cold," I say. But I'm trying to remember what it is about the 20th . . . then it comes to me, and suddenly, without question, I know that I *am* different.

The next day—the day Eddie recovers enough to go to practice—my cold is worse.

"It's because you're thinking too much about flying to Europe for that weekend," says Lil. "Stress. Sometimes it's better not to think things through too much. Better just to do them."

But I can barely get through the day. The manual I'm working on is boring, and my mind wanders— to the Eiffel Tower, to Greg's Paris restaurants and three-piece suits. I sneeze constantly on my way to pick up Peter at the lab. Seeing my puffy face, he says, "Poor Wheels, you look terrible. Come, I'll show you the lab. It'll cheer you up."

How this is supposed to cheer me, I'm not sure, but I'm too weak to resist. He shows me beakers and Petri dishes, computers and high-tech instruments. "We're not working on a cure for the common cold here," he says, after he's shown me all through his lab, "but somewhere, in a lab just like this one, someone is." He touches my crimson nose. His long eyelashes are growing longer. I realize this is because his face is coming closer to mine. I think he is going to kiss me. I wonder how I will breathe. I remember Lil saying it's better not to think things through too much, just to do them. So I do.

"I had to do that before you go flying off to your boyfriend," he whispers afterward, holding me close to him.

"I'm not going," I mumble into his shirt.

"You're not?"

"It's the weekend of Eddie's state finals. I want to be there." That's true, but I don't tell Peter that I'm bothered by Greg's statement that one child might not "get in the way" too much. I only lean into Peter's chest.

He kisses me again. His closeness must have an antihistamine effect, because, though we kiss for a long time, I am able to breathe.

"What about the Eiffel Tower?" he asks, rubbing my back.

"Some other time." I realize that I do not actually believe in the Eiffel Tower. It's a picture in a travel brochure, but I don't believe it exists. Suddenly I identify Peter's aftershave as Old Spice—strictly family-style stuff. It seems to me that I've learned something about "family style" that Peter has known all along and Greg may never understand. For me, Peter and Eddie and Lil are real—not the Eiffel Tower.

He has a warm, searching mouth. I tell myself my decision to stay is based on momentary physical attraction, on the trembling in my legs and the bright place on my back under Peter's hands. It has nothing to do with long-term commitment. It has nothing to do with love. But I find myself wondering why I need Continental cuisine when I can have Lil's cooking. I find myself wondering what will happen if Eddie decides to run track in the spring. Who will remember his arch supports?

༈

THIS APPEARED IN *MCCALL'S*, OCTOBER 1987

KINKS

Kayla had been sick and wasn't well yet, and her temper was sharp as knives. She was tired of being weak, tired of looking rotten. Tired of being lied to ("Oh, Kayla, your color is so much better!") Tired of missing work. And at the moment tired of her hairdresser, Nick, who was pretending he knew how to straighten her hair.

"My main concern is to keep lotion off those damaged ends," he announced, dabbing gingerly when the idea was to get good coverage.

"Damaged ends, hell. You're nowhere near the ends. You have to put it on thick. You're supposed to work fast." Kayla had the kinkiest hair of anyone she knew. Once, an inept stylist had left her with a crew cut, and since then she'd straightened it herself. But when Nick offered this time, she brought him her straightener because she was too tired to say no.

Moving unhastily, Nick parted her hair into sections, applied cold-creamy goo onto new growth the consistency of Brillo. "Almost finished. Then we'll leave this on for a while."

"No! Only fifteen minutes, or my hair will break! You have to follow the time chart!"

"Ah —ze time chart." He tried for a comic accent, gave her a patronizing smile. Before now she'd found him pleasant enough, a petite, balding man with unhealthy yellow eyes and a fashion sense developed in the tropics. Today he wore a loose Hawaiian shirt with electric orange flowers and royal blue leaves that pulsed under the shop's fluorescent lights. Kayla shivered.

"Something wrong?"

"I'm fine."

But was she? Chills had been the plague of her illness, every night and sometimes during the day. She'd run a fever and endured a nagging pain in her side. She'd shivered even when she was wearing sweatshirts, couldn't sleep, watched her hair grow dry as sand. The infection had lasted all winter, resistant to antibiotics, to vitamins, to bed rest. The pain was not debilitating, just terrifying. What if it signaled not an infection but something worse? What if it grew sharper? Never went away? Sometimes she'd awaken clear-headed and lie helpless while it crept back, its intensity building like the volume on the radio. She hadn't worked for so long that she'd run out of sick leave. "Getting better *is* your work," her husband assured her.

"Harder than going to the office, but lower-paying," she quipped. They pretended they didn't miss her salary.

Then, two weeks ago, the ache in her side suddenly disappeared. And, more gradually, the shivering— until now. She clenched her teeth to make it stop.

A Barbie doll face floated into view—Bonnie, the

manicurist—pink, pouty lips and a reedy, petulant voice. "Oh, you're taking out all those curls! If only I had curls like that without having to do anything for them."

"You wouldn't want this, believe me."

Bonnie sighed. She rarely had customers, so she was forever wandering the shop, offering the customers compliments and coffee. Friendly as a puppy but always in tight bodysuits and slacks, never any bra. Two haircuts ago, Nick had revealed that Bonnie was his wife. Wife! Brains of a moth, trashily pretty, under thirty. Nick was fifty, easily. His hands froze in mid-air as he admired his wife's perm. An ashier blonde than before, soft new waves. His own handiwork, no doubt.

"Concentrate," Kayla told him. "Time's almost up and you haven't smoothed it yet."

Setting his applicator brush on the counter, he seized a wide-toothed comb.

"No! You're supposed to smooth it with your fingers. Not comb it. Not pull it. It says right here." She snatched the directions from the shelf.

"With your fingers? Really?" All innocence. He put down the comb.

"Hurry, Nick. I mean it."

"This won't take long." He began stroking the sections with gloved hands. Imperiously, he turned to Bonnie. "Check my appointment schedule, will you, hon?"

Bonnie scurried off, obedient, completely under the man's power. But Kayla was the fool who'd let Nick loose with enough chemicals to burn her hair to the breaking point. Which he seemed about to do. Her heart thrummed frighteningly at the thought.

"Relax, hon," he said.

Relax? Imprisoned in her chair, about to go bald, didn't she have every right to be tense? After months with an ache in her side, chills skittering up her spine, pain that exhausted her to tears—on top of that, a naked scalp?

"Now!" she demanded. "Rinse out the straightener now."

She tried to stand. A slight pressure forced her down: Nick's fingertips, insistent on the top of her head. "Take it easy. No problem. Some people leave this stuff on for hours."

"Some hair is coarse! Mine is fine. It'll break." Her heartbeat bruised her ribs.

"It's not fine, it's medium," he said. "Almost done."

Above her, one of the fluorescent lights began to buzz. The air was thick, hair floating up from the floor, releasing an unhealthy, chemical odor like the antiseptic for hospital rooms where someone had died. On Nick's shirt, the orange flowers beat like garish hearts. She felt dizzy.

"Hurry, Nick," she said again.

Languidly, he continued smoothing. She pictured her stubbled head days hence. Breathe deeply. Inhale. Exhale. This is nothing to die over.

But why, as soon as people got some advantage over you, did they turn the knife? Rejoice in the fine treachery of power? While she was sick, she'd made herself stumble out to get a birthday present for her husband, Dan. Her side had nagged at her, she'd had a fever. The saleswoman stared at Kayla's check, asked for her license, took the documents to her superior. Raked Kayla with her eyes—the baggy pants (she'd lost ten pounds), sunken cheeks, lifeless hair. She'd almost fainted from exhaustion.

"There," Nick said.

"Done?" she gasped.

Of course, done. What did she think?

"Mrs. Dodson was scheduled for three," Bonnie called from the front of the shop, "but she just canceled."

Nick's expression flattened, a punctured tire. At the shampoo bowl he tilted Kayla's chair back so quickly that her neck bounced on the rubber lip of the basin.

"Use the neutralizer after you rinse," she instructed over the rush of water. "The straightening doesn't stop till you neutralize."

"Oh."

"Lather two or three times."

In the distance, a phone rang.

"Mrs. Dodson again," Bonnie called. "She wants to reschedule for Saturday morning."

"Fine."

"The neutralizer," Kayla repeated. At the edge of her vision, a pair of nipples strained against the fabric of a bodysuit. "We have that yard sale," Bonnie mewed.

"So?" A dollop of shampoo hit Kayla's head. "You can handle the yard sale yourself, can't you?"

"Keep track of customers and make change both? Not really."

Well, of course not. It was a miracle if the girl could make change at all.

"I can't leave Mrs. Dodson flat," Nick said. "Let me think. Tell her you'll call back." Then there were only Nick's fingers rubbing, the smoosh of neutralizer shampoo in her hair. This was better. Her heart rate slowed. Eyes drifted shut. What luxury, being tended to without the ache in her gut, the chills, the constant fear. Icy rinse water woke her. She jumped.

"You okay?"

"Just startled. I think I dozed off."

"They often do." Nick sounded pleased. Kayla shivered. Nick turned the water hotter—a little act of kindness. She wouldn't have thought him capable.

Her husband, Dan—now, he was kind. Pretending they didn't need her paycheck. Holding her when she got chills. Warming her.

As the hot water warmed her now.

When your hair falls out, fool, you won't feel so cozy, she told herself. But she felt lulled, comforted.

Bonnie's voice broke her reverie, hopeful and pert. "Maybe we could pull the ad out of the paper."

"No. It's too late. Don't be silly." Nick jerked Kayla's chair upright, flung a towel around her head. He sank his fingers into the towel and dried roughly.

Kayla shifted away, escaped in the direction of his styling booth. Nick and Bonnie trailed her, the tension between them like a knife poised in the air. Nick jammed the diffuser onto the end of the dryer, turned it on, wielded it like a weapon. Bonnie crossed her arms and watched. The sourness of their anger drained Kayla the way her illness had. Until you lived with pain, you had no idea. A quick, sharp jab shuddered through her side and then was gone. Couldn't the two of them fight later?

"I have to call her back now," Bonnie said.

"In a minute." Nick pointed the dryer at Kayla's neck. She picked up the hand mirror to look at the back of her head. Oh, Lord. The dry places near her scalp were paper straight. The ends were straight. But in the middle, Nick had missed a whole section. Straight at the roots, then kinky, then straight again. She looked like something out of a side show.

"You didn't get it all," she accused.

The dryer hummed; he couldn't hear.

"Straight, curly, straight," she shouted.

No response. He was looking beyond Kayla into the mirror at Bonnie, who dropped her arms and stalked away. For a second he went as white as powder.

I'll be damned, Kayla thought.

Which just went to show you could never tell about someone else's marriage. You could hardly tell about your own. At her sickest, she'd actually asked Dan if he'd ever had an affair. If she was going to die, she might as well know.

"Of course not. What do you think? When would I have time?"

"Well, if you ever do, I'll leave you. It's even retro-active. If I find out you had an affair ten years ago, I'm still leaving."

"Not to worry," he'd told her.

Bonnie plunked down at the manicure booth. Nick

stood straighter. "You can't imagine what a pill she is," he said.

"Bonnie?"

"Mrs. Dodson. Gets her hair done every week. Not a time goes by that she doesn't want to change her appointment."

Ah. Regular income. Not easy to give up, no matter the inconvenience. Nick set the dryer in its slot and picked up the curling iron to shape her bangs. In the end he couldn't afford to lose Mrs. Dodson's business, yard sale or no, any more than Kayla could afford to be out of work. Pitiful to be reduced to that. The reason people exerted their power, she supposed, was because they had so little. And against illness, none at all.

Even so, she didn't forgive Nick the frizz.

Stepping back to examine his work, Nick finally noticed the kinks. Flitting around, flowers throbbing on his shirt, he lifted a round brush, tugged at the curl. It straightened out, then snapped back. He gave up, blasted her with spray. Pulled off her smock. In a week or two, the kinky hairs would probably fall out along with the straight ones.

She wouldn't pay him a cent. This is totally unacceptable, she would say. They moved toward the cash register. Bonnie, filing her nails at the manicurist's station, didn't look up.

This is totally unacceptable. Heart thumping again. She hated scenes.

"All right," Nick said loudly. Kayla startled, but he wasn't talking to her. He was calling to Bonnie three feet away. "Phone Mrs. Dodson and tell her I'll take her Saturday, but not before noon."

Bonnie looked up, puzzled.

"I'll help with the yard sale and come in later," he said. "Yard sales are always over by noon."

Bonnie beamed.

Totally unacceptable, Kayla rehearsed. Outside, children biked by, their cherry and lime helmets bobbing above gawky bodies. In the cold spring sun, they looked like a parade of lollipops.

"Oh, look at you!" Bonnie cried, approaching Kayla, arms outstretched. "Straight except for that band of crimping around the middle. What a neat new look."

Crimped like a damned circus freak. "It's awful," Kayla said.

"I'll only charge you the same as a haircut," Nick defended.

"Oh, it's wild," Bonnie enthused, scrunching a handful of frizz in her fingers. "Really wild."

Wild. Like a tiger. Like an orangutan.

Nick looked wary. Kayla sighed. She had no energy for this. If she went bald, it would not be because of sickness, only because of a beauty shop incident—a trifle. Nick's fault, but so what? He had offered because he needed the money. She had accepted.

She opened her purse, rummaged for her wallet. Maybe she wasn't well, not really. Maybe her lack of pain was temporary, a gift, on loan. But wasn't it always, in any life? Having known such misery herself, why should she make him miserable?

In the bright sunlight that poured into the reception area, Nick's shirt looked even more horrid than before. So cheap and flashy that it might be his very life pulsing there, blooming against his chest. She smiled because there seemed no reason not to.

"Thanks so much, Nick," she said, and pulled bills from her wallet—more than she intended—and handed him a ten dollar tip.

ॐ

THIS APPEARED IN THE (RALEIGH NC)
NEWS & OBSERVER, MAY 27, 2001

BULLFROG AND MOONWALKER

The year Kammie was fourteen, she and her brother, Nathan, came in from junior high one day to find a note on the kitchen table saying Mom was at their aunt's apartment and would call later to explain. When she did, all she said was she and Dad had problems they had to work out before she came back. *If* they could work things out.

"It's not as if you and Nathan were babies," she said. "You can cook dinner for yourselves. You can throw in a load of wash."

"Mother, I don't believe this. What problems?"

"Remember how you said there were certain things you couldn't discuss with a mother like me? Well, this is something you don't discuss with children. It's just that I need a little distance right now. We're not going to be able to work it out with me staying in that house."

Kammie felt a little woozy; she couldn't believe her mother was saying this. This was the same mother who had a fit when she heard that Kammie's friend Darla had a boyfriend who smoked—who went on a tangent about Kammie keeping secrets from her.

"Kammie never told me you went with someone, Darla,'" Mom had said at the time.

Darla laughed. "I tell my mother everything." And Kammie, trying to smooth things over, said, "You're not the kind of mother you can tell things to," meaning only that Mom wouldn't really care about hearing, she'd only care about the smoking and the boyfriend. Smoking was bad, drugs were worse, getting boy-crazy too young was senseless. "I got married at twenty-eight and I've never been sorry," she would say. "Do everything you want before you get married. Boys can wait." She acted as if people like Darla's mother didn't exist, who could listen and not necessarily give a lecture afterwards.

When Darla left, Mom said lightly, "Tell me something, Kammie. You never tell me anything." So Kammie knew that though her mother pretended to be joking, she was hurt. And so when Mom moved out of the house, Kammie felt partly responsible for the lack of communication.

"At least let us know when we'll see you," Kammie said.

"I could take you to the school dance Friday night, if Dad'll pick you up after." Mom never liked to drive late at night. The headlights made streaks on her glasses, and she liked to go to bed early while their father stayed up late. Kammie wondered if that was part of their problem.

When Kammie got off the phone, Nathan had the stereo blasting and was sliding backwards across the kitchen floor with his shoes off, moonwalking as if nothing unusual had happened. "That's it, isn't it?" he said. "I've really got it now, don't I?" For weeks Nathan had been trying to moonwalk the way Michael Jackson did on television. The idea was to slide backward on the toe of your shoe so fast you looked weightless, floating, though Nathan never did.

It was typical of him to be dancing even though Mom had left. All he ever thought about was himself. Usually he turned "Billie Jean" on the stereo while Mom was cooking dinner, and moonwalked in front of her so she could hardly move. He'd get his socks filthy and flail his arms around as if he was engaged in some kind of struggle. Instead of getting mad at him, Mom would say, "He's only in seventh grade, this dance means a lot to him" or "Yes, that's a lot better than yesterday," even though it wasn't.

"Nathan, you know why you always have to pretend to be Michael Jackson?" Kammie asked. "It's because you're such a twit."

When their father came home, carrying a pizza, Nathan asked in his usual diplomatic fashion, "What's the matter with Mom? Female problems?" Dad sometimes joked that "That's how women are, Nathan. Female problems."

Mom always replied, "Male problems, Nathan. Females problems are caused by males." But tonight Dad didn't want to joke. "Maybe she just needs a couple of days," was all he said. He looked at Kammie. "Do you want to help out at the office tomorrow after school?" he asked. "We could use you."

Kammie thought he was trying to make up for Mom's leaving, so she said "No thanks" and stuffed some pizza into her mouth. Usually Kammie liked working in her father's engineering firm. She liked getting paid minimum wage and she liked talking to Bernice, the secretary, who had shiny black hair and green eyes, and who acted as if she really appreciated Kammie's coming in. But that night Kammie said, "I can't work if I'm going to have to cook dinner tomorrow. You can't count on Nathan."

The next day, she could hardly keep her eyes open after school. Even before her mother moved out, Kammie had started feeling tired in the afternoon. Mom said it was because she needed to take vitamins with iron now that she had her periods. Mom set the pills out every day, but Karnmie always forgot. She dumped her books down and put a TV dinner in to cook while she watched General Hospital with Nathan. Usually Nathan did his homework after that, and Kammie watched the reruns of Charlie's Angels until Mom came in and made her turn the TV off. Mom said Charlie's Angels was sexist trash. But that day, Nathan put his Thriller album on instead of studying, and moonwalked around the kitchen while Kammie ate her TV dinner.

"Pooter gave me a moonwalk lesson in the cafeteria today," Nathan said, sliding backwards to the music. "He taught me exactly how to do it. Watch. I can really do it now." '

"Beat it," Kammie said. The TV was on in the family room, and the stereo in the living room. The kitchen was a sound chamber. "Just beat it," Michael Jackson sang. Nathan smiled and shimmied and moonwalked out.

Kammie finished the fish cake and potato puffs in her TV dinner, then threw away the metal tray with the peas still on it. Nathan said the peas in TV dinners looked like rabbit turds. Back in the family room, Kellie of Charlie's Angels was being gagged and blindfolded by a jewel thief. Mom said the only way to redeem Charlie's Angels would be to make the heroines thirty years older. She had a strong opinion about everything. Usually Kammie started to wake up after she ate, but on that day she fell asleep the minute they put Kellie into the getaway car.

* * *

"You know, I wasn't asking you to work in the office out of charity," Dad said later in the week. "Bernice is out, and we could use the help. You could use the money."

"Yeah, but there's all this laundry." Actually Nathan was doing the laundry while Kammie watched TV and waited for Mom to call each afternoon, to see how the kids were getting along.

"We're all right. What're you doing?" she would ask,

"Working a lot," her mother told her.

Mom had a part-time business writing brochures and newsletters. She said she liked it because it allowed her to be in the house if someone was sick. Darla said Kammie's mother was very traditional.

"I miss you guys," Mom said. Kammie wanted to say, why don't you come home then, but she didn't. "Are you eating all right?" her mother asked. "Are you cooking?"

So far Kammie had fixed hamburgers and spaghetti with sauce from a jar. Kammie liked to cook, probably more than her mother did. Mom didn't eat potatoes or a lot of other things the family liked, though she always said in any family you were bound to have differences over food. This was part of her "prices of family life" lecture. And though she got mad when she set out a bowl of stewed tomatoes and Nathan said, "Yuk, it looks like barf," Mom always thought Dad's jokes about her food were funny.

One Sunday, Mom had a coffee cake in the oven, with cinnamon and coconut and sugar on top. When she opened the oven to check it, the cake was half-risen and misshapen, puffing out of itself the way her cakes usually did. Seeing it, Dad sprang up from the Sunday papers and quickly pulled Mom away from the oven, yelling, "Don't worry, Connie, I'll save you!"—holding his arms out, pushing her out of the kitchen, into the family room and down onto the rug, landing on top of her the way you'd land on top of somebody if a bomb was about to go off. Mom was laughing so much she could hardly breathe. Then Dad got up and brushed himself off, saying, "With complete disregard for his own safety, he used his body to shield her from the most horrible, the most unthinkable . . . " He took a deep breath. "I ought to get the medal of honor for this." A little while later

Mom served the coffee cake, but she was still laughing too hard to eat. Kammie couldn't believe that had happened just a couple of weeks ago.

"Mom's picking us up for the dance and you're bringing us home," Kammie told her father on Friday. She had spent all afternoon cleaning her room so it would be nice when Mom got there. She used to keep it neat, but lately she had been so tired that her blow drier, curling iron, towels from her showers, and most of her clothes landed on the floor. Mom never said anything, only closed the door whenever she passed by. Kammie even dusted the furniture before opening the door and turning on the light.

* * *

Dad looked at her blankly when she mentioned the dance. Then he recovered and said, "I hope you remember what I told you about dancing with boys."

Kammie didn't think that was very funny right now, but she said, "Don't worry, Dad," and smiled a little, just to be polite. When Kammie was getting ready for the first junior high dance of the year, her parents asked her if girls danced with boys or with each other or what. Kammie said you could pretty well dance by yourself to the fast dances, but to the slow ones you had to dance with a boy, what did they think, you could hardly dance with a girl. The girls put their hands on the boys' shoulders and the boys put their hands on the girls' waists.

Mom looked at Dad and said, "Oh Daniel, I don't think she's old enough for that." smiling as if

Kammie was some little twit. Then Dad said, serious-ly, as if he were going into one of his father-daughter talks, which Kammie hated, "Did I ever tell you what happens if you dance with boys?"

Kammie rolled her eyes and put her hands on her hips. "No. What?"

"You turn into a bullfrog," her father said. Her mother giggled.

"I guess that's what happened to you, then, Mom," Kammie said.

"Oh no, your father never danced with me. He was never a dancer. Maybe once, at the wedding." She patted the wrinkles around her eyes. "These are from the stress of raising children."

Later that night, both Mom and Dad wanted to know how the dance was, but instead of asking out-right, Dad looked into Kammie's face as if he were examining her for a rash and said, "Yes, I can see she danced with boys. The slight bulge of the eyes." Ordinarily Kammie wouldn't have told, but since she couldn't help laughing she said, "Only one, Steve Johnson." and her mother said, "Oh, him. Well, you ought to be safe."

Mom didn't come in when she picked them up for the dance. She honked the horn in the driveway. In the car she didn't say anything about bullfrogs, only asked Nathan and Kammie if they had a little extra money for a Coke.

"I could use an extra five," Nathan said.

"Fat chance," said Mom. "Nathan, I hope you're helping with the laundry." Nathan had his own unique way of folding clothes, but he was helping. "Have a good time," their mother said. "I'll see you guys later."

"Does that mean she's coming home?" Nathan asked after she drove away. "Or she's not? Or what?"

* * *

On Saturday, Dad took Nathan to swim practice in the morning and Kammie to dance lessons at noon. Then they all did the grocery shopping, though none of them really knew what they needed since Mom always shopped. Sunday they were reading funnies in the kitchen when their father put the paper down and said, in a voice just a little too loud for the room, "I've thought about it and I've decided you're old enough to know why she left. I hope you understand this is just between us, just inside the family."

"Yeah, sure," Nathan told him. Kammie felt prickly the way she did when he was starting one of those father-daughter talks.

"Remember the other week when I had that public hearing after supper?" their father asked. Kammie did. It was the last time she'd worked at his office.

Bernice, the secretary, had been excited and flushed, trying to get everything ready on time. Nathan nodded as if he remembered, too, though Kammie was sure he didn't. Michael Jackson had just burned his hair off while doing a Pepsi commercial, and all Nathan cared about was getting Mom to buy him a copy of *People Magazine* with pictures of Michael Jackson in the hospital. Mom had said absolutely not, *People Magazine* was not something she'd ever buy for herself, and if Nathan was too undisciplined to save his own money for things like that, he would have to do without.

"Well, that night Bernice brought some papers down to me at the court house," their father said. "And after the hearing we both went back to the office to put them back in the files. This is something we do all the time after a hearing. It's normal procedure."

Kammie and Nathan both nodded. "While we were in the office, Bernice's husband came down. He started pounding on the door, which was locked because it was after ten at night. When I answered, he came rushing in insisting I was having a love affair with Bernice.

"I want you to know this was absolutely untrue," their father went on "The only person I've ever had a love affair with for the past sixteen years is your mother."

Nathan nodded again and his eyes got big. Kammie felt a little sick.

"Anyway, Bernice's husband called us both a few choice names—I won't go into that—and then he grabbed her car keys from her purse, for what reason I can't tell you, and stormed off.

"You can imagine how upset Bernice was," he said. "So I drove her around a little and let her talk about her problems. Then I took her to her friend's house to spend the night, and came home. That's all there was to it."

Kammie thought she really might throw up; she shifted so there wasn't any weight on her stomach.

"It turned out that by the time I got home, Bernice's husband had called here and told Mom he found me in bed with Bernice. Of course that's absolutely ridiculous, but Mom had no way of knowing I was just driving Bernice around all that time. It was probably a mistake." He started folding up a piece of newspaper. "I guess she's still not convinced. That's why she moved out. But I want the two of you to know: I was telling the truth."

Nobody said anything else for a long time. Kammie still didn't feel very good, but finally it was so quiet that she said, "You sure got yourself into one this time." Her father laughed a little then, more like a snort.

*   *   *

On Monday, Mom asked if Kammie wanted to go out to the mall after school to look for shoes. Her feet kept growing; she had to get shoes every couple of months. Kammie said okay and Nathan, who liked to shop for about ten minutes until he could ask for a hot pretzel, said if Kammie was going, he was going, too.

"Nathan, you have to be patient," Mom said when they got to the mall. "We don't always find Kammie's shoes in the first store we come to." What bothered Kammie was the way her mother was acting exactly as she always did. Nathan said, "Fine. I'll go into Waxie Maxie's, and when you're finished, you come and get me."

As soon as they left him, as soon as they were walking down the center of the mall beside the little planters of tropical trees, Kammie said to her mother, "He told us why you moved out."

Mom just kept walking as if Kammie hadn't said a word, and turned into Kinney's, which they usually avoided because most of the shoes were too narrow for Kammie's feet. Sure enough, the sneakers she tried on didn't fit, but she saw exactly the shoes she really wanted, pink canvas flats with a crepe sole.

"Be serious, Kammie," Mom said. "You know how practical they'll be?"

"Oh yeah? How practical is it for you to move out on us when nothing even happened?"

Kammie put the pink shoes back on the display rack and ran out into the dimness of the mall. She didn't want Mom to catch up because she couldn't talk, her throat was too tight. She wasn't going to cry there in the middle of everything, in front of people. But Mom found her and fell into step.

"Did I ever tell you I was engaged before I met Daddy?" she asked after a while. Kammie shook her head no; she could do that without crying. "I was engaged for a year and a half," her mother said. "We were supposed to get married. Then I found out he'd been seeing someone else. Other people knew about it. I was the only one who didn't. I decided I wasn't going to stand for that again. That was the one thing I wasn't going to stand for. I didn't need any man that badly. I still feel that way."

Kammie's throat loosened a little and without

meaning to she sighed so loudly her mother could hear it. "Come on," Mom said, touching her shoulder to turn her around. "At least try those pink shoes on."

The shoes fit because the canvas stretched so much, and Mom bought them for her. Back at Waxie Maxie's she bought Nathan an old Jackson Five album featuring Michael Jackson as a little boy. When they got home, Kammie dumped the shoes on the floor and said to Nathan, "We're taking advantage of her. She would never buy me these shoes if she hadn't moved out. She wouldn't have bought you that album."

"So?" Nathan said. On the stereo, Michael Jackson was singing "Oh baby, give me once more chance." Nathan was making a pretend microphone out of his fist and singing along with the record.

"Shut up, Nathan," Kammie said. "Did you know she was engaged before she met Dad?"

Nathan stopped singing. "Yeah?"

"You didn't, did you? We don't know anything about her. Do you even know where she went to college?" Nathan didn't say anything. At the mall, when their mother bought the Jackson Five album for Nathan, she said Michael Jackson was about ten years old when those songs on the record were popular. She was a young woman. Kammie had seen pictures of her mother young, but she didn't remember them well. Mostly she thought of time as something that went forward from now—to when she, Kammie, would be grown. Mom never mentioned her own youth and so Kammie never thought it would be interesting. But maybe Mom didn't talk about it because it *was* interesting, just like Darla's boyfriend's cigarettes. She sat in the family room without even turning on the TV, listening to Nathan pretend to be Michael Jackson, thinking: that's why she didn't get married till she was 28, because she was engaged to someone else. She would never have imagined that.

When she tried to picture her mother young, she got a hazy figure in an amber light, the color you would paint if you wanted to show things that happened a long time ago. She imagined Mother listening to Michael Jackson and maybe dancing with a boy. She tried to imagine some boy giving her a ring, kissing her, and then going out with other girls. She couldn't picture those things clearly. She thought how all the things Mom lectured about—watching Charlie's Angels and not getting boy-crazy too young—everything she had opinions about, probably started back there in that amber light, where Kammie couldn't really see. She wondered what else had happened that Mom didn't tell her. It would be embarrassing to know. But it bothered her that her mother was living in her sister's apartment right now, instead of at home, because of things that happened back there in that amber light.

* * *

Bernice had quit. "If she hadn't, I would have had to fire her," her father said. "You can't have a secretary with a crazy, jealous husband."

"So she wasn't just out last week, she was gone for good," Kammie said.

"Yes."

"You're not even seeing her, then!"

"I was never seeing her, in that sense," Kammie's father said.

Kammie's father was interviewing other women to take Bernice's place. In the meantime, there was no one to answer the phone. Finally Kammie did go into the office one day because she felt sorry for him. A lady with a frizzy perm came in to interview for the job. "Come in, Mrs. Tannenbaum," her father said, very stiff and formal, nothing like he was at home. Kammie remembered he had been that way, formal, with Bernice. She believed that he had not had a love affair with her. She could not imagine him joking with Bernice the way he did with her mother. She couldn't imagine him kissing her. Now that she thought of it, she wasn't sure her father liked Bernice very much.

She thought she'd tell her mother that. But when her mother called, she didn't ask about Dad, or even if Kammie was watching Charlie's Angels, or if anything was new with her friends. It used to be that whenever Kammie said anything about her friends, especially Darla whose mother had been married three times, Mom would say that divorce was so easy now, so common, that before you got married you had to decide this was an absolute commitment you were making for the rest of your life. She made it sound like some horrible duty. But Mom didn't say a single word about divorce or commitment during those phone calls. And when Kammie thought about her parents on the family room floor laughing about the coffee cake, or talking about her turning into a bullfrog, she saw that her mother's actual life with her father had nothing to do with commitment or duty, but with something else entirely, that had gotten its start in the amber light. So she figured it wouldn't help to explain about Bernice.

One afternoon, Mom was there when they got home from school. Kammie would have let it pass, but Nathan asked right away, "Are you here to stay?" and their mother nodded. Then Nathan went to the record player and put on his Thriller album and said, "Look, I learned to do the moonwalk."

Later Mom went upstairs to unpack her clothes and Kammie followed. "I was getting tired of cooking every night," she said.

Her mother smiled. "It's a thankless job, isn't it? Maybe now you'll appreciate what I go through around here."

"Oh Mother." Then because she couldn't help it, she said "If you're staying, I guess that means you believe him."

Mom put a hanger down onto the bed and looked at Kammie as if she might give one of her lectures. But all she said was, "I wasn't there that night, was I? I suppose I'll never really know."

"I guess not," Kammie said. She thought she should say something right then about her father and Bernice, how formal he was with the people at work, but she couldn't say it straight out, just like that, so she didn't.

When Dad came in he put his arm around Mom and might have kissed her except that Nathan turned up the stereo and yelled "Look!" and started dancing around in front of them. Having demonstrated the moonwalk already, he got down on the floor to break dance, spinning on his back and then rocking across the rug on his belly.

"What's this? Is he having a convulsion?" Dad asked. Her mother laughed. Dad started dancing Mom around, doing some old-time step and swinging her under his arm. Right then they looked very young to Kammie, still back in that amber light. When they finished dancing, Dad leaned against the refrigerator and Mom sat down on a kitchen chair, catching her breath and laughing. Kammie was going to pretend nothing was happening, but at the last minute she was so full that she said, "Mom you better look in the mirror."

"Why?" her mother asked, putting her hands up to her face.

"Because you're beginning to look like a bullfrog!"

֍

THIS APPEARED IN *VIRGINIA COUNTRY*, APRIL 1985

TRIAL BY ALTITUDE

It was August, 90 degrees in the parking lot of the Denver airport, and Jake's daddy Sam was smiling as he heaved Jake's suitcase into the back of the van, saying, "Before this day is out, son, we're going to have a snowball fight."

"Sure, Dad. Snowballs."

"Wait and see." Sam's weight-lifter's muscles pumped, and his teeth gleamed in the glossy mountain sunshine as he slapped the side of the van companionably. "Borrowed from a friend," he said. A woman friend, Jake feared. One set of seats was folded down to make room for a tent, sleeping bags, canteens, groceries and such. Sam and Jake were headed to Steamboat Springs, where Sam worked in a sporting goods store, but on the way they'd camp overnight in the mountains. Jake's mother, Leslie, disapproved. "Oh, I see, a father/son ritual," she'd said on the phone. So Sam waited until Jake got off the plane to announce that their ritual father/son cookout would be preceded by a hike to above the tree line, "to see what snow feels like in the middle of the summer." Though it was only marginally cooler in Denver than it had been in this morning's dripping Virginia heat, Jake noted that the snow-capped peaks of the Rockies did indeed rise impressively in the distance. He was 12, just off his first solo flight. Two weeks in Colorado lay before him. Snowballs? Why not?

They drove north from Denver to Fort Collins, then west into the mountains, his daddy talking all the time. "I bet your landing was rough, wasn't it? That's because of the thermal currents coming up from the valley floor. The heat gathers there all morning and then rises up. That's why it's rough if you land in the afternoon.

"But you'll need a sweatshirt when we get up beyond the tree line. You have a sweatshirt, don't you? Well, hell, your mother packed you, didn't she? She probably put in your winter coat."

Jake laughed because she nearly did. His mama said living in a pocket of warm air along the Virginia coast gave you a false sense of weather. Every place else was colder. His mama's boyfriend, Albert, said, "Let him be, Leslie. It isn't that cold in August, even in Colorado." Albert was in a good mood because Jake was leaving.

The road ascended into the mountains, into spectacular scenery Jake had seen before only on postcards. The sky was so blue and the trees so green that they seemed almost unnatural, more like a movie or a dream. Or else no sleep last night was catching up with him—being keyed up, flying west, gaining two hours. He got this hazy, detached sensation sometimes when he was tired—or bored in school, in a hot slant of sunlight, hearing a teacher drone—or getting hit by air-conditioning in summer after swim workout, after walking home in the heat. The sensation wasn't unpleasant, just weird. And very possibly the first step toward craziness. He couldn't afford to be crazy, not now. He said to himself, this is actually happening right this minute. I am here seeing these mountains. His daddy was talking about the jagged peaks, high and uneven because they were so young, geologically speaking. Concentrate, Jake thought. Sam pointed to the tree line—an actual line almost straight around the mountain at a certain height. "As if all the trees got together and decided they just wouldn't grow above that point." Jake laughed, and then the detached feeling went away.

"Depending on my schedule, I'm hoping we can go on one of those white-water rafting trips while you're here," his daddy said. Talking, talking. Sam had been in Colorado only since spring, and in Florida and Arizona before that. He didn't get to Virginia often, but when he did, he took Jake water-skiing or deep-sea fishing or to the batting cages and the beach every day. They ate picnic lunches and suppers at Taco Bell, and when Jake arrived home tanned and happy and too tired to talk, his mama criticized. "Your daddy means well, but he's too unsettled and too rough." Her idea of an outing was a movie with Albert.

"They say the rafting trips are for tourists and pretty tame," Sam said. "But it might be fun."

Better than a stroll around the park with Albert, Jake thought. He began to feel excited and a little afraid the way he always did when his daddy was around. By the time they reached the turnoff for the campground, he was completely awake.

"There," Sam said, pointing to a mass of snow on a peak above them. "That's where we're hiking to." Jake followed the finger upward, beyond a stand of dense trees to a harsh rock-and-grass incline leading to the snow. Sam showed Jake his topo map. "We're at eighty-six hundred feet," he announced, "and about to go up." Except in an airplane, the highest Jake had ever been before was 5,000 feet, when he and his mama drove the Blue Ridge Parkway,

They set up the tent first. Sam showed him how to hammer in the tent pegs, tie the knots. His daddy probably did this all the time. They gathered firewood to use when they came back from their hike. "Ten of three," his daddy said. "Just time to get up and down the mountain before dinner." Sam slung two canteens of water over his shoulder and instructed Jake to tie his sweatshirt around his waist for later.

The trail began with a footbridge over a stream of water, shallow and fast-moving and so clear that the smooth oval stones beneath it seemed almost magnified. "The Laramie River," his daddy announced.

"Looks like a creek. Too small for a river."

Sam laughed. "In the West, this is a river." And then, seriously, "The water all looks clean out here. But never drink from these streams. There's stuff in them that makes you sick." Poisoned water! Adventure! Jake knew his mama would hate the idea of streams that could make you sick.

The trail led through a field of wildflowers, then up the mountain, on hard-packed dirt and rocks, switching back and forth as it snaked upward between the trees. At first it was wide enough to walk two abreast. "There's a waterslide you'll like in Steamboat. And a big pool," his daddy said. "There's a boy your age in the condo next door."

When the trail steepened and narrowed, Jake fell behind, watching the canteens bob on Sam's narrow hips, watching his sturdy, muscular arms swing, tanner than Jake's own arms though Jake was in the sun all summer. Sam's legs were sturdy, too, and covered with dense brown hairs above the running shoes he always wore. Jake would be just as muscular; he'd start lifting weights next year, soon as he was old enough to use the weight room at the Y. Sam kept talking, glancing back to make sure Jake heard. Then, as if it were a normal question, he asked, "You get along okay with Albert?"

"Yeah, fine." Albert was a photographer, a vegetarian, what Sam would call a pussy. Jake didn't say Albert had moved his dark-room in. The day he set up all his trays and equipment in the laundry room, Jake and his friend Matthew swiped six bottles of chemicals and buried them under some trash in the dumpster outside the apartment. Albert might think they were lost in the move, or he might suspect, but he'd never know. "Have you been messing around in here?" Albert asked after Matthew left. "There were some bottles. Right here."

"I didn't see them."

Albert squinted and glared. "How about keeping out of here then? With all this stuff in here."

"What if I'm doing laundry?" Jake never did laundry.

"Seriously, buddy," Albert said. "How about making like a tree and leave?"

"An old joke, Albert."

"Not a joke, Jake." When Jake's mama wasn't around, Albert didn't even bother to be polite.

Jake's plan was to tell his daddy about Albert little by little. Nothing judgmental. Just facts. The things Albert liked to do—eat Chinese, take pictures, spend Sunday mornings in bed with Jake's mama. He'd let his daddy make up his own mind about whether Jake ought to go back to Virginia or live here in Colorado. Sam got so quiet that Jake figured either that he was thinking about Leslie, which seemed unlikely, or that walking had begun to occupy him. At least it had begun to occupy Jake. Despite the switchbacks on the trail, the path was steep. They were in the trees and couldn't see much: the tree line must be straight above them. Jake was a little winded; thirsty, too. He'd have taken a quick drink, but Sam had the canteens. Why was his daddy carrying both? Jake wouldn't ask to stop because they'd been walking only maybe half an hour. The air was already cooler, just as Sam had predicted. Soon he'd need his sweatshirt.

It was odd being so thirsty without being hot. Why was his mouth so dry?

"Take it easy the first couple of days," his mama had said. "People need time to adjust to altitude. Don't let him take you on one of his Olympic marathons."

Maybe he was adjusting to altitude. He pictured the drinking fountain outside his homeroom at school, pictured water coursing out in a thick cold silver arc.

Abruptly, in front of him as if he'd read Jake's mind, Sam stopped and shrugged the canteens off his shoulder. They'd come around a bend. A mountain was visible in the distance. The snow seemed not so far above them. A flat-topped rock hunkered above the trail.

"Up here," his daddy said. They scrambled up and sat on the rock, surveying the trail below them and the mountain in the distance. Jake waited for his daddy to open the canteen and offer it to him. Jake drank for a long time.

"Tired?" his daddy asked.

"No," Jake lied. He handed the canteen to Sam, who drank and gave it back. Jake drank again. Then he slipped the strap over his shoulder. "I'll carry this one," he said.

His daddy nodded and jumped down from the rock to the trail, a long way, maybe seven feet. Jake felt he had to jump down, too. Leslie had made him wear hiking boots with no spring in them. He shoved off, hit the dirt trail hard but kept his balance. His daddy watched him. He wished for running shoes like his daddy's.

"How's the swim team coming?" Sam asked, walking off again.

"Okay," Jake said. Another lie.

"What's your best stroke?"

"Freestyle." He was better at breast-stroke but didn't want to say he got disqualified every time for doing a scissors kick somewhere in the race. He never felt himself doing it, so getting d.q.'ed was always like being kicked in the stomach.

"You can't expect to win your first summer," Sam said, striding out now, making Jake work to catch him. "The first year you have to race against your own times and against the clock. Second year you start worrying about the competition."

"Yeah, I guess." He didn't say that most of the kids had been on the swim team since they were nine, three years ago. Nobody started at twelve. How could he ever catch up? He was swimming because Jake's grandma said, "That boy is raising himself, alone in that apartment while Leslie works and then sees that man." That man. Besides, Jake liked raising himself. Making his own peanut butter sandwiches, playing video games. But Sam and Leslie and his grandma were of one mind: "You need a summer sport, Jake." Next thing he knew he was signed up for the swim team. The pool was in walking distance. Practice was at seven in the morning. The chlorine left his vision blurred and his head stopped up. After the first month he could win in practices but never in meets. He lost because of clumsy starting dives, an inefficient stroke, getting disqualified. Going fast had nothing to do with it. He detested swimming.

His daddy pointed at a break in the trees where they could see mountains in the distance again. Dark clouds had gathered behind the peaks. "Let's hope we get up there before it rains. It almost always rains in the afternoon at this time of year." As if they'd chosen to hike in rain deliberately. "Thunderstorms sometimes." His daddy winked.

Jake was out of breath again. Already. More than before. His boots were weighing him down. His daddy got farther in front of him. His mama used to complain that when Sam was walking or biking, he'd forget anybody was behind him. When Jake was little, she said Sam's bike got so far ahead that she didn't see him for hours. "Why does it always have to be a race? If I want to go twenty miles, why does it always have to be fifty?" Her voice grew shrill and high then, which Jake didn't like. "Why does it always have to be an endurance contest?"

He was thirsty again, though it hadn't been five minutes since they'd had their drink. He took a swig from the canteen without slowing down. Drinking and walking at the same time made him more out of breath and didn't satisfy his thirst, either. A laughing couple passed, coming down the mountain, descending toward the shush of the Laramie River, perhaps dipping cupped hands into the clear water, marveling at how each oval rock seemed highlighted on the riverbed underneath, as if in one of Albert's photographs. No one would believe anything toxic could grow in such clear water. It would taste cool, delicious. False.

Since he couldn't drink and walk at the same time, he concentrated on things outside the dryness in his mouth. Rocks embedded in the packed dirt of the trail, the pale leaves of the aspen trees, their white trunks. The sound of his own breathing.

He was getting cold. If he put his sweatshirt on without stopping, the act would take more air from him. His daddy was walking fast. He tried to remember heat coming off the blacktop in the airport, to draw warmth from it.

Another stream now. Above the water, the air shivered. They balanced on rocks and went across. On the other side, a scout troop had pitched tents and built a fire. A corner of red plaid flannel protruded from one of the tents—the inside of a sleeping bag. Jake imagined pulling the cloth around him, catching his breath, being warm.

Sam waved at the scouts and kept going. Jake wasn't just winded now: his head felt foggy, too. Not detached, as in the van earlier. No, this was a fog of sickness. His stomach was jumbled: he shouldn't have taken the drink back there. He didn't feel well at all. Sam moved fast, not looking back. Jake remembered his mama giving up biking, staying home, her anger and restlessness filling the apartment like fever. Sitting motionless except for her teeth against her nails, biting away. Her disposition snappy and mean. Jake knew even then she'd quit biking because she was weak. His daddy left because of her weakness. Albert was weak, too. When Sam went around a bend and couldn't see, Jake stopped a second to catch his breath. It didn't help: he was too sick. He couldn't understand why he wasn't in better shape after swimming all summer.

His nose had started running. He wiped it with the back of his hand. His hand came away red. Blood. He'd never had a nosebleed in his life. The light dimmed and brightened through the trees, depending on the movement of the clouds. From the distance, far away, came the rumble of thunder.

He wiped the bloody hand on his sweatshirt and went faster, getting his daddy in sight. Sometimes they came around and saw other mountains, just briefly, jagged against the sky. They had been walking—how long? An hour? Two? Jake squinted at a far peak, trying to assess the angle of the sun. He couldn't judge. He was still on Eastern time, confused by the foreign pattern of clouds and brightness.

His nose was bleeding, his stomach jumbled, and now his hands tingled, too. His hiking shoes weighed more than they had at sea level. "Me, I'm an ocean person," his mama said, claiming some people liked to live near the ocean and others in deserts or mountains. "It's as if in a certain environment, they automatically feel right at home." Jake didn't care about the ocean now that he had to swim every day at the pool. Where there was ocean, there was Albert. But in the ocean the danger was not from the water but other things—vicious fish or vicissitudes of weather. Here the mountain itself was treacherous, the cold dry air; the piercing light.

His daddy stopped short and whistled through his teeth. Jake caught up. The trail had ended; a huge clearing opened ahead. "Look at that. An avalanche must have come through."

Before them lay a forest of downed trees. Slender whitish trunks, some kind of fir. Every tree for a hundred yards across had been completely uprooted in the avalanche's path, flattened utterly. Above the expanse of trees was bare slope, steep and rocky. The tree line. Patches of snow. Behind the peak, the clouds were dark as the rock. A few raindrops splattered down. Sam sat down on one of the tree trunks, patted a spot for Jake, opened his canteen and drank. Jake was too sick to be thirsty. In a minute he was going to throw up.

"You all right?" Sam asked.

"Fine."

Horizontally across the line of downed trees, the trail picked up again. Sam eyed it, then looked up. Jake saw what his daddy had in mind. The tree trunks provided hundreds of footholds, as steep as the slope was. "What do you think?" Sam asked.

"We could go cross-country," Jake said. "Straight up."

His daddy stood, pleased. Jake had no time to catch his breath. The air made his lungs burn anyway. He swallowed to keep his lunch down. He stood. Not weak like his mama and Albert.

Sam made his way across the tree trunks, graceful in his running shoes. Jake followed in slow motion, boots heavy, stomach really sour now. Drizzle misted his face and hair. Not a lot of rain, but cold. It might not be really happening, except that the rain was so cold.

He had to be careful where he put his feet. The tree trunks were wet and slippery. Sometimes they were so close together that he had to step on top of them. Other places the trunks were farther apart, and he could step over them and put his feet on the ground, torn and furrowed by the violence of the avalanche. His daddy moved faster, lighter, looking up at the snow.

Then his daddy stumbled, pitched forward slightly, then back. He seemed to sit rather than fall. His shoe was wedged under a tree trunk. "Oh, shit," he said. Sitting on the wet ground, knee bent, he wrapped his arms around the hurt leg, resting his head on the knee. "Shit," he said again.

"You hurt?"

"I twisted it." Sam pulled down his sock. The ankle was already beginning to swell. "I'm all right," he said.

Jake helped his daddy up. "Can you walk?"

Sam tried to put pressure on the ankle. He grimaced. "Not really, but you can always hop down a mountain." He tried to smile, but his face went gray and rough. It was as if he didn't have a suntan.

Jake remembered something he'd forgotten. When he was four, his daddy broke Jake's wrist.

Sam was whirling Jake around above his head, letting him fly on outstretched arms. The hot green twilight blurred into a single splash of color. Sam circled faster. Jake closed his eyes. He was dizzy and the world was apart from him.

Then a single slice of pain brought him back. He screamed. It was the first pain that made him think he was living solely in the part that hurt, that all his life had knotted and clumped into the few inches between hand and forearm. His daddy didn't stop right away. He thought Jake was having fun.

Now Jake asked, "Are you okay, really?"

"Sure." Sam sat down again. "Give me a minute."

"You want to wait a while?" Jake asked. He knew what he had to do.

"You don't need to go after help," his daddy said. "I can get down."

"I don't mean that." Jake pointed up the mountain. Beyond the fallen trunks the trees stopped. Beyond the tree line it was 200 feet to the snow.

His daddy regarded him proudly, Jake thought.

"You go ahead," his daddy said. "I can wait."

Jake felt air stabbing his lungs as he made his way across the remaining tree trunks—hot metal points of air. His lunch and his heartbeat were in his throat. No matter. If his daddy wouldn't keep him, who would? Up. The trees gave way to bare ground. Across patches of thin grass, outcroppings of rock. The incline almost 45 degrees. A steady rain now. Slipping over the wet rocks. Not really walking anymore—more like crawling. His daddy had known it would rain. Leaning forward, clutching the grass, clutching for balance at whatever protruded from the ground.

Dizzying movement in his stomach. In his head. Sick.

Up.

Kneeling, crawling.

He clung to a rock. Red drops of blood dripped from his nose.

Chest on fire. Head whirling. Then a wave of weakness. He couldn't move. His mama said take it easy, but she never said that altitude would light candles in his lungs, make the air spin around him, turn his stomach, force blood from his nose. If she had, would he have believed it?

Maybe he was dreaming. He'd never felt so bad inside a dream. But no, the rock was cool beneath his cheek. Finally he turned his head to the side and threw up.

In front of him, in a circle of dirt, a dandelion bloomed. Dandelions grow above the tree line, he thought.

If you could think of something outside of yourself, you were all right.

He squiggled along a little, on his belly. Above him, snow. Glistening, even in the rain.

Strength trickled back into him.

Put him on his feet. Hard shoes digging into the hillside. Holding on as if to the side of a building. A wall. Inch by inch. Foothold to foothold.

Up.

Detached now. His daddy was a speck among the fallen trees below. He imagined a hiss of air, air on the plane, hissing from the overhead nozzle, thick and luxurious, whole milk after a diet of skim. He breathed that air.

Belly to rock, wet, cold. At the end he couldn't see his daddy at all. He didn't know it would be so simple. Reaching up, higher than he had ever been before, he opened his hand to whatever it would grasp, and found he was clutching the snow.

ॐ

THIS APPEARED IN *VIRGINIA COUNTRY*, VOLUME XIV,
NO 3, FALL 1991

RETURNING TO NORMAL

That winter, there were some very cold, very sunny afternoons during which Carrie Johnson delayed picking up her children at the baby-sitter's house and went out into the air for the purpose of physically exhausting herself. Leaving the junior college where she taught English, she would return home to don slacks and thermal sweat shirt and then jog for perhaps a mile through the suburban development where she still lived. (Russell, her ex-husband, had rented an apartment.) Winded, she walked until she revived, then alternately jogged and walked until she had covered perhaps five miles, only to turn and repeat the process on the way back home. There she showered, changed into her work clothes (this to convince the sitter she was coming directly from school) and picked up the children. The object of these excursions was not cardiovascular fitness, not the desire to be alone, not communion with nature: only physical exhaustion. This she usually achieved.

Why did she do it? Partly because that winter the shape of her existence had been finally stripped bare. The divorce final, the first months of confusion over, her job secure, now suddenly her life spread out before her as a great yawning chore, unwelcome and unrelieved. She no longer missed Russell: The marriage had been too bad for too long, faltering since Steve was born six years before and worse after Krista. But single life presented her with overwhelming mechanics—dealing with unreliable plumbing, with the trips to the doctor for Krista's ears and the stark realization that there was no one to help. The women in the development had quickly dropped her after the divorce. Her best friend Wilma lived 60 miles away; her parents were two hours south. Her one remaining ally was Jim Anders, recently divorced himself, who taught in the history department.

The summer had passed: a blur. Fall was only slightly better. She worked, cooked, did laundry, shopped, went back and forth to the sitter's house. At Christmas she visited her parents because she knew she could never get through it alone. One day in early January as she stopped for a red light, she observed a scene that shattered her reserve. A mother, waiting with her kindergarten son for the school bus, laughing and fidgeting in the bitter air to keep warm, suddenly stopped and pulled the boy's cap down over his face. Surprised, he squealed with delight. Carrie could not remember the last time she had shared a moment of spontaneous mirth with her children. Driving away, she saw that the grass had gone dormant since she had last noticed, giving the landscape an almost unbearable bleakness. The

January world mirrored perfectly her own internal state: a palette of rich color now drained to dull browns. So she had started running—exhausting herself. Between the exercise and the pressing busyness of her days, she lived in relative numbness.

Occasionally, briefly, her protection vanished, seared off by raw anger: when Russell's support check was late, when the electric bill came, and once—only once—because of the children. Waking early one morning, she had stood barefoot on the winter-cold floor, stirring white sauce and Cheddar cheese into a huge pot of macaroni, enough for the evening's meal and then some. She set the finished casserole on the bottom refrigerator shelf to be baked after work. Moments later Krista had appeared with the casserole in hand. "I want macaroni."

"Oh Krista, not now." But before she could cross the span of floor between them, Krista had lost her grip and dropped the bowl onto the linoleum, cracking it neatly in two. "Oh, damn," Carrie said. "Krista, I've told you never to take things out of the refrigerator. Never. Damn. Oh, damn." And she landed a smack sharply on her daughter's arm. "Don't ever do that again. Ever!" Like a fishwife.

Krista, wailing, retreated to the kitchen table to wait her out. When she tired of crying, she stopped, chin set, the sturdy dark-eyed survivor even at three, and said to Carrie firmly, "Don't hit me any more." Carrie felt a sudden wash of pity, of shame, and then nothing. She went to her daughter and put her arms around her gently. "I won't, Krista, I won't." The appropriate gesture, but sham: She was already numb.

In those months she came to know the rhythms of her body all too well; peaks and valleys of a graph. Once a week she longed to sleep with a man. Once a week. Jim Anders, her friend, her confidant, with whom she shared divorce stories, became her lover. After Russell took the children on Saturday, after she had cleaned and shopped and made her life presentable, Jim would knock on her door with a bottle of wine tucked under his arm, to cook dinner with her and talk and make love.

"I never imagined we'd end up in bed," she told him once. "I would have considered it . . . incestuous." He had nodded, awkward as she.

She often fell asleep with her head still on his shoulder, the two of them like children free-falling through some frightening gap in their lives. When he left after breakfast, she was grateful to him in some mild way, for providing something to cling to: the cloth monkey, the surrogate love. Refreshed, she would go out to run. The children arrived home from their father's on Sunday afternoon, upset from their change of routine, but her mellow afterglow stayed with her, letting her feel that she could cope with everything, that her raw edge had been buffed smooth.

January passed, and February. March was distinctly milder. She shed her thermal sweat shirt for an ordinary one. The early crocuses bloomed. Her sense of impending springtime left her so restless that she mapped out a regular course for herself, as if to impose order on the unsettled season.

"You sound as if you're trying to make your body atone for your poor bruised spirit," her friend Wilma told her on the phone. "I wouldn't trust it, Carrie. You can't live so much in your body."

But she did. And then one day a dog bit her.

The dog bounded out of nowhere, a huge shepherd, dragging the chain that usually held him. He growled, his territory invaded, baring his teeth. Thinking to calm him, she quickly halted and let her arms hang limp at her sides. He was having none of it. He bit her in the forearm, then retreated, still growling. Whether it was from stopping so suddenly or her shock at being bitten she didn't know, but the edges of her vision slowly went black and then she fainted, something she had never done before in her life.

A neighbor, returning from work, helped Carrie sit up and took her home. She knew the dog's owners and used Carrie's phone to reap assurances that the dog had had its rabies shots. Carrie did not even have the energy to shower. She called Jim and asked him to pick up the children and give them their dinner. Then she fell into a dazed sleep. The next morning she woke with a terrible sore throat, her resistance suddenly gone. Jim took the children to the sitter and told Carrie she must do two things: get a tetanus shot and call her parents. Her mother was there by the time he brought Carrie home from the doctor.

"It's good to see you, even if it's not under ideal circumstances," her mother said. Cushioned by her fever and the familiar childhood pains—the aching throat, the sore neck—Carrie gratefully gave up: watched her mother do dishes, watched the children bask in their grandmother's warmth. She allowed herself a long sleep. It occurred to her upon waking that she had collapsed. And having collapsed, she could begin to recover—an act that had been impossible before because she had had no concrete low point from which to reach up. When, on the fourth day, she found herself complaining long distance to Wilma about her mother's interfering ways, Wilma laughed. "That just shows you're getting better. I hope now you won't depend on your body so much."

Perhaps, Carrie thought, there was some wisdom in this. When her mother left, she began dropping the children at the sitter's early so she could run in the morning and have her afternoons free for them. She ran for three consecutive miles and was home and showered in less than an hour. She enjoyed it and was no longer exhausted.

But it was a slow healing, fraught with lapses. Steve lost several baby teeth, and she, frazzled from work, often forgot to replace them under his pillow with coins.

"Mom, I lost a tooth yesterday, but the Tooth Fairy didn't come," he said more than once. Groaning inwardly, she invented bright excuses: "Maybe that's because I set my Tooth Fairy trap. I looked in it earlier, and there were some wings and bones."

"Oh, Mom," he would say.

Once, swamped with ungraded mid-terms, she forgot two nights in a row. "Did you look everywhere?" she asked when he informed her on the second morning. "Did you look under your pillow?"

"I even looked on the floor," he said wearily.

When he went to brush his teeth, she replaced the tooth under his pillow with a dollar. "I think maybe you'd better look again," she called. And, when he emerged with his find, explained that the Tooth Fairy must be running late.

"Then maybe we can see him out in the yard," Krista exclaimed.

"I don't think so. Actually I've heard that after daylight the Tooth Fairy turns into a worm."

"Oh, Mom," said Steve.

"And you know if he turns into a worm, a bird might eat him and then we'll have the Tooth Bird."

"Oh, Mom." He picked up a pillow from her bed and hit her with it, solidly across the back. She picked up the other pillow and returned the gesture. Krista brought a third pillow in from her room. Forgetting the ungraded exams, forgetting breakfast and her determination to run, Carrie defended herself with what she thought was a certain expertise.

It was then the middle of May.

Shortly after that she began seeing Jim Anders only at school. She met another man, and then a third. A woman from the college became her friend. Later, she was to gauge her return to normal from the morning of the pillow fight, that leap from the edge of hurt back into the rough-and-tumble center of her life.

꒳

THIS APPEARED IN *MCCALL'S*, JANUARY, 1981

Ellyn Bache is the author of nine novels, including *Safe Passage,* which was made into a movie starring Susan Sarandon, a collection of stories that won the Willa Cather Fiction Prize, and a nonfiction journal about sponsoring refugees. Her 2011 novel, *The Art of Saying Goodbye* was a SIBA Okra Pick and Book of the Year Award nominee.

The mother of four grown children and grandmother of 15, Ellyn grew up in Washington, DC but has spent most of her adult life in Maryland and the Carolinas.

Visit Ellyn online at www.ellynbache.com